Hunger.

That's what Abby felt. Hunger. For knowledge of him. For the chance to get closer to him.

Either she'd gone insane, or Cameron had the ability to hypnotize her with his wolf power, because she grappled with a spectacularly idiotic, completely suicidal compulsion to have the itch forming down deep inside her scratched by a razor-sharp claw.

The highly erotic vibrations he gave off were the epitome of a perilous death trap.

"What do you want?" she demanded in frustration.

He replied in a voice like soft, sifted gravel. "I was wondering if perhaps you have a death wish?"

She'd known better. So why did her body want to meet the animal in him?

WOLF HUNTER

LINDA THOMAS-SUNDSTROM

Published in Great Britain 2015
by Mills & Boon, an imprint of Harlequin (UK) Limited,
Eton House, 18-24 Paradise Road, Richmond, Surrey, TW9 1SR

© 2015 Linda Thomas-Sundstrom

ISBN: 978-0-263-25417-4

89-0515

Harlequin (UK) Limited's policy is to use papers that are natural, renewable and recyclable products and made from wood grown in sustainable forests. The logging and manufacturing processes conform to the legal environmental regulations of the country of origin.

Printed and bound in Spain
by CPI, Barcelona

Linda Thomas-Sundstrom writes contemporary and paranormal romance novels for Mills & Boon® Nocturne™ and Mills & Boon® Desire™. A teacher by day and a writer by night, Linda lives in the West, juggling teaching, writing, family and caring for a big stretch of land. She swears she has a resident Muse who sings so loudly, she often wears earplugs in order to get anything else done. But she has big plans to eventually get to all those ideas. Visit Linda at lindathomas-sundstrom.com or on Facebook.

To my family, those here and those gone,
who always believed I had a story to tell.

Chapter 1

It was only moonlight. A damn luminous light show...

But Abby Stark stood frozen in a pool of it.

A choice four-letter word slipped through her clenched teeth.

Tonight's recon should have been routine. It was too late to second-guess what had gone wrong. One move now, no matter how slight, and whatever was out there in the dark, whatever had stopped her in her tracks, would find her. Breaking the silence by talking into her cell phone would mean attracting any number of bad guys roaming the area.

She couldn't afford to be caught with her pants down in this notorious Miami park. Her mind brought up the words *dead meat*.

The thing out there in the dark, too close for comfort, didn't even begin to fit the term *bad guy*. Its presence left an eerie wave of ripples in the air. Otherness rolled across her skin in waves.

This visitor was not human.

Big freaking surprise.

The thing heading her way was trouble with a bite. A large male, her senses confirmed, and charismatic enough to affect her from a distance. Not just any old monster, either, according to her gut reaction. Something special. Encountering his vibe had been similar to slamming up against a brick wall face-first.

Damn it, had he come close enough to see her?

Was he paying attention?

Don't move.

Flicking her gaze from right to left brought up nothing out of the ordinary. Then again, most of the planet's darker things were difficult to catch a glimpse of in the darkness that bred them.

Adding to the problem was the rain of coldhearted moonlight highlighting every move she'd dare to make—like a circus spotlight pointed in her direction when she was supposed to be in stealth mode.

Step right up, folks. See the girl who's about to have her ass kicked.

Moisture began to gather in the valley between her breasts. Sweat dampened her forehead. Her skin burned beneath her black fatigues because her engine was revved but stuck in neutral.

How screwed was she, on a scale of one to ten?

There was nothing to be done now, Abby supposed, short of wishing for backup, though she couldn't decide what would be worse—being caught by a monster, or having her father's team of elite monster hunters know she'd been found by one of those monsters.

That's what her father called the man-wolf hybrids that had recently claimed this park. *Monsters.*

Her head came up.

The night rustled as if something had just punched its way through the dark. More nerve endings fired as Abby strained to see what approached. This guy had turned the tables, making the watcher a target, rather than the other way around.

She didn't like anything about this.

Sensing Others was what she had always been good at, yet she'd been inexcusably late to this particular party. The hot flashes burning through her were a telling sign that she'd found the very thing she'd been seeking tonight. *Werewolf.* A beast that also might have found her.

Unfortunately, this sucker's presence seemed strong. It might even be a full-blooded beast, though she'd never come across one in the fourteen years she'd spent scouting for her father's team. If not one of the mysterious Lycans, this Were's pedigree had to run parallel to that status. The older the bloodline, the stronger the wolf.

Who are you?

Abby fisted her hands.

To her relief, her watcher wouldn't be a full-fledged beast tonight, since the moon wouldn't be full for another twenty-four hours, though he'd be close enough to being a beast to have set off warning signals.

Her nerves were virtually singing.

Show yourself, wolf. I know you're there.

Abby hoped he wouldn't actually take her up on the offer. Not a creature this potent. Real toughness, a trait she'd inherited from her father, fell short of the mark when dealing with big male werewolves, a fact brought home by the ribbon of fear weaving its way up her spine over the thought of how excited this Were would be tonight, so near to a full lunar phase. He would be restless.

Hell, she was restless. And puzzled.

Whether werewolves were furred-up or not, her intuitive sense of them remained the same. She could pick Weres out of a crowd. She'd always known they were around. But the intensity of the spark igniting deep in her belly at that moment, when stumbling upon this guy, also resembled some sort of messed-up sexual craving. That was new. Brand-new.

Mixed signals between fear and lust? Had to be, because no way in hell could feelings of lust be right.

I'm no amateur, you beast.

I've been around.

In her father's private and very personal war on werewolves, a war that had started with greed before escalating to be so much more, she had been more than useful.

The going rate for a wolf hide chimed in at five hundred dollars in the European black markets. For a fully morphed werewolf pelt the dollar decibel moved over, altering that sum to a full ten grand. In another category altogether came rare, pure-blooded Lycan pelts, skinned before the wolf shifted back to its humanlike form. The grand total for remnants of the king of beasts was fifty thousand bucks. Enough to build a swimming pool.

But Sam Stark's war on Weres went deeper than dollar signs. The bigger, darker motivation for werewolf haters like her father outclassed thoughts of money and reaping vengeance on a nasty criminal element that had been feasting on humans in Miami and elsewhere for quite some time. Sam's motivation came under the classification of genocide. The elimination of beings unlike himself.

The goal of the TTD, an acronym for Take Them Down, was to cull all mutants with moon-tweaked genetics from the population—creatures that could pass for human some of the time, but weren't really human at all.

Abby didn't like the bad stuff. She never accompanied the team when they hunted werewolves, and didn't care to witness what they brought back. Her awareness of Weres had grown more intense as time passed, and now seemed almost personal.

Heck, she was the last person to understand how that

intuitive connection to Weres worked, but hoped it didn't go both ways. All she had ever wanted was for werewolf violence against humans in her own backyard to stop. And here she stood, being stalked by one of those same hybrids from a species doing real damage around town.

So, who is going to show up, and what will you do?

Without a completely full moon, Weres looked like everyone else, with human heads, shoulders, arms and legs. Some of them would speak English.

In human form, wolfmen were tall and tautly muscled, with plenty of supersize capabilities, such as being able to smell her from several yards away.

Like this one must have.

Would he eventually appear in his human skin cocoon? Fake being a jogger? Play at acting like just another guy out for a midnight stroll in a park that no one in their right mind would trespass in alone without an Uzi—unless that mindless sucker happened to be her, with a very special agenda that made dangerous places her job sites of necessity.

This park was a nightmare.

More human bodies were found each year in public parks than anyplace else in Miami, outside of the city center. Bodies turned up without bullet holes or knife wounds, trashed by bite marks and the deep grooves of razor-sharp claws—wounds the Miami PD had no way to explain because not everyone knew about monsters, or that they actually existed.

The Starks knew.

So did handfuls of other people.

Hunters from all over the world came to Miami to join her father's underground big-game hunting expeditions. Some of those people actually believed they were doing God's work.

I know what you are, wolf.

I know you're there.

Reality hit hard. Odds being odds, Abby had figured that someday this kind of accident might happen. In all those years of service to the TTD, she'd never gotten within a couple yards of any big Were. She had never allowed herself to.

Now what?

This one was getting closer by the second—close enough to make her blood simmer. The initial quake of recognition that had rocked her backward splintered into smaller quakes. Her knees felt gummy. Her skin was hot. Weres were often volatile and always dangerous. Right then the sense of danger seemed extreme.

Come out, damn it. Let's get this over with.

As Abby saw it, she was fresh out of options. It would have been useless to try to outrun a strong male when chasing prey is what they did so well, and this guy's presence alone had nearly knocked her off her feet. There hadn't been time to find cover after her initial awareness of him. Currently, she stood in the open, completely exposed.

Why don't you come out?

Are you toying with me?

At that moment, Abby hated the moonlight that ruled these beasts more than ever. She hated everything about the moon.

Shit. How far was she from help?

She'd been cornered between two of the walls separating one of Miami's megamansions from the east end of the park. Although she had been in worse places numerous times, being stuck in the open and drenched in moonlight didn't help her chances.

Attached to her leg, above her right boot, a knife rested in its sheath. Her cell phone was keyed to her father and the rest of his hunters waiting for news at her father's bar.

Short of using the blade, throwing the phone at a beast in man form would be an unconscionably girlie thing to do.

For the record, I haven't been that kind of girl for some time now, she wanted to shout.

"Damn moon. I hate you."

"In that case, this is probably the last place you'd want to be tonight," a deep masculine voice returned from the shadows.

Contact.

He had spoken out loud.

Pulses of pure adrenaline, fierce and feral, skittered through Abby, producing a series of massive electrical jolts. Her stomach twisted into knots. Her teeth slammed together. Staring at what stepped out from under the trees, her hands flew to her neck in an automatic gesture of self-defense, as if in man form or not, her visitor might go for her jugular.

And God help her, part of her untimely inertia was due to the fact that her impression of this guy, from afar, hadn't been wrong.

This sucker was one hundred percent intimidating.

Chapter 2

Abby stared in shocked silence as the Were in his human incarnation advanced in a balanced combination of hard angles and mounds of lean muscle.

He stood tall enough to tower over her, and was twice as broad. A first glance proved him to be brutally handsome. His energy was electrifying. Looking at him kicked the scalding Miami summer temperature up several notches and turned her shudders seismic. Her heartbeats thundered in a way that any Were worthy of its species would be attracted to.

Searching, she saw nothing wolfish in his outline, though an aura of Otherness radiated from him like visible radio waves. His casual, almost nonchalant stride screamed of combustible energy tightly contained in a human casing. His long limbs and wide shoulders were topped by a tanned sculpted face and thick chin-length hair that fell somewhere on the color spectrum between gold and bronze.

Oh yes. This guy was a breed unto himself, and completely unlike anything she had come across before. He was a magnetic combination of rugged and elegant.

Too gorgeous to be human.

He wore a blue long-sleeved shirt rolled at the cuffs to expose sun-kissed forearms. An open collar showed off more skin. His jeans were faded, and she caught a flash of heavy black boots, though he advanced soundlessly with his gaze riveted to her.

Abby felt color drain from her face. *Mesmerizing* wasn't the word to best describe him. *Magnificent* seemed a better choice. Also *deadly*. This beast, with his incredibly honed body outlined by the tight, fitted shirt, moved toward her little circle of light with the grace of an animal…because he was an animal, at least in part. And the overtly masculine, almost hypnotic physical details that described him were likely some kind of built-in bait for reeling in prey.

The devil always lay in the details. Her father had warned her about this many times.

Never get close to the enemy.

Hell, she'd just smashed that golden rule to smithereens through no fault of her own.

Beneath her outward quakes, Abby's insides trembled with a mixture of fear and defiance and something else she didn't dare address—that new thing that had no business showing up alongside this large golden wolf.

Hunger.

That's what she felt. Hunger. For knowledge of him. For the chance to get closer to him.

Either she'd gone insane, or this guy had the ability to hypnotize her with his wolf power, because she grappled with a spectacularly idiotic, completely suicidal compulsion to have the itch forming down deep inside her scratched by a razor-sharp claw.

The breath she exhaled after holding it for so long was

steamy. Aside from her need for self-preservation, and against her better judgment, this werewolf in his human form affected her in ways that were totally wrong. The highly erotic vibrations he gave off were the epitome of a perilous death trap.

She got that. She knew better. So why did her body want to meet the animal in him? What possible explanation could account for her absurd desire to fold herself into his heat?

"What do you want?" she demanded in frustration.

He replied in a voice like soft, sifted gravel. "I was wondering if perhaps you have a death wish."

The world went white-hot beneath this Were's unwavering gaze. Moonlight seemed to amplify every sensation rippling through Abby, all of those sensations pointing to him. No doubt about it, her sexually suggestive reactions were as dangerous as the Were himself.

She'd never been an out-and-out rebel, really, she thought now, though she had lived on the edge, more or less fending for herself since her mother died of a prolonged illness when she was a kid. In the past, she'd had no reason to flaunt her father's strict authority, since he had provided, if not earnest affection, a roof over her head.

So, was there an actual rule about people having to do the right thing at the right time, or only what was good for them?

Breathlessness made her light-headed, a symptom of anticipating more trouble to come. Needing air, unable to stand the silence, Abby spoke in a voice shakier than she would have liked, given that werewolves, as with other predators, could ferret out fear.

"Death wish?"

He nodded. "Everyone in Miami is familiar with this park's unfavorable mortality statistics."

Inner warning signals went off again. Red flags waved.

If she couldn't outrun this sucker and he wished her harm, she'd have to fight.

Keep him talking. Gauge his intent.

Was he a member of the pack killing people out here? The way he rolled his shoulders reminded Abby of how much muscle lay under that cool blue cotton, and how that muscle would soon adapt to a new shape. If not an organic werewolf, known from Sam's lectures as a Lycan, he'd have to have been bitten by another werewolf, and that bite had injected the wolf virus into his bloodstream. Human and wolf particles had fused to form a freakish new entity.

Did this guy's raw, undulating maleness stem from the kick of some mystical ancient virus in his bloodstream, or had he always been a heartthrob?

"I know about the park," she said.

She hadn't really looked closely at his face. It was bad enough that the bronzed skin beneath his chin, exposed between open buttons, beckoned to her with the lure of the forbidden.

Would his flesh be smooth, so close to becoming a wolf? Abby cursed the urge to press her fingers there to find out—an action that would probably add one more body count to those unfavorable statistics he'd just mentioned.

Keep strong.

Resist the craziness.

Never get close.

"Then you do know this park is probably the last place a woman should visit, alone and at night," he said quietly.

"Only women?"

"Anyone."

"Am I alone?"

"That seems to be the case."

Abby gestured at him with a wave of one hand. "You don't count?"

Sarcasm didn't make her feel better about her predicament. The Were's eyes remained on her in an uncomfortably intense way, giving Abby the impression that he could see through her clothes and down through her skin to the place where the sparks of her crazy curiosity about him glittered.

She hoped to God he couldn't see that.

Stomach tightening into a ball of uncertainty, and with her body temp soaring to a disgusting degree, she waited for what might come next, facing the Were, whose specialized internal furnace would soon fuel a werewolf's shape-shift.

"You do know that bad things sometimes hide in the night?" he cautioned with no threatening move in her direction.

"Are you one of those bad things?"

"I could be. How would you know?"

"Well, then, I guess I'd better go before you have a chance to provide the answer."

"That might be a good idea," he agreed.

Movement, though, was impossible. Turning her back to this guy would be a bad idea, no matter how friendly his approach had been. Big reminder: though he looked like a human, and talked like one, he wasn't.

Feeling the weight of the cell phone in her pocket, Abby tried to remember that Weres weren't the only treacherous faction in town. Her father, Sam Stark, was as deadly as any werewolf and quite possibly twice as lethal, since Sam had no tolerance for anomalies like this one, and his hatred was usually backed by an element of surprise.

She wondered what color this guy's pelt would be. Bronze, like his hair? Golden, like the rest of him? With moonlight reflected in each strand of his sleek, slightly mussed mane, whatever color of wolf he turned out to be would amount to tons of cash for the Stark accounts if the team found him. He'd bring a small fortune and it shouldn't be any concern of hers. This wolf and others like him hurt people when the moon was full.

How close to the surface is your wolf tonight? she wanted to ask. *Are you a killer?*

Any of those things spoken aloud would let him know she had pegged him for a hybrid, taking things from bad to worse in a hurry. The team's plan had always been to drive Weres like this one into the open, into the moonlight that betrayed what they were, and strike fast, strike hard. No mercy.

But this wasn't a killing night. Tonight her job had been only to locate some Weres. See who was around.

"And I found you," she whispered as her interest in the gorgeous Were reached broiling status internally, as if her mind and body were engaged in a war of ethics, while the big fellow on the edge of the light continued to prove how good his acting skills were.

It was a standoff. *Checkmate.*

Who would make the first move?

Daringly, Abby let her gaze drift upward to his face before immediately wishing she hadn't. His features were chiseled, with high cheekbones and a full mouth. He had a strong jaw and arched brows. She refused to meet his wide-set eyes.

Daring to speak again in a voice husky with strain, she said, "What are you waiting for?"

After a long pause, he replied, "Why don't I walk you home?"

Abby shook her head. "Don't think so, but thanks all the same."

"There could be others out here, much worse than me."

"Really? Much worse?"

"I can assure you of that."

"Then why are you out here?" she asked.

"I like to walk and think."

"In the dark?"

"Yes."

"Here?"

He shrugged.

"Maybe you're some kind of danger junkie," she suggested.

"It's a possibility. What about you? Is danger your drug of choice, or were you trying to get somewhere and got lost?"

Unclenching her hands, Abby then fisted them again, rattled by the stilted repartee. The heat, both hers and his, had become suffocating. He had a gaze like a frigging laser beam that wouldn't let up or miss much. The sixty-four-thousand-dollar question was whether this guy would try to hurt her, or not.

Why don't you make your move?

"Danger isn't really my thing," she said.

"Yet here you are, in a place that attracts it."

"Not for long."

Listening hard, Abby separated the layers of city noises. Cars paraded down the boulevards in the distance. The faint buzz of insects reached her from the trees to her right.

The air was filled with the smells of dry, sun-drenched pavement and the bitter odor of crushed grass and leaves. Above those things something else, some other scent, surfed the night air. She tagged it as the not-so-sweet odor of the unseen.

Her scalp pricked. Her racing heart gave an extra thump. This Were's wolf was close to the surface and getting stronger. Whatever lay inside him that she had easily connected to wasn't going to go away with a bit of conversation.

Something else bothered her, needled at her. If this guy was an Alpha, he'd have a pack close by.

Her odds in favorably dealing with the situation plummeted. At the same time, her morbid fascination for the wolfman kept Abby focused. She wanted to know so much more about him, and about what went on here. Her appetite for those things grew by the second.

Abby held herself tightly to keep from squirming. If Weres like this one possessed animalistic superpowers, he'd have already noticed that she had become a heat-sensing Geiger counter for the very thing that should have had her screaming. Her fevered flesh and skin-ruffling gyrations were the equivalent of inviting the fiery hand of death to slide between her legs.

Hell with that. Due to his looks and masculine vibe, this Were probably had a harem of women willing to take him in. He didn't need one more willing supplicant. Besides, wolves and humans did not mix, except when those things in an anomalistic fashion resided within one being.

The situation sucked. All outcomes seemed dire. Whatever outlandish thing was taking place between this werewolf and herself had gummed up logic. He was seducing her without any effort on his part at all. He didn't have to be blatant about it because the seduction worked. All he had to do was stand there, looking like a sexy hunk.

Stupid girl. Stupid, stupid girl. Get out. Get away.

You, she wanted to shout to the creature across from her, *are the very thing my father and his teams despise. There has to be a reason for that.*

Lifting her chin defiantly, Abby backed up a step. *This is the final test. Will you pounce?*

As it turned out, he didn't do anything of the sort. Instead, he calmly asked her a question.

"Why do you hate the moon, if you don't mind me asking?"

The question was as unexpected as the earnest ring of curiosity in his voice.

"You said you hate it," he reminded her.

"I hate what the moon does to people," Abby said.

Her companion glanced up at the light. "You don't find the moon beautiful?"

"Its beauty is deceitful, as beauty often is."

If he got the point and the allusion to himself, he didn't show it. He took a step toward her, closing some of the distance separating them and setting off another round of sparks that burrowed well below Abby's waistline. He continued to study her face as if whatever he sought there might be important.

What did he want? An apology for the atrocities her father and his team had inflicted upon his species? Did he want revenge, when he had to know how many humans Weres had killed in Miami in the past year alone?

In hindsight, she should have covered up the logo on her T-shirt that advertised a bar that just happened to also be a field office for Sam Stark's hunters. She hadn't taken the time to change, in a hurry to get outside, away from the crowd. Maybe this guy had already made note of it, which would be bad news.

Move, Abby. Hesitation is no longer an option.

No wolf could be allowed to discover where the team kept court, or seek to uncover the source of her own unusual connection to their breed. Those were secrets for keeping behind closed doors, under lock and key, especially when facing a Were male of this caliber.

Damn it, the spell he had put on her had to be broken. Her murky, inexplicable attraction to him had taken her too far off base. She had feared this kind of face to face for a long time.

Use the phone. Make that call.

Yes, and what would she say to her father if he answered the phone? That she'd screwed up this time? That she'd been mesmerized by a wolf? There was no way Sam's team could find her like this, feverish and out of commission, when so many others expected her to be a chip off the old guy's block.

Plus, all of a sudden she wasn't so sure about wanting the team to find the Were across from her who was too damn pretty to be a rug on some billionaire collector's floor.

"Got to go."

She needed to hear the urgency in her voice. The muscles of her upper back twitched. Although her heart rate again spiked, she didn't go anywhere because backward wasn't the direction she really wanted to take. Every molecule in her body strained to get closer to the wolf in his human skin, while her mind struggled to find a way out of this standoff that made sense.

Do the smart thing. Turn and sprint. Hope he won't follow.

Why hadn't she at least tried that?

Was he touching her? No. Yet she felt as if he were.

Could he be holding her there physically with his wolf aura? *Yes. Hell, yes.*

This wolf was the real deal, times ten. And he was what? Being *friendly*? They were having a *chat*, as though the word *species* didn't matter?

If this Were internalized her scent, or any other of his cousins trapped her with a purpose the next night, she'd make the obituaries, or worse. One swipe of a claw or a bite that deeply pierced her skin and she might become one of them.

Considering that she survived at all.

Abby's lips parted for a speech she didn't make. Without thinking she inched toward this Were like a bug drawn to light, her body, independent of her mind, urging that forbidden touch as if part of her actually wanted to burn. As if the secret guilt she had built up over the years about the whole hunting scene, as well as the lectures from her father, the loneliness she'd endured for so long and the image of werewolf pelts hanging from ceiling beams, would burn with her.

Swallowing the lump in her throat, Abby waited for sanity to intervene, hoping it would hurry.

"Will you let me go?" she asked breathlessly.

"Of course you can go. Though I really would like to make sure you get where you're going safely."

An offer of safety from the scariest thing out here?

As if she was supposed to believe him.

"Nights here are always dangerous," he said. "Tonight feels especially tense. Do you sense that?"

"Why care about me at all? You don't even know me."

"It's what I do."

"You make a habit of accosting women in dark places, and then woo them with the promise of a compromise?"

"I try to make sure that no accosting goes on, actually."

"Are you some sort of vigilante?"

"Something along those lines, yes."

"I don't recall asking for your help."

"Can you assure me that you know the difference between looking for danger and actually finding it?" he countered. "No one comes to this park after dark for fun or shortcuts. Not even if they carry a knife."

Okay. So she hadn't really supposed he wouldn't know about the knife, scent being one of a werewolf's strongest attributes, and silver being repugnant to them. But why hadn't he hidden his knowledge of the knife, when it couldn't be seen? The forged silver blade would be a wolf's worst nightmare if it touched skin. No human could have smelled it.

Maybe that knife was why he hadn't made his move.

Tilting his head slightly, he said, "Something about you drew me to you, if you want to know the truth."

"Yeah, like I haven't heard that line a million times," she said. "I work in a bar."

No matter how hard it became, she had to keep reasonably calm, at least on the outside. A frightened human's scent, she'd been told, was a veritable aphrodisiac for hyped-up hybrids.

But how did their sense of awareness translate to a human that might not be frightened enough and, instead of fear, held an illicit fascination for this one?

"Are you really so fierce, I wonder?" he asked.

"You have no idea."

"You've no need for company?"

"Not yours."

He shrugged his broad shoulders. "Then go, and I'll watch your back."

"Or stab me in it."

"Direct, but way off the mark. I don't have any reason to harm you. And you have the knife."

"Maybe the weapon deters you?"

"Honestly, I like to think of myself as one of the good guys. What does that knife say about you?"

It was a good question. Because of it, Abby's conscience nagged. What if he turned out to be okay, after all? There were decent folks along with the bad in most cultures, though her father had not once mentioned that possibility with werewolves.

She did know about this good-bad thing in other animals, though, being an animal control officer three days a week. There were nice dogs and bad dogs, and she had quickly learned how to tell the difference. Telling signs started with the eyes.

Could that ability translate to decoding good and bad Weres?

Who was he really?

How different was this Were's world from hers?

What did it feel like to carry a fully formed wolf inside, and be part of such a dangerous minority that had to hide from the masses?

No one had explained those things to her, because no human she knew had the answers. Her father killed werewolves on sight. If he had interrogated any of them, she'd never heard about it.

Here was her chance to find out about the so-called enemy, and she couldn't afford to take that chance. Not out here. Not like this, when it had become increasingly obvious that she wasn't thinking properly.

Will you really let me go, wolf, or is this some sort of cat-and-mouse game?

Time to find out.

"Well, then, I'll be on my way. I'd like to say it's been fun…" Her sentence faded when he took another step forward, bringing his heady physical powers of persuasion with him.

Abby widened her stance defiantly, her body exhibiting more visible signs of distress. The mere fact that she had questioned herself and her motives for being here meant that she'd started to cave. The Were knew this. Animals zeroed in on weakness. His silence told her he recognized what her body wanted in spite of her arguments to the contrary, and in spite of their differences.

He would have noticed her flushed face and averted gaze. He'd feel the return of heat she gave off and intuit with his wolfish senses about the very private spot between her thighs that had seldom been accessible to anyone, yet had become a quaking mass of need for a stranger.

Not just any stranger.

What was wrong with her? Who could interpret the idiocy of what she'd been thinking and feeling? One more step, and she'd feel his breath on her face.

This is not okay.

"But you'd be lying." He completed the sentence she had left dangling, in a tone that wafted over her like a length of fine, drifting silk. "About the fun."

"Yes," Abby admitted. "I'd be lying."

She knew right then and there that it was too late for escape. Electrified excitement charged through her. Moonlight sparkled around them like a desert sandstorm, dulling the edges of reality, making closeness to a wolf seem viable. Making sexual fantasies with one seem viable.

Hell, possibly she did have a death wish.

And God…his eyes, drawing her to return his gaze, turned out to be gold, like the rest of him. A light, pure gold.

"I won't hurt you. Go on. Take off." The gruffness of his voice suggested that he might be sharing her inner turmoil.

"If you follow me, you'll know where I live. I can't allow that," she said.

He held up both of his hands in a gesture of placation. "Then I'll just wait here. I won't follow."

Abby's left hand hovered over the pocket that held her cell phone. Her right hand straddled her right thigh above the knife by her boot. But she didn't use either escape route, imagining she already felt his heated breath on her cheek.

Up close, this guy was outrageous. He oozed male masculinity and owned the term *raw animal magnetism*. This wolf was sex on long, lean legs, and seduction by design. He smelled like a man, not a monster. Drifts of aftershave, damp cotton fabric and musky male moistness floated in the air.

She wanted him in a really bad way, and there was no excuse. Her chest hurt. Bones ached from standing at attention. Her heart felt as if it had been squeezed, and not one breath she took in seemed sufficient to fix her oxygen deficit. It had been a long time since she'd been this close to anyone of interest. Her life had been that of a loner for reasons that necessitated never allowing anyone in.

At her father's bar, she had remained more or less camouflaged, which made coping skills in dealing with her inner angst so much easier. She did her job. She did what she was told to do in order to be left alone afterward. Alone time away from Sam Stark and his gang had always been a reward.

Did it take a creature so unlike herself to make her desire something more? Someone not completely human who had to understand what it was like to feel out of place?

Damn it, she had caved. Someone had to pull her away because she couldn't do it herself. The dichotomy of what she had been taught versus what they had going on here ratcheted up the tension of her internal tug-of-war. There had to be some good with the bad, and she wanted proof of that.

The pulses of desire passing through her were richly intense. Just looking at this guy was a treat and a pleasure. Doing anything more, however, might be suicidal.

"You have the police on speed-dial?" Her companion pointed to her pocket. "In case you meet someone else out here who's not so accommodating?"

Another surprise. The concern in his tone sounded genuine.

An inexplicable flush burned its way up Abby's neck and into her cheeks. The exposed triangle of flesh at the base of this guy's neck had become like a glimpse into a world completely foreign to her—a world that was off-limits, new and untried, yet something she suddenly and desperately wanted to find out about.

Would he act on her show of weakness at last? Take advantage? Push her over the edge?

Abby briefly closed her eyes.

Despite everything in her life so far, and while knee-deep in danger, she wanted very badly to see what lay beneath his baby-blue shirt.

She wanted to know what made this Were worth so much to the team, and why he hadn't yet hurt her, when the people in her life wouldn't have given him the same consideration.

More than anything, she desired to run her tongue along the crease of his lips, drink deeply from his Otherness and truly indulge in the flavor of night. She would get those longstanding questions about his species over with, once and for all.

Right now.

"Perhaps you'd like me to go first?" he asked soberly. "The sooner you're out of the area, the better. That's a fact."

He raised a hand as if he'd touch her, then let it fall before he did. Hoarsely, and as though the words stuck in this throat, he said, "My advice? Run away, little girl. Run fast."

On quaking legs, Abby stubbornly stood her ground. "You first."

His sigh struck her like a soft caress. "All right."

When he took a step back, the strange bond that had sprung into place between them stretched tight.

"Good night," he said without leaving her or turning away. The bastard just stood there, his golden gaze riveting.

Perhaps sensing how the mood had changed, he shook his head and smiled warily. Though misplaced, the smile dazzled, lifting the corners of lips Abby fantasized about licking, and making him seem way more human and approachable.

Suddenly, she felt like the animal here.

His unexpected exhibition of lightness seemed a confirmation, a mutual acknowledgment that the link that had sprung into place between them had grown red-hot and all-encompassing for no apparent reason, other than that old adage about the craziness of animal attraction.

That smile made something inside Abby shatter. Pieces of the reasoning process scattered like confetti. Sparks imploded down deep inside her with an interior fireworks display, creating a craving for this Were like no other, a craving the equivalent of a wave of primitive primal need.

Swearing beneath her breath, Abby realized that she truly hadn't finished with this Were. She knew with absolute certainty that the treacherous moon above their heads that was nothing more to most people than a silver disc orbiting the earth was now about to become either her keenest enemy...or her future lover.

Fully aware of the risks, and discounting the consequences, she took that last stride forward...

And looked up just far enough to see the surprise on the gorgeous Were's face.

Chapter 3

"What the…?"

Cameron Mitchell took a good look at the woman standing before him and frowned. She was within touching distance, and he hadn't put her there. The woman had gotten right up in his face.

Her actions were a complete surprise, and not wholly unwelcome. His feelings for her had come on strong from the first glance, and as unlikely as it seemed, her feelings appeared to parallel his. Still, acting on those feelings would be a huge mistake.

They were strangers, talking because of the way these immediate attractions went. Though the urge to touch her was impossible to resist, and he didn't want to resist, he did have to maintain control. She wasn't the reason he patrolled the park, and was, in the end, a distraction.

Still, his groin ached over the lushness of her scent. The inhuman parts of him swirled in reaction to the way she licked her lower lip after speaking, with the tip of a small pink tongue. Looking at her made the wildness trapped inside him long for release, and there was only one way to solve that problem.

Crazy woman! She telegraphed her willingness to break down barriers in a way that even the dullest senses could have picked up on. But the heat signature that had drawn him to her in the first place would also be a homing beacon for other Weres in the area, and a lightning rod for lunatics.

He couldn't have her. The sooner she got out of range, the better. He had to let her go. Discounting others in the area, there was no way to predict what might happen if he acted on his sudden addiction to her, or if she might end up getting hurt. Though his wolf wasn't in charge tonight, it hovered close enough to be in favor of taking this opportunity.

And the wolf's motives, he had discovered, were unreliable.

Hell, woman, I could be one of those criminals. I could be lethal.

She had to know how easily she could be overpowered by a larger source. Surely she understood that this park was off-limits for a reason. She had confessed to knowing the awful statistics.

She eyed him keenly in return with an intelligent emerald-green gleam that suggested she was no fool. Her defiant stance lent her a certain air of capability. Yet she had been alone at night in a place where no other human dared to trespass. This meant no one would probably be coming to her rescue, and that if he desired to give in to the force of his rising libido, she'd be his for the taking.

He put a hand to his forehead, hoping to stall those thoughts, and posed a string of silent questions.

Why are you here?

Why this odd attraction?

Unable to help himself, he studied her.

For all her defiant attitude, she was small. He topped her by a full head or two. She had a hard-muscled sensuality that cut into him as though she had wielded the blade near her boot—the blade that sang to him of its presence as if it were alive.

She wasn't a classic beauty or the stuff most men couldn't forget after a first glimpse. No hourglass curves, big breasts or blond curls. Lean, taut arms were exposed by a sleeveless black shirt. Baggy cargo pants hid the sculpted lines of her legs. Straight, shoulder-length hair, a brilliant shade of auburn with purposefully dyed dark black tips, seemed to him an edgy color combination.

She moved again, closer.

Damn her.

Her fragrance intensified, filling his lungs with each breath he drew in. Every woman had her own unique smell, but this one…this one smelled like candy.

One touch. Only one.

He pressed his palm to her cheek and waited to see her reaction. Her eyes blazed. His own reaction wasn't so simple. The beast inside him began to unfurl, adding depth to his illicit desire to possess her. His need to circumvent control began at a cellular level and dug in deep.

"Don't you get it? I can be dangerous," Cameron said to her. "There's something about you."

She did not reply. How could she, after that confession? Neither did she run.

Which made matters worse.

Her skin felt like velvet, an intoxication that streaked through him. The fact that he hadn't been with a woman for a long time came home to haunt him. He hadn't indulged since the damn gangbanger he'd been cuffing in a raid bit him, changing his life forever.

I'm in control. I can do this. Stay firm and see to her safety.

He chanted that silent internal directive several times before deciding that she had to do the moving. He couldn't be trusted. Not completely. Not so close to a full moon.

How do I make you go? Scare you? Be the bully you had expected me to be? Maybe another touch will frighten you into doing the right thing.

Testing that theory, Cameron let his open hand linger on her cheek, almost able to hear time ticking away. Yet she didn't take him up on the invitation of a hasty retreat.

He felt so damn beastly.

A roar of conquest rumbled in his chest as his heart changed rhythm to adapt to hers, lifting and falling in a series of vertical spikes. With utmost willpower, he fielded an oncoming rush of adrenaline.

The nameless woman's legs were apart, with her feet planted. She had fisted her hands at her sides. Her teeth were clenched. But in her eyes lay another kind of unspoken invitation.

When his fingers slid slowly downward, she flinched as if she'd been stung, and blinked slowly. The level of her defiance in the face of rules governing two strangers meeting in dangerous places made his needs escalate. Cops were adrenaline junkies out of necessity, but this situation flowed out of the box. He was hot for her and wanting closeness. Any kind of closeness.

A growl erupted from his throat unchecked. Hell, he hadn't meant to do that.

The woman beside him swayed in reaction to the sound. Her delicate face lost some of its color. Long lashes fluttered. Her chest rose and fell quickly with each new breath. But she stood there with her pulse racing hard enough to lift the skin beneath her right ear, movement that caused the two small diamond studs in her lobes to sparkle.

When she finally moved, it was in a way Cameron truly

hadn't expected. She stepped closer, pressing her chest to his, her hips to his. Suggestively.

Her eyes were on the top button of his shirt. She kept her gaze there while her body telegraphed quite clearly what she expected to happen.

Cameron swore. Restraining himself took real effort and came close to being the hardest thing he had ever attempted, after being a cop for five long years. More than anything, he wanted to throw her on the ground and prove just how dangerous he could be. His wolf liked the idea.

"You haven't gone," she said, speaking now through seductively moist parted lips.

"Neither have you." The blood in his veins thrashed, racing toward the places already erect and ready for action.

"I'm thinking about going," she said.

"Maybe you should think harder."

She shook her head. "My advice to you is to take it or leave it before I change my mind."

Another streak of heat tore through Cameron, magnified by surprise. What had she just said?

She had no qualms about this? About sex with a stranger who could have been anyone, and was, in actuality, so much more?

"I don't know what game you're playing, or what you're up to," he said, "but I just told you I never accost women in dark places, and I wasn't lying."

"Okay. Leave it, then."

Cameron stared down at her, his stability tumbling. Finding this female had temporarily taken his mind off pressing problems. Imagining what he'd like to do to her was a luxury. But finding her alone in this park on a night like this—especially on a night like this—made all those sinful thoughts unacceptable.

Several gangs called this place their home turf. The whole area stank of wolf gone mad, and those mindless badasses, minus the fur, were out tonight and always up to no good. No werewolf could resist the play of moonlight so near to a full. *He* hadn't been able to ignore it.

He could barely ignore this, or her.

Despite his eagerness, and after a monk-like few months, mating with this woman, on this spot, just wasn't possible. He was what he was, and had been for a while. Wolf particles had been introduced to his bloodstream, creating and sealing a wolf to his system, leaving him unstable.

It had taken days of severe agony in order to recover from the initial nightmare of the bite that had made him a hybrid. In his mind, the image of the hyped-up bastard that had chomped on his arm remained fixed.

He might have lost his mind completely for a few of those terrible days afterward. Nothing of that existed now, other than the brief remembrance of uttering prayers about needing to be put out of his misery.

Yet he had survived. And closeness to others had become impossible, at home and at work. He stopped returning the stares from women on the street, and made no dates. He quit having drinks after-hours with the guys on his beat. All that withholding was paramount, and out of necessity, until he found out as much as he could about his present state, and about the control necessary to maintain it.

He existed now in werewolf infancy, with no way to anticipate what might happen if his emotions got involved. What if he hurt a woman by accident?

So you, he wanted to say to the female with the shining green eyes, *are the ultimate temptation.*

Until he knew everything, and maybe not even then, he wasn't relationship material. And it was a given that a one-nighter with a pretty woman in a notoriously feral park wasn't a win-win for anybody, under any circumstances. This close to a full moon, any thought to the contrary would be pure lunacy.

If you knew what resides at my core, Green Eyes, and what I have become, you would run off, screaming.

I hate what the moon does to people, she had said.

Those words still echoed in his mind.

Its beauty is deceitful, she'd said.

Looking at her now, he wanted to say, *If you only knew what deceit actually is.*

His wolf stirred, raising goose bumps on the back of Cameron's neck. The wolf was searching for an early way out. This wolf, Cameron feared, might want to bite somebody back.

Oh yes, I want you, both man and wolf agreed when eyeing this woman, though in spite of the physical need pounding through him, he had told this woman he was a gentleman.

No joke.

Still, he had to admit that she possessed a streak of wildness unlike anything he'd encountered in a female, and this sparked his pleasure buttons. Part of him voted to take her up on her offer of closeness. Heck, most parts did. He was hard in all the right places and aching to act.

Didn't everyone need company on a dark summer night? Even a monster?

As the scent of female hormones floated in the moonlight, Cameron's heart thundered. Her face was dewy, and enticingly damp. The slightest flush of pink had returned to her cheeks. Those large emerald eyes, slowly lifting to the level of his neck, his jaw, and continuing upward, were wide open. Her generous lips opened as if she'd say something else or take back what she'd said about him either taking her up on her offer, or leaving it.

He almost wished she would take all this back.

Cameron ran his hand over her black T-shirt, his heated

palm sliding slowly from the rounded collar to the swell of her breasts. The shirt was thin. He felt her fullness as if there were nothing between his hand and her skin. And indeed, she was lacking undergarments that would have taken precious time to remove.

The raised buds of her nipples were an erotic discovery and a telling symptom of her heightened state of arousal. She was exotic, narcotic, and had become his drug of choice on a moon-filled night.

After all, the whole gentleman thing only went so far.

The sting in his fingertips announced the closeness of claws that had no business intruding on tonight. A ghostly shudder of lengthening ligaments tickled Cameron's spine as his baser side pined for release, when in reality, he and the wolf were one, and inseparable.

The feisty woman's heart beat frantically beneath his hand. She dripped with the same moonlight that would soon issue a command for him to trade one shape for another, and the light made her features appear more angular, and riddled with shadows. She was moonlight personified…and he was going to use her. Because, swear to God, she looked as if she could handle what he wanted to do to her, and like it.

Stroking upward from her breast, wedging himself tighter against her, Cameron allowed the beastly cravings some room, just this once, and angled his ravenous mouth toward hers.

Chapter 4

His face came close. Their breath mingled. The stranger's supple mouth closed over hers with a kiss that made Abby stagger.

She let him touch her. Let him kiss her. Their closeness was combustible. With that first meeting of their eyes he had become the *need*. The *must have*. Rampant desire for him ruled her, fed her, drove her toward a storm of emotion that wanted him inside her. Nothing else would do.

She couldn't allow herself to examine the reasons behind this sudden irrational craving.

So, really…who was the animal here?

She kissed him back, giving in to the sensations. His hot, demanding, talented mouth rendered her breathless. When their tongues touched, a blistering dance began between mouth and lips and bodies straining to get at each other.

He tasted like midnight. Like moonlight on a mountaintop. Like a howl of wildness echoing through a vast valley. And a lot like the physical manifestation of greed. No human connection could be like this, she realized. None ever had.

Her mouth clung to his, nipped at his. As the kiss went from dry to damp, moving quickly toward savage, Abby raked his lower back with her fingernails, wadding up his shirt to get at the taut flesh beneath, desperate to make him pay for what he was doing to her. Both of them needed to share the pain of accessing the forbidden.

His skin radiated the heat of a hundred bonfires, burning, singeing. His mouth piled fire on top of fire in an overlapping grid of flames. Being close to him was a pleasure that existed in a land beyond thought and consequences, falling into the realm of her pure carnal fantasy.

Maybe this was why werewolves were feared. Because of what they had to offer.

His masculine body felt solid and rock-hard against hers. His embrace became an all-consuming bliss. She pulled at his shoulders and wrapped her hands in his hair, wanting to be closer to him still, processing the danger as sublime.

Her feet left the ground. Air whooshed out of her lungs as her back hit the grass. Her companion dropped to his knees and stretched out on top of her, as breathless as she was.

And this felt good.

Writhing beneath his weight, Abby tore at him with trembling hands, her fingers finding his waistband, and beneath it more fiery skin that simultaneously burned and beckoned.

Hell, in a minute, she would howl, even if she didn't know how.

When he paused, she formed challenging words against his lips. "What's wrong? Did you get an *A* in self-control?"

In answer, a growl rolled from his throat and into her,

its vibration the biggest surprise of all. As if that growl had tickled something hidden inside her, Abby felt the rise of her own voice, coming from a place she hadn't known existed.

The sound she made shot through her, emerging as an echo of his. Her body twitched in shock.

"Well, well," her sexy companion whispered, his golden gaze boring into her. "I suppose that makes things infinitely easier."

He lifted her up before his remark had time to register, and set her on her feet. He peeled her T-shirt over her head, then ripped open his shirt with a pop of pinging buttons. Warm hands eased her pants and underwear over her hips, and down her thighs.

She was naked, and quaking in anticipation of his next move. But he stood there, looking at her with a gaze that nearly did her in.

Damn him and the moonlight he rode in on, she was not going to beg.

He sidled up to her at last, the heat radiating off his shirtless chest like that of an inferno. His arms encircled her waist. Their chests met with a jarring impact. They were going to do whatever it took to address this raging passion. There would be no stopping it. She was in the arms of the enemy, and had willingly crossed enemy lines.

The scratching sound of a zipper opening stirred Abby's blood. His hands stroked upward over the curve of her buttocks, and up her spine. His fingers splayed over her rib cage. When he elevated her again, she wrapped her legs around his waist.

Her boot heels dug into the backs of his thighs. The boots and the knife in its leather sheath were all she had now, but notice of those things distanced as the glorious cock he settled her over took all remaining breath away.

She clung to him as she slid down his length, the pleasure of having him between her legs exquisite and extreme.

"I'm not afraid of the night," she said without knowing why. "And I'm not afraid of you."

"Not afraid? Then that makes one of us."

The white-hot Were backed her against a tree for balance, and pulled off her boots. He glanced at the silver-bladed knife attached to her calf.

"The knife stays," Abby said. Then the ability for speech left her.

Not satisfied with their bodies locked together in a way he couldn't manipulate, her lover took her again to the grass. He perched above her, and with one hand found the moist, quaking spot he needed to again enter her overheated depths.

Abby opened for him, wanting every last bit of what he had to offer, and unwilling to wait. He sank into her with a thrust that stretched her to her limits.

Abby gasped and threw her head back as she took him in, working to draw him deeper, while at the same time accepting his drowning kiss. Sensations overwhelmed from two sources at once, flowing gloriously from her mouth to what lay buried between her thighs.

The taking wasn't an easy one, or time-consuming. Foreplay belonged in the bedroom, between real lovers, and this was something else altogether. This was nuts.

Her Were entered her again and again, hard enough to tickle the sensitive spot already close to a climax. Spasms began to build that forced her hips into him, urging him on as she closed herself around him.

Having him inside her was at once heaven and hell and a mistake she might live to regret, but it was exciting. When he withdrew, Abby dug into him with her fingers, drawing blood with her nails to again make him pay for being a beast, the enemy, and for his part in this crazy liaison.

Thoughts flashed by at lightning speed. She'd never see him again. A few stolen moments were all they had. If her father found out about this moonlight tryst, he'd kill her with his bare hands.

The scent of blood filled the air. His blood. A sound of surprise slipped from his throat, though he didn't stop kissing her. His response to her fingernails was to thrust into her deeper, over and over, building a rhythm that made Abby see stars.

Unable to hold off what loomed so close to the surface, a cry of growled pleasure tore from her. Her eyes fluttered open. Abby found herself again looking into his beautifully inhuman eyes, and the intensity of the connection she found in them brought more lightning and tripled the emotional storm.

She cried out again as he hit the place that had never been touched, never been found, so deep down inside her. The look in his golden eyes as he did so pierced her soul, knocking down barriers she had long held in place to keep emotion at bay.

She opened that last little bit…and came.

Arching her back, hit by a sizzling, fiery orgasm, Abby bucked off the grass as each successive wave of deliciously vicious pleasure overtook her.

The world drifted in whirling flashes of bright, multicolored cartwheels that mirrored the moonlight. Sound ceased. Breath suspended as her body went rigid in the throes of a ceaseless, endless ecstasy. The man providing the pleasure held himself motionless, pinning her to the orgasm without easing up. Like her, he fought hard for each labored breath.

"Yes," he whispered, encouraging her to give in to the pleasure. "Yes, little wolf."

She crested wave after wave of ecstasy until the waves finally began to recede. It seemed like hours before the shudders ceased and the orgasm faded. Her breath finally returned as the spasms fled. Her limbs slowly regained feeling. But Abby kept her eyes shut, afraid to open them, afraid to look at the man, the stranger, the creature, who had made this incredible thing happen.

What would she possibly say? *Given what you are, we should have used a condom?*

Nevertheless, she had no way around it. She had to face him. Face this. She had to get up, get dressed and walk away.

He wasn't there when she opened her eyes. She saw only a dark stretch of moon-dappled grass that made reality come crashing down. She was on her hands and knees in the dirt. Her knees were aching. Her palms were scratched. Their mating session had taken on aspects of the surreal.

He hadn't gone. Abby heard him breathing. Her ardent lover curled around her, with his bare chest pressed to her back. They had changed positions sometime during this exotic escapade, and had gone after each other like two animals rutting.

His arms were wrapped around her waist. Both she and this creature were slick with sweat and completely silent in the aftermath of what they had done.

How right her father had been about some things, she thought. Weres were dangerous. They were treacherous without having to kill someone in order to earn that reputation.

"Are you okay?"

His question sounded oddly out of place. The resonance in his tone pulsed in her ears. She expected him to get up and walk away, having had his fill of her. *Thank you, ma'am.*

Abby could not think of a single verbal jab or witticism to reply with, though she opened her mouth to try. Damn him, his question had been nice.

It was time to get up and get away.

What had she done?

Sliding out from beneath her lover, Abby got to her feet. Feeling only slightly self-conscious about being naked at midnight in a public park, she muffled a startled cry as a piercing pain ripped through her right thigh, hurting so badly, she sagged back down to her knees.

Muscles seized. Her vision began to tunnel. A haze of inky darkness descended as strong arms swept her up and a voice whispered, "It's okay. I have you. Curse this damn park and everyone who has ever set foot in it, because I knew there would be trouble tonight."

Chapter 5

Abby's eyes fluttered open to a moving tableau. Earth, grass, trees passed by, everything wrapped in a startling, stinging round of pain.

She gasped and sucked in a lungful of air.

"It will be okay," a familiar voice soothed. "We'll get help."

More pain crashed over her. But as Abby breathed in the night air and steeled herself against the discomfort in her leg, she realized the discomfort wasn't life-threatening, and that whatever had happened had merely come as a shock.

"You'll be all right," the voice repeated. *His* voice. The man who was also a Were.

Her wits returned. The landscape wasn't moving. She was, caught up in his arms. The Were carried her. She wasn't out of it enough to fail to realize that she was completely naked, and to remember that she and this guy had just shared a round of mind-numbing sex. Her lungs were filled with his scent. Her mouth felt swollen. Beside the pain in her leg, she ached deep down inside.

Had she passed out? Fainted? If so, it would be a first.

Glancing sideways, Abby saw that *he* was dressed, and that her clothes dangled from his closed fists.

"Put me down." Her voice sounded fairly strong and demanding.

The golden beast stayed infuriatingly silent.

"You forgot my boots," she said without looking up at him. "And I've forgotten the magic word. *Please* put me down."

"It would be better if you directed me where to take you, if that isn't to the closest hospital." He spoke in the same sexy voice that had first roped her in, though it now carried a trace of anxiousness.

"What happened?"

"You've been shot."

"What?"

"You've been shot, and we need to get help. We need that leg bandaged. I can't just set you down if you can't walk out of here. I can't take that chance."

He gave his head a toss to move the glossy curtain of hair that had fallen to cover half of his face. The gesture tweaked another ache deep inside Abby.

"We weren't wrong about this park and what goes on here," he said. "I'm sorry you had to take the brunt of that. You shouldn't have been out here in the first place. Spending any time here…well, both of us should have known better."

Frigging park. She'd actually been shot after making the biggest mistake of her life so far? Was that some sort of Karma?

"Bullet?"

He nodded. "Only grazed."

"Who would do that?"

"The shot was probably meant for me."

That announcement didn't make Abby feel better or provide a clearer picture of what had just happened. She glanced around again, wondering who would shoot at this guy without the onset of a full moon.

She didn't like what came to mind.

Could it be a gang warning them to keep off their turf? Other than that, who prided himself on being a kind of guardian angel for the darker areas of Miami, knowing what sort of things inhabited those places?

Good old Dad.

But Sam Stark and the team in residence this month hadn't mentioned coming out tonight. They had nothing to gain from hurting anyone in human form, and none of them possessed the ability she had to detect species other than their own. There was no reason for the team to hunt. Plus, her father wouldn't have missed a target. As a sharpshooter, Sam's marksmanship was first rate.

Abby turned her head to thoughtfully scan the dark to the east of where they walked.

Couldn't be Sam. Unless her father had in fact been looking for her, and had taken a potshot at the man keeping her from doing her job.

Unless Sam had witnessed the sexual escapade and been angry enough to get that point across.

In that case, maybe her father had meant to hurt her.

She checked out her leg and the raw skin on the outside of her thigh. Blood hadn't pooled there, so it was, in fact, only a graze. Still, it stung like hell, and her nerves hadn't calmed down much.

Can't be Sam.

Nevertheless, she couldn't be entirely sure.

The object of her sexual fantasy continued to hold her. If her father remained in the area and took better aim now, he'd have a twofer. With the next shot, Sam would lose an important piece of his business on the one hand, while bagging a Were with the other, without knowing his daughter's lover was Were. The same beautiful wolf that actually appeared to care about what happened to her, and might even care more than her father did.

How would she explain any of this at a hospital?

"I can walk," she said.

"How fast?"

"Fast enough."

Broad shoulders strained against the fabric of his open shirt. When the Were turned his head, Abby felt tension ruffle through him that made her senses stir uncomfortably.

"We've lost them for now. Too many others patrol the sidelines of this one section of the park for gangbangers to willingly trespass so close to the boulevard," he explained.

"Yet they're not gone."

That remark earned her a sober glance.

"No," he agreed. "They're out there somewhere, waiting."

"For what?"

"Possibly to try another shot, better aimed this time."

"Why would they go after you, if, in fact, they did?" she asked.

"You mean a reason that didn't involve getting lucky with you?"

The remark sounded like forced lightness—an excuse that didn't work, a cover-up that sent Abby's mind into overdrive.

She tried again. "Who are you?"

"Just a guy."

"Oh no. Not just a guy. It doesn't take a genius to know that."

When he didn't respond, Abby said, "Okay. Listen. We don't owe each other anything, like sharing names, phone

numbers or Sunday dinners." She glanced at the surroundings for the source of his nervousness, shoving aside her
own discomfort.

"I don't feel anything remotely like the kind of pathetic
female in need of carting around or being rescued from
her own mistakes," she said. "I can manage a grazed leg."

When he looked at her questioningly, a prickle of fear
underscored Abby's sense of balance. Uncertain about
whether this guy's closeness caused the flutter in her belly,
or if something else wasn't quite right, she gritted her teeth.
The icy chill at the base of her neck brought up a fresh
round of anxiety.

In contrast, the shirt pressed against her hip and shoulder felt soft and silky. Abby recalled all too well the
smoothness of the Were's back beneath it, and how she
had marred that skin with her nails.

Holding up one hand, she saw blood under her fingernails. She remembered the heat-tempered smell of blood
in the air. That had been his blood. Now, the scent of hers
mingled with the memory of his.

Another jolt of pain struck, slightly milder this time
and ending up as a dull, persistent throb that Abby had
to compartmentalize. Danger lurked. They had to get out
of the park.

"Put me down and I'll be on my way. You don't have to
take me anywhere. You aren't responsible for what happened, and don't have to wait around to get to know me
better."

"That's a bit presumptuous, don't you think? Imagining that I'd want to know you better?"

"Actually, I can feel how much you'd like that."

He didn't smile. Though he was hard enough beneath
his jeans for Abby to feel the ongoing state of arousal that
told her how much he might appreciate another round of

death-defying sexual antics on any available surface, the Were's expression was deadly serious.

"Someone's coming," she guessed.

"Yes."

No way could she ask whether that someone was human, or something other than human, because that would let the cat out of the bag regarding her ability to detect Weres.

"I can walk," she repeated. "I promise."

He looked down at her, his face a mask of doubt.

"Promise," she said.

He stopped walking long enough to set her on her feet— reluctantly, Abby thought. Although her leg protested when she put weight on it, luckily it didn't give out.

Grabbing her clothes, ditching the embarrassment of being naked and upright, Abby tugged the T-shirt over her head.

"Who is out there?"

"No one you'd want to meet," he replied.

"I noticed you took the time to get buttoned up."

"Two naked people would have created quite a scene when we reached the street." His eyes met hers. "I hurried."

Upon closer scrutiny, her midnight lover was on guard, his angular features shadowed. He didn't like whatever he sensed in the dark.

"How many are there?" Abby yanked on her pants.

"Enough to make us want to clear out of here as fast as possible."

"So, you actually were trying to get me to safety?"

His sad expression made his face seem older, though no less appealing as he said in the manner of a confession, "What I've done is to let them know about you. I knew better, but you…" He let that fade and started again. "You were a surprise."

Those words dug into Abby's psyche as if there were two meanings inside them, if she could only comprehend.

She felt tense and unable to explain to the Were she'd just thrown caution to the wind with that she knew who and what was out there in the dark as well as he did. She kept tight-lipped about mentioning that she knew about him.

Possibly her father had also been there moments before. Maybe the TTD scoured the area for reasons other than locating her, and had made a mistake. However, the new presence suggested an oncoming storm of Otherness.

Forgetting her recent decision to keep some distance from the creature beside her, Abby leaned against him to button her pants. That simple touch went a long way toward robbing her of what little breath she had left. He was hard, hot and way too good-looking for any decent thoughts to prevail.

"Oh hell!" Pushing away from him, Abby centered her weight. She had to concentrate on the moment, and whether she could really rely on a wounded limb to get her out of there. If so, it would be a miracle.

"Hell, you say? I'll second the sentiment." Her lover grasped her hand. "But I'm not ready to visit the land of fire and brimstone quite yet. And neither, I'm guessing, are you."

"You got that right," Abby solemnly muttered.

Cameron took off at a run, pulling the woman with him, relieved to find out how fast she was and that she wasn't going to question him further or complain.

She kept up, her barefooted stride soundless on the grass and her slender arms pumping. The only evidence of her injury lay in her limp. She breathed heavily through the bruised mouth that he'd have given a lot to kiss again right that minute if he didn't feel responsible for her safety. Thoughts about responsibility made anything having to do with her body off-limits, except getting it the hell out of there.

Four manned-up wolves were on their trail, and had ventured into protected property, potentially drawn by the woman's scent now that he'd sexually enhanced it a thousandfold. Still, it was more likely they were after him for his part in patrolling a place they called their own, with his intent to keep them far from the busy Miami streets. For the past two months, his nightly prowling had created an invisible fence between them and the unsuspecting population.

Were those wolves dangerous? Seemed like it. But what more could happen to him after his last meeting with the fanged-and-clawed crowd? Besides, he'd taken a vow to protect and serve this city, and had to live up to that vow.

Also, at the moment, the need for a quick escape saved him from having a real conversation with the woman beside him.

Although telling her what he did for a day job, his name and rank, might have eased her mind, because people usually trusted cops, confessions at this point might also have made things worse. If regretful of the brief time they'd shared, she could file a complaint. She might cry foul over the same actions she had helped to initiate.

The situation was tricky. What would the department say about his after-hours patrol, on his own time? How would he explain it, when in no way did it make sense to allow his comrades or Internal Affairs a closer look at him or his nocturnal activities?

There were secrets to be kept on both sides of this mistake in the park, and zero chances for a future relationship with the woman he had hold of. The task was to get her to safety, then back off, forgetting wicked thoughts about her sleek, naked thighs and the kind of pleasure he'd discovered between them.

She'd been a distraction only, a kink in his plans. He needed to find other Weres for reasons that went beyond revenge. He needed information about his new state and what he could expect down the road. This park seemed like the only place to find those things.

And, he added in thought with a sideways glance at the woman beside him, the truth was that there had been someone else out here minutes ago. Werewolves, even while in their human skin, seldom used guns, and he'd smelled the metal.

"Are you coming?" he asked.

The woman beside him looked paler, and still limped. Her hair streamed behind her as she ran. She didn't look directly at him. Cameron's heart thudded annoyingly as he gripped her hand tighter.

For the first time since that vow with Miami law enforcement, he felt as though he had more than just a casual stake in the outcome here. Tonight, his investigation and the woman it had brought him felt personal. Was personal.

Racing between a line of young palm trees, a sign of the approaching streets ahead, Cameron chanced another look at his passionate, nameless lover, and found her expression questioning. God bless her sleek little hide, no hint of fear showed on her face—only a kind of steely determination.

She was indeed much more than she seemed. She was, in fact, a tough little thing.

Too bad for us, whoever you are.

Hell of a lot of bad timing here.

In the back of his mind lay the question of whether the immediacy of their connection meant something. The look in her eyes, and the way those eyes had seared into him, suggested there might be more in store.

A nagging suspicion suggested that he had better find out what this connection to her meant and if, after all was said and done, he truly would be able to forget her. In the meantime, because she had sidetracked his intention to capture and interrogate another Were tonight, his personal quest for information about himself had been put on hold.

Chances were good that they'd get off easily and chock tonight's events up to nothing more than a casual, if unusual, event that happened to men and women all the time, all over the world. Casual sex between strangers. Case closed.

Snapping his teeth together so hard that his jaw burned, Cameron said, "Fire up, woman," to the enigmatic female by his side, and increased his pace.

Abby's legs felt weaker than normal and in need of a break. She'd just had a lover between them, and evidence of that was an ache that spread outward from her womb like cracks in a breached wall.

Her breathing was harsh, her chest taxed. Over the sounds she made, she heard their pursuers. At least two of them, and maybe more. These were Weres the one holding on to her didn't want to meet, or didn't want her to meet.

The park was brimming with monsters tonight. The one gripping her hand dialed back his speed after calling for more of it, considerately matching his stride to hers. Leaving him would have been a good idea, if it weren't for the other creatures not far behind that likely had the scent of her bloody leg in their noses.

Every few seconds, she stole a glance at her lover, wondering as she watched his shirttails fly and his bare chest muscles ripple, how anyone on the bad end of society, including his own gene-spliced alternate species, could possibly expect to deal with him in any confrontational circumstance.

She felt the power in him, and had taken some of that power inside her. Remnants of that energy washed over her now, and yet every move he made seemed angled to make him appear human. Nevertheless, could an angel hide its wings for long? Could a devil hide its horns? A werewolf was a werewolf, and she had just been intimate with one.

Oh yeah, and guess what? She had liked it.

"Don't slow down on my account," she said as they rounded a corner. "I can take it."

Her mind clung to the thought that if she had mistakenly accused her father for her wound, and didn't call in soon, Sam would come after her for real—maybe not out of fatherly love for his daughter, but out of a strong business sense. There had never really been much love or admiration between them. Hardly any at all. Actually, none at all.

With her fingers securely curled in the Were's hand, they raced past a brick wall that had seen better days and smelled of moss, finding an alley of palms. Dogs barked behind the tall fences, pinpointing Otherness without having to see it as she and the wolf passed.

Although the uneven earth here made sprinting difficult, Abby was determined to shake the Weres on their trail and remove herself from the picture. She was eager to pretend tonight never happened, and hopeful that the guy next to her would do the same. She had tucked into her mostly boring little life of being an animal control officer by day and a bartender by night.

All for the best.

When she got back to the office, she'd report the bad guys like she was supposed to do and pray that this big, beautiful Were would take his moonlight shift someplace else. She'd be convincing. She would get over this, and forget about him. The grazed leg she'd keep to herself.

Without a hint of warning, her companion slammed to a halt. He spun her around to face him and said soberly, "Go. Now. Don't look back."

"I can…"

"Now." It was a command. "You do know your way? You weren't lost?"

"I know where I am." Abby barely got that out before again feeling his breath on her face. Her eyes closed as his mouth met hers almost angrily, and in the manner of someone who might never get enough of what he'd found. His tongue swept over her teeth, and across her lips. She kissed him back.

Lord help her, this wasn't over. *Can't be over.*

The kiss lasted only seconds before he tore himself away. Letting go of her hand, he gave her a shove.

"Go," he reiterated. Whirling from her, he began walking, not away from the creeps following at a distance, but toward them, with his head lifted and his long stride purposeful.

The sheer weight of his larger-than-life presence filled the night as Abby watched him go. Her heart did not stop its infernal pounding.

Sensing her hesitation, he stopped only once to glance back. Across a span of withered grass their gazes met. He didn't acknowledge a similar reaction to the one that had her reeling, or let on that he felt the same. Blood striped his shirt. Her fingernails had put some of it there. Her injury had done the rest.

Mirroring the twitch that set his shoulders, Abby finally spun around. Without reaching for her phone or making the call that might have sent the team scrambling, and maybe even helped this one lone wolf in the short run, she sprinted for the road.

She'd take no chances. This big Were was nothing she'd be willing to share. He'd be her secret. Her very private secret, added to so many others.

On the plus side, she might have been a fool tonight, but at least she wasn't going to be a dead one.

The TTD motto served her well here.

Live to fight another day.

Chapter 6

Cameron felt himself distancing from normal human perceptions of his surroundings, as though his humanness danced on a last remaining thread of control.

Angling his neck, he heard a crack. Then another. But this wasn't a night for the beast to exert itself to a full extent—at least, as far as he knew. So whoever was out here would be in the same boat, minus the badge tucked inside his pants pocket.

As if he had wished them into existence, the miscreants came around a corner in single file, which would have presented him with an opportunity to gain something of an upper hand in a fight, if it weren't for the fact that they had moved too close to a busy street for a fight to go undetected.

"Are you boys heading in the wrong direction?" he called out.

"What direction would that be?" the shaven-headed guy in front responded.

"Oh, I don't know. Toward trouble, maybe?"

They didn't laugh. Halting a couple yards away and meeting shoulder to shoulder in a united front, as animals in the wild sometimes did when eyeing a potential meal, they studied him impersonally with flat black gazes. The odor of wolf gone bad hung heavily in the air.

Cameron held up his hands and kept his voice light. "Just doing my job. Keeping the streets safe."

The tallest of the gang, wearing a torn white T-shirt and baggy pants, took the initiative. "Why don't you do your job someplace else?"

Cameron shook his head. "No can do. This is my beat."

"You're a cop?"

Cameron shrugged.

"A filthy badge-carrying pig?" The speaker turned to his companions. "I thought I heard him squeal."

The other three gangbangers chuckled on cue, cut off when the lead dog spoke again. "Or was it the girl that squealed?"

Cameron's hands opened and closed, readying for a skirmish. "What girl would that be?"

"The one you let get away. The naked one."

"Well," Cameron said, "I'm wondering what that has to do with you."

"That bitch needs riding. She's been broken in."

Cameron squeezed his hands tighter, sure he felt one claw spring through his fingertip, though that couldn't be right.

"Go home, boys," he said. "There's plenty of help here on the street if I whistle, and I'm sure you have better things to do than wait for what will happen."

"We'll make a deal," the leader of the unholy pack said. "You stay away from this park, and we'll let you off with a warning this time."

"Why? Are you hiding something out there?" Cameron asked.

"That's none of your business. You might be a cop, but we know what else you are. We can spread the word."

"Really? What am I?"

"A freak," the guy said. "And all alone out here most of the time."

Cameron nodded. "Does that make us cousins? Should I feel warm and fuzzy?"

"What you should feel is scared."

"Scared of you?"

"Us, and others like us who can be your worst nightmare."

"Sorry," Cameron said honestly. "My worst nightmare has already come and gone."

He realized someone was approaching from the street behind him before he had finished the statement. An authoritative voice rang out. "Is there trouble here?"

Recognizing the voice, Cameron called back, "Davidson, is that you?"

"Mitchell? Yeah, it's me. Stegman is in the cruiser. Do we need to call him?"

Cameron eyed the pack of animals that looked at the moment like any Miami southside street gang with too much attitude. He smiled. "So, what will it be, boys? A truce, for tonight?"

"That would be a shame," the tall guy replied. "Because I really feel like fighting, and the odds are in our favor."

"The odds, I think, will be slim, since cops also carry guns."

The big dog waved the suggestion away. "It just so happens that we eat guns for breakfast."

Cameron nodded. "We'll do some damage, though. I'm sure your pals here will agree that you might want to take your games elsewhere."

"We don't play games," the lead dog snapped.

"Then maybe you should consider it," Cameron warned, though it became obvious by the way the gang advanced, and the way they simultaneously reached for whatever they had tucked into their waistbands, that the damn hybrid idiots weren't going to take his advice.

Davidson, a veteran cop and as smart as cops came, trotted around the corner. The poor guy had no idea what was in store, or that Miami could actually produce something worse than a street gang claiming public territory for their own.

If Cameron's claws weren't aching to spring a full night ahead of time, he might have been able to warn his badge-carrying brother of the danger ahead. But he looked down at his hands to make sure the sensation wasn't real as the mindless Were pack barreled forward with the force of a battering ram.

Chapter 7

Cameron leaned up against a warm wood-paneled wall and scanned the room with half-closed eyes. The night outside those walls called to him. His skin twitched in reaction to the light floating through the open doorway. Answering that call was imperative, as soon as he could.

Like most pubs in Miami, the room around him was dim and smoky with an undercurrent of sweat and booze and too many men crammed into a small space. The odors fermented in his system, making breathing difficult.

He counted fourteen law enforcement officers in the crowd, plus a handful of detectives. Seven of those in attendance he knew by name; the others weren't associated with his beat. The rest of the bar's occupants were regulars, by the looks of things, and quite at home in the well-worn ambiance of the place. He, on the other hand, was a carefully managed mass of nerves.

Each of the men in his party were on their fourth or fifth raised glasses in honor of a fallen comrade named Stegman, the victim of the ongoing war between law enforcement and raunchy street gangs on the south side. That's what they thought, anyway.

All of them had patted the shoulder of the man who had been responsible for taking their comrade's killers down. Cameron's shoulder. The shoulder aching to be free of shirts and praise and small indoor spaces because something far more primitive than the almost-constant hunt for bad guys existed outside the bar's walls. *Moonlight.*

Madame Moon was full tonight and whispering to him like a lover. She taunted him mercilessly with the call of the wild, and he had to maintain a calm outward appearance at the moment, despite his growing anxiety. But centered within the chaos of his life rose a spiraling vortex of insatiable longing for freedom and for the chill of silvery light on hot, bare skin. Hunger had become a ravenous beast in itself, unpredictable and always insatiable.

"Hey, Mitchell!"

A creased-faced, gray-haired officer who went by the name of T. Garrison gave Cameron a friendly punch to the left biceps. Cameron smiled and touched his arm as if the guy had a powerful swing.

"We owe you for what you did. Davidson told us the story of how you chased those guys." Garrison gestured exuberantly. "Next drink is on me. So is the one after that."

In their off-duty drinking, these guys were doing justice to multiple bottles of fine Irish whiskey. Cops took care of their own, seriously mourning their fallen brothers and realizing every day that they might be the ones never to make it home from work.

They cared. Cameron sure as hell had to give them that. But he didn't feel like a hero and preferred not to be treated like one. He had done what he had to do to keep a lot of people safe, and had, with Davidson's help, removed four messed-up thugs from the mix. The only good thing here was that Davidson hadn't known what they really were.

Like most of these guys on the force, he did his job—just in a slightly different way, with extra hours and the added bonus of special senses. Still, he hadn't been able to save the man they were toasting. He couldn't tell anyone in this room what those gangbangers really stood for, and what they'd had in mind when they'd geared up for a fight.

And here, in the crowded bar, fewer than twenty-four hours later, Cameron felt claustrophobic.

"Barmaid," Garrison shouted. "Another round for this man."

Though Cameron smiled his thanks, he hardly heard the offer. A fresh scent rode the breeze by the door, causing his surroundings to blur, taking Garrison's friendly face out of focus. When added to the blistering heat of the summer night and the fall of light crossing the threshold, the fragrance came across as being something important to identify, something familiar and heady.

Roses. Also another scent that stirred Cameron's baser instincts as he inhaled deeply and looked around the room for the source—a search that stopped near the long length of gleaming mahogany wood across from him.

Cameron's heart gave a thump that he felt all the way to his boots. His wolf gave a whine that twisted his gut. Not quite sure if he could be imagining this, or if one beer had been one too many, he blinked and took a second look, his insides roaring, adrenaline surging.

Female pheromones, light as dandelion fuzz and seductively alluring, rode the room's darker male buzz. Those pheromones came from the female standing behind the bar. Not just any female, either. Oh no.

A riot of mixed emotions hit him all at once, as did an

instantaneous pulse of interest. Blinking slowly, Cameron choked back a growl of surprise.

Of all the bars in the world… Hell, he had walked into *hers*.

What are you doing here?
Get out.
Go away.

Abby had noticed him the minute he'd entered the building, and reacted with a grunt of stunned surprise.

Among the crowd of cops and detectives jammed into every corner of floor space, she perceived the big Were as intensely as if he was still inside her, on their hands and knees in the grass.

Swearing out loud, she doubled over to recuperate, repeating unladylike oaths several times more. This had to be a dream. Her worst nightmare. The Were whose name everyone here chanted couldn't possibly forget the sight or scent of the woman he'd called his little wolf in a moment of shared passion. She hadn't been able to get him out of her mind for one single minute.

Above the heads of the others, his height stood out. His unnaturally good looks caused her heart to stutter, as those looks had the first time she'd set eyes on him. This second sighting didn't lessen the impact. Her thighs quivered uncontrollably. The space between those thighs thrummed as if interior body parts were warming up for a repeat of their mutual sexual assault.

He was there, ten feet away.

The big bad wolf had found her.

Unsure of what to do, Abby feared that any move might give her anxiousness away. But she couldn't tear her gaze from him.

"Damn. You're a cop?"

His hair, too long for a cop's usual tidy look, kept her

from viewing his face clearly—that incredibly, inhumanly beautiful face that had been like a sucker punch to her solar plexus.

And the body.

God, that body.

His taut bareness had been tight up against hers, hard, willing, and slick with sweat from the exertion of their mindless coupling.

"You can't be here. Not now."

He wore black and white tonight, another bit of irony that paralleled his hybrid state. A crisp white long-sleeved shirt hugged his chest. Black jeans perfectly defined his incredible physique. Again, his shirtsleeves were casually rolled up over his forearms, showing off some of the corded strength she had tested firsthand.

She saw no evidence of the blood that had marked him the night before, or signs of cuts and bruises signifying the fight he must have been headed for after pushing her away. Yet tonight he soaked up accolades for having been part of something big that had happened after she left him.

A Were and a cop.

How could that happen?

She felt dizzy with the realization that he stood under the same roof. As she continued to stare, the passing moments seemed suspended from time.

Cameron Mitchell. She mouthed the name, remembering the taste of his wolfish Otherness and the exquisite talent of his mouth and body. His job might have explained his presence in the park, but how about his willingness to take her on there? Sex in a public place wasn't a usual cop routine, she was fairly sure, and could, in fact, get him sacked.

So, had the chances he'd taken been instigated by a simple slip of morals, or by the wolf curled up inside him? Without a full moon over their heads, had Cameron

Mitchell's animal side required him to let off steam in a sexual way?

What about her part in that?

Abby finally managed to look around at the rest of the sea of faces. She recognized a few. Though the Miami PD often frequented this bar, *he* had never been here, and shouldn't have been there tonight for reasons beyond her own embarrassment. Her father mingled with the regulars, three stalwart hunters among them. The back room held guns and rounds of ammunition that no wolf pack could withstand.

If Sam and his hunters somehow knew about the Were in their midst…if her father saw her reaction to him, or something she did gave this Were away, the game would be on.

The moon was full tonight.

That goddamn moon.

As far as she knew, there would be no way for a werewolf to avoid it. Silver light would suck the wolf right out of its nesting place and make that wolf prowl.

Bad news.

She chanced another glace at Cameron, so bloody perfect from head to boot. Though her acting skills were decent, she doubted they'd get her through this. Already, her breath was ragged and forced, and her pulse soared. She hadn't slept or eaten since her return from the park the night before. Her injured thigh, bandaged tightly beneath her jeans, throbbed like a son-of-a-gun.

She was about to lose it, and had to get away from him soon.

Trembling hands made her drop a glass, which earned her a frown from her father. She smiled back at Sam and shrugged, knowing she couldn't afford to draw more attention to herself. On this night, both Cameron Mitchell and Sam Stark played at being one of the boys.

The energy in the room was high, and escalating. The cops in attendance were well on their way to becoming sodden. Hunters eagerly awaited the midnight hour so they could get their kicks. And Cameron Mitchell wasn't as human as he looked.

Abby scanned the doorway, where moonlight streamed across the threshold. More light seeped through slats in the shuttered windows. These things were catnip for wolves, and also a kind of perpetual poison. And it seemed obvious, by the swiftness of her own reactions, that she wasn't immune from either thing—that bloated moon, or the creature across the room that now stared back at her as if he'd seen a ghost.

Yes, it's me. So what?

She'd been made, found, identified. Turmoil churned inside her, souring her surroundings. With this incredible Were's presence breaking through what defenses she had left, the only viable option she had was to scurry away and hide. And he wasn't going to allow that. His eyes made that quite clear.

Setting her cleaning cloth down, Abby met those eyes. A rush of adrenaline pounded through her. Leftover sparks that had never fully died out sent waves of inexcusable lust for him coursing through body parts he had already conquered as the intensity of the inexplicable connection to him resurrected within her.

Her breasts strained at her shirt, taut and aching. Her panties moistened with the desire to again have him inside her.

Turning from the sight of him, breaking eye contact, Abby stepped toward the hatch in the bar, ignoring a patron calling her name. When she looked back, *he* was beside her, having moved too quickly with nonhuman reflexes.

"Abby," he said in a casual voice that took her by surprise. "Nice name."

Gold eyes, darker indoors but no less bright or piercing, waited for her to again find them. Tightness closed around Abby's heart. Her throat went dry.

How, she thought fleetingly, hadn't anyone else noticed his unusual eyes?

"I'm sorry." Her gaze dropped to the mouth that had simultaneously tortured and pleasured her. "Do I know you?"

"Maybe not. But it's still a nice name."

Damn him. The memory of his lips nipping at hers threatened to get the best of her, as did the recall of his first thrust into her accepting, malleable body. In the forefront of her mind sat an acknowledgment of his appetite for passion that had seriously moved things inside her.

Abby moaned softly.

"I've been looking for you." His tone had turned unbearably intimate.

"All of your life?" she countered wryly, her pulse banging in time with some distant, inaudible beat.

"You never told me your name."

"You never asked."

"Or where you live."

"So now you know."

Seconds of silence passed, loaded with tension.

"I searched for you all day, covering most of the bars on the west side."

She had mentioned working in a bar. Thankfully, he hadn't noticed the logo on her shirt. Did that mean fate had brought him here, or just plain old bad luck that a downed cop's friends had chosen this place to honor their comrade?

Abby waved at the crowd. "I hear kudos are due for your nocturnal heroics."

He didn't reply. He wasn't the type to brag.

Abby lowered her voice. "You found the guys following us?"

"Ah, so you do know me."

She gave him a serious look.

He nodded. "I did find them."

"They didn't hurt you?"

"I've covered up the battle scars. Another cop wasn't so lucky."

She said with a sorry attempt to modulate her tone, hoping her aggravating breathlessness wouldn't show, "Why did you search for me when the deal was to move on?"

"I didn't know we had a deal."

"Then you terribly underestimated me."

Abby had the feeling he wasn't saying half of what went through his mind. Then again, neither did she. She was two for two on the danger scale, and quickly upping the ante.

"Would you like to talk, Abby?"

"Isn't that what we're doing?"

"Abby," he said again, as if tasting the name.

Though she felt a throb begin at the base of her spine in anticipation of what he might say next, Cameron Mitchell didn't follow with anything important. In fact, he allowed her a few seconds to get a grip on herself instead of the edge of the bar.

Abby tried to center herself. Grinding her teeth together to keep from shouting, she pressed both hands over her hips to smooth not only her shirt but also the twitching body beneath it—reactions that were a complete giveaway as to his effect on her.

"Well, here I am," she said. "What now?"

"We talk in private. That's a start."

"You're a hero, and these guys want to be with you tonight."

A hero and a gentleman. An irresistible combination.

"You're resistant," he observed.

"I'm trying to ignore you, and you're not making it easy."

He said nothing and continued to study her.

"There were two of you out there?" She wet her lips with the tip of her tongue before biting down with her teeth on the lower one.

"Three, in the end, when other cops arrived," he said.

"And you were doing your job by watching the park. It actually was a real job?"

"Yes."

"I'm sorry," she said, "for what happened. That other cop was a friend of yours?"

"I consider all of them friends."

Abby acknowledged that response with an inclination of her head, and waved at the door. "You'll be back out there tonight?"

Moonlight is what you'll need. Your secret is out.

"I'm out there nearly every night," he confessed. "Working overtime has become a habit on nights when I can't sleep."

"But not in uniform. You didn't wear one last night, and you're not wearing one now."

"I'm on my own time."

"Patrolling that park to look for bad guys, alone, increases the odds of getting hurt," she pointed out.

"Maybe. It is, however, a necessity."

He had answered hesitantly, as though he had disclosed more of his secret than he'd meant to. Abby supposed that everything he said could be taken two ways, because this was a creature straddling both worlds. Cameron Mitchell had one foot in this one, and the other foot someplace foreign, and straight out of myth. Would any purely human soul truly be able to understand what that felt like?

Would Sam, if he knew that a Were could be a cop?

Abby wanted to shout out to her father that Cameron Mitchell was one of the good guys, after all. The fact that there really were good Weres was a validation of her former theory that now made her feel sick.

How many others like Cameron Mitchell had her father's team captured unquestioningly with the shoot-on-sight method of hunting? Had Sam ever taken the time to find out?

"Some of the people in this bar will also be out there tonight," Abby said meaningfully.

How much could she give away with Sam looking on?

"Guys who aren't cops, but have a similar agenda."

Had Cameron understood her cryptic remark? He glanced at the crowd over his shoulder.

"Possibly more of them than you know," Abby cautioned. "For reasons other than the reasons you might expect."

A secret in return for a secret. He'd go away and avoid the park tonight, and she'd only have to live in private with the fact of what she had done the night before, with him.

Did this veiled warning to him about the danger in this room fall under the category of helpful werewolf hints?

"You're not talking about yourself, I hope." An edge of concern returned to Cameron's voice as he turned back to her. "You wouldn't go outside on a night like this?"

"Nope. I'm not in need of another good lay, since the last one was decent enough to last me awhile."

Cameron Mitchell studied her openly, blatantly, not caring if anyone noticed. His face showed no emotion. His tone was carefully managed. "Meet me in an hour."

"No." Abby slammed a glass down on the bar. With all the noise going on, no one in the crowded room paid attention. Each successive round of drinks meant that voices got louder. More people had come in, blocking Sam's view of her flushed face.

She couldn't breathe.

"Meet me," Cameron Mitchell repeated.

"Bite me," Abby whispered. "Oh, wait, you did that already, plus a whole lot more."

He seemed to think over her remark. She expected a growling reply that didn't come, and let loose a sigh of exasperation. She was sweating, a sign of her body rebelling against this test of her willpower. She fielded the urge to hurdle the bar and either jump into this Were's talented lap, or sprint for the door. High drama either way. Endless trouble.

He wasn't helping. He caused her internal chaos.

No. That wasn't exactly true. She had brought this on herself, by being unable to resist him last night.

No way she was going to find out what he would be like tonight when moonlight hit him, though—the same moonlight she had always detested for its role in twisting monsters out of their napping places. Moonlight that also had the power to affect her in strangely personal ways that she would not dare mention to the wolf across from her.

Nor would she be clearer about the danger awaiting this Were tonight. Sam had a lot of friends, a couple of them nearing where she stood transfixed by a creature they had hard-ons to hunt.

Her lips moved, though she wasn't sure what she'd say until she heard it. "It's quite ironic, you know, that you've come to the one bar in Miami that you should have avoided at all costs."

As Cameron Mitchell searched her face in a replay of his riveted attention of the night before, Abby counted her heartbeats without having to press a finger to her neck. The suspense of this meeting mounted. Emotions flowed as if a tap had been left open. She felt anger, fear, love, hate, longing and lust—all there at once as this man's eyes continued to hold her hostage. His gaze was both fire and ice, disconcerting and suggestive, taunting and sympathetic. His golden eyes were equally strange, and utterly familiar.

"I know what you are," she said.

That surprised him. The mouth that had pleasured her so completely and adeptly nearly twenty-four hours earlier opened. But he didn't speak. Instead, he carefully scanned the room before returning his attention to her. Then he raised an eyebrow questioningly.

"I knew last night what you are," Abby said. "I knew what followed us out there, and what those gangbangers who killed your friend really were."

The room seemed to darken once she'd gotten that out. Movement slowed. Voices dulled to a background murmur. None of that was real, though, and only the effect of meeting this wolf again so soon, and in less than stellar circumstances.

Did she want to speak to him of things beyond this terse confession? Yes. In another minute, though, her father would come over to see why she hadn't filled orders, and who this guy was. If luck was with her, after one look at his daughter—at the pink face and the visible quakes—Sam might merely assume her to be ill, and cut her some slack.

Or else he might put two and two together and come up with *wolf.*

Swiping at the trickle of perspiration sliding down the side of her face, Abby wondered what would happen until then. Possibly another standoff between Cameron Mitchell and herself?

She felt so damn hot. And the wolf who was a badge-carrying member of the Miami PD had gone mute.

More than any of that, the thing she feared more than all the guns in Miami lay just past that doorway, up in the sky. Like a giant magnet, the moon whispered to her as though she were one of the moon's cult, and as though that light ruled what flowed in her veins to some minor degree.

"Abby."

She tossed her hair, unwilling to listen to anything her

one-night stand had to say. The dilemma of what to do next was an excruciating one. If she stayed still, the hammer would fall. Being near to this Were made it too difficult to keep herself in line.

She felt jazzed, wired up—not all of that due to the fact that she had toyed with a wolf and was dealing with the consequences. The bigger fact here was that she had been scouting for Weres for so long, she might have started to feel like a wolf herself.

"All right," Cameron said, his voice low, his tone inquisitive. "You know I'm a cop. I should have told you last night. The circumstances were…"

Abby interrupted, shaking her head, meeting his eyes. "Wolf," she whispered.

His eyes widened. A frown creased his brow.

"You are a goddamn werewolf, Officer Mitchell," she said. "How's that for insight?"

Chapter 8

The way his expression changed gave Abby no pleasure. It made her sicker.

"You have to get out of here," she said, following up on her announcement. "Not all of these guys are your friends. This bar also hosts people who hope to be your executioners. Hunters. Werewolf hunters."

Cameron didn't blink, grin or laugh outright. Neither did he protest what might have seemed to ninety-eight percent of the people in Miami like an outlandishly ridiculous statement. Instead, he rested his hand on hers, on the bar, and the shock of his touch ripped through Abby all over again.

She was going to drown in that touch.

"Yes. Okay." She drew her hand away. "Part of this is my fault. You tried to push me away. I know that. My resistance was low because I'd been looking for you for a very long time."

"Looking for me?" he said.

"Someone like you."

"What do you think you know, Abby?"

"Plenty. So do the hunters."

He had to know what effect he had on women, and what they would want from him, she thought. Going through life looking the way he did had to attract women in droves. Factor the hidden wolf vibe into the rest of his molded perfection, and no female in heat would stand a chance.

This cop was trouble, and she had opened her legs to let it in. But she had come to her senses. This, for obvious reasons, would never work out.

People in the room had shifted position. Meeting her father's sideways glance, Abby tried to smile back. Her elevated body temperature had become a nuisance. Her sleeveless shirt felt damp. Sam had a keen eye for those kinds of reactions in her. If this continued, she'd have no recourse but to either escape or give this wolf up to the team.

Yet if she ran, and this particular cop followed her, Cameron Mitchell's human semblance, his recognizable outline, would burn away—fried to a crisp and turned inside out before coagulating into a new creation. *What then?* she longed to demand of Cameron. *Will you remain a gentleman?*

This was irony at its best. Her will wanted one thing, and her body another. One dangerous dalliance in the night, and this werewolf had rendered her permanently under his spell.

What could be worse? They were surrounded by officers in this bar who had no idea what went on beyond the realms of their imagination, and were in close proximity to her father, who might have been a hair away from realizing what stood under his roof. For Sam Stark, having a daughter lust after a wolf would be the ultimate sacrilege. Mind-blowing stuff.

What she needed was a dark hole to crawl into.

"Officer Cameron Mitchell." Testing her voice, Abby looked up at him. "Not only one of Miami's finest, but one of the city's best-kept secrets."

The next sound she made came perilously close to being a gasp of despair.

"We need that talk, Abby." His comment seemed devoid of the emotion tearing her apart. "Agree to meet me in an hour. You pick the place."

Officer Mitchell, king of beasts, again rested his hand close to the one she used to brace herself against the bar. Abby counted the inches between their fingers. Hers were shaking. Any second now, she'd fail at this terrible calmness game. If he touched her again, it would be over.

"Abby, look at me. Who knows? Who else knows what you think you know?"

She couldn't have answered if she'd wanted to. She was all choked up.

He persisted. "Which of the men present tonight know about what you called me? Who did you tell?"

"I can't say anything else."

Cameron was too close, too hot, too wolf. She desired all of those things, all over again. Mostly, though, she wanted him to live.

Forget him. Escape. Run.

Those were useless thoughts, since she couldn't escape from herself and her feelings.

Sensing her father watching, waves of chills rolled through her heat. Abby sucked in a lungful of the bar's stale air and blinked to get her bearings. As she saw it, there was only one way out of this.

Raising her hand, she slapped Cameron's lovely face hard with her open palm. With the same hand, she shoved aside the glasses lined up in front of her and said loudly,

"I don't think so, but thanks all the same, Officer Mitchell. I'm taking my break."

Unable to think about what she was leaving behind, hoping her father would chock this little scene up to a rebuffed attempt for a drunken stranger to get to know her better, Abby rounded the bar, waited until her father had turned away, then ran for the door.

Cameron started after her with his heart in his throat.

The little idiot had left the pub and had run right into the street. Cars rushed past. Tourists strolled by. She didn't seem to care.

A big hand stopped him before he got to the sidewalk. The hand belonged to a detective he didn't know, one he'd missed in the crowd since he hadn't been paying attention to anything other than Abby.

How the hell had he missed this, though?

"You're not leaving?"

Wolf vibe reverberated through his arm from his shoulder on down, and so fiercely, Cameron checked a rising growl. His insides immediately scrambled. Like loaded switchblades, his claws sliced through his balled-up fingertips until he forced his wolf down.

This detective stopping him was Were.

Jesus, there were others like him on the force.

Rather than easing up, the detective kept hold of Cameron's arm with a grip like steel. Each second that passed as they faced each other transferred a dizzying array of indecipherable wolf messages to Cameron's confused brain.

Not only Were, his senses told him; this guy had known the word *Were* for a while, and wore that species easily.

The detective was tall, with brown hair that curled over his ears and a pair of intense, deep-set eyes. He had a deceptively lean build, and wore a black T-shirt, jeans that had seen better days, a beat-up leather jacket, in spite of the heat, and had a shiny gold badge pinned to his belt.

A werewolf detective. Cameron hadn't imagined this. It's what he had been looking for, hoping for. Like him, there were other good guys.

He wanted to clap the guy on the back, and shake his hand. A hundred questions needed answers, and this detective probably had some of them. But his attention went to the door Abby had run out of as if she'd left a trail of breadcrumbs impossible for his hunger to resist.

The compulsion to go after her tore at him, stronger than any bond he needed to make with a like-minded wolf. And though he had no idea why, or what it meant, he knew his need for wolf company had to be put on hold, at least temporarily, until he found Abby again.

Affixing a wary smile on his face, Cameron shrugged. "I've got a date. Something nice after all this."

"Ah." The detective's eyes brightened as if he understood completely. "Now that is a worthy excuse for leaving the party."

"Nothing else could tempt me away."

"Well, then go to it, man. And give her a kiss for me."

Cameron's grin had already slipped. The emotions tied to seeing Abby again, right that minute, were making his senses go haywire. Being so close to another male Were doubled the current dilemma.

"Mitchell," he said to the detective eyeing him closely. "Name's Cameron Mitchell."

The detective nodded and responded in kind. "Matt Wilson. Homicide."

"I have to go," Cameron said.

"I can see that," Matt Wilson remarked. "I assume we will meet again soon. Until then, you will take care? We wouldn't want any more trouble tonight."

"I'll be sure to do that. And, Detective?"

"Yes?"

"Watch yourself in here. I'm told that, besides us, other things in this bar aren't what they seem."

The detective's eyes reflected his acceptance of that piece of information as Cameron pushed past him.

On the street, just outside the building's front door, moonlight hit Cameron in the face, sending shudders of anxiousness through his system. Grimly, he dived for the shade of the awning, fighting the urge to rip off the clothes that would be a hindrance to a much larger shape.

Catching sight of Abby in the distance, he muttered a choice, official, police-regulation well-accepted four-letter word. Setting off at a brisk pace, weaving in and out of the people lining the sidewalks while keeping beneath overhead cover, he followed Abby, waiting until he reached an old line of trees before daring to unbutton his shirt.

I know what you are. Her words rang in his mind. *I knew last night.*

Moonlight slanted through branches, adhering to his bare chest and burning like gelled fire. After the first loud crack of overstretched sinew, his vision began to narrow. But he held on to his human shape with every ounce of willpower he possessed, knowing this would be what Abby needed to see.

Half a block ahead and moving west, Abby appeared as no more than a dark outline. Gaining on her, Cameron called out, "Abby. Stop. Wait."

By refusing to look back or slow down, she made it quite clear that she wasn't going to listen. Cameron prayed that he'd be able to hold off on the imminent shift a while longer, but running felt good, and chasing Abby felt even better. Wolf was in the air and in his throat, coating his insides, seeking to be free.

He tried again to reach Abby. "Talk to me, damn it!"

She turned a corner. When he reached the old stucco

wall near that intersection, Cameron saw a puddle of black draped on an open trash can. It was her shirt. Farther down the alley, he found her shoes—sandals, covered in an animal print.

Abby, what are you thinking? What are you doing?

Upping his pace, Cameron's anger began to simmer. He'd barely had the time to properly handle his own problems, let alone taking on hers, and it was obvious that she not only had her own issues, but didn't want anything to do with him.

Well, all right. If she preferred things this way, so be it. He'd leave her alone. He would go back and find that damn detective. Clearly, what she'd said in the bar bothered him in a way he just didn't get. She had known about him all along...and had been intimate with him, anyway?

Did that make her nuts? Completely off her rocker?

Maybe she had made up all that stuff about the other people in the bar.

Werewolf hunters. There actually were such things? And with two Weres present in the crowd, plus a room full of Miami's finest?

It was possible, he supposed, for that place to be a hangout for another kind of criminal, one he hadn't anticipated. Hell, killing werewolves wasn't illegal, since hardly anyone knew of their existence.

"Abby, how are you involved with those kinds of people?"

Remembering the streak of wildness he'd seen in her, picturing the short-handled silver knife strapped to her leg, Cameron again swore out loud. "You're a wolf hunter, and that's why you were in the park."

The realization kicked at his stomach, impossibly painful.

He added aloud, "That's ridiculous. If you knew about

me, for real, you wouldn't have met me out there. You wouldn't have dared to..."

Cameron couldn't finish that statement. Logical thinking had flown out the window, pushed along by questions that swirled so fast he couldn't pick one out of the bunch. But it was no wonder that Abby didn't want him to catch up with her. Having sex with a Were had to be the biggest mistake of her life. A seriously unforgivable faux pas for a hunter.

"So, why did you do it?"

Let her go, you idiot. You can smell trouble, and she's at the epicenter.

His wolf pressed against him with a fierce rebuttal. One sharp claw sprang from his index finger, and this time Cameron didn't bother to tuck it back. He wasn't fooling anyone with the would-should-could-haves. He had to catch Abby. For whatever reason, and despite solid arguments to the contrary, he had to see her again. He had to kiss her again.

Hearing the first crack of vertebrae, Cameron fought against the impending change. "No freaking time for that!"

After dealing with Abby and what she might know, he'd find that detective what's-his-name. Wilson.

Matt Wilson.

His alternate world was closing in, but Abby's scent got stronger, picked up by the wolf parts of him about to take over. She had tossed to the ground a fragile, lacy piece of clothing that she hadn't worn the night before. A dainty black bra with thin ribbon straps lay curled up near his feet, looking like a line in the sand that he couldn't afford to cross.

That lacy thing further messed with his resolve to remain in human form. Every man, he told himself, would have been an animal with a thing like that in his sights.

"Abby," he whispered, having a fair idea of where she'd

go. He also had an uneasy feeling that perhaps she didn't shun him at all, and the discarded clothes were indeed a detailed map meant to lure him along. If so, he might have sorely underestimated Abby.

Then again…

No. It couldn't be.

The other reason for shedding her clothes didn't need to show itself. The theory suggesting that, like him, Abby needed the room and freedom of being without clothes in order for her wolf to take over.

Cameron nearly stopped dead. His head swam with thoughts.

Hellfire, if there was any conceivable way he might have been right about her during their first meeting when he'd called her his little wolf, Abby also had a secret that could get her killed tonight with hunters and wolves on the loose.

Was that why she had coupled with him in the park? It was a case of like attracted to like? Two animals sniffing around each other?

Absurd.

What kind of werewolf hunter had wolf particles in her bloodstream?

But the more he thought about it, the more viable that theory became, until Cameron wanted to hit something, anything—a tree, trash can or the side of a brick building. Still, emotion had to be kept under control in public. It was a sure bet he wasn't the only beast on Miami's crowded sidewalks. If he and Wilson could blend in with normal people and go virtually undetected, then werewolves could be anybody and anywhere.

One of them could be Abby Stark.

Icy prickles washed over Cameron, producing a gut-wrenching desire to drop his human shape and get on with it. Shafts of moonlight laced the ground everywhere he looked, and he hadn't completely mastered the ability to manage the beast in taxing situations. He'd only dealt with this fucking problem for a few long months.

"In the thick of it now, Bud. Welcome to your new life."

After reaching to pick up Abby's underclothes, Cameron jumped the curb. Leaving the relative safety of the shadows of the buildings, he sprinted along the pathway she'd taken that led back to the park, hoping with every fiber of his being that he would find her before the moon truly found him.

Chapter 9

"**M**ust. Get. Away."

Abby couldn't get enough air into her lungs, and wondered if she ever would. If she stopped running, she'd have to face Cameron Mitchell again. Tonight, she'd see what the moon did to him. Tonight, her father would be in killing mode.

The moon seemed closer than usual, but not large enough for the kind of damage it would inflict. Streams of light lit the way from the street to the park, urging her on.

She ran from tree to tree in a zigzag pattern, hoping to avoid being tracked by others, knowing Cameron could easily catch up, getting away from the hunter-infested bar.

Because of the diligence of her escape route, he also might be able to beat the lure of cascading moonlight until he had cleared the streets. At the very least, she owed him that for helping her last night to get out of the way of some very bad guys. The horror was that someone else had died in her place.

The question on the table now was whether she actually wanted him to find her, or if it was enough to have lured him away from danger.

Terrified, and trying to ignore the gnawing in her stomach, she felt Cameron's wolf stirring within him as strongly as if it stirred inside her. In their moments of intimacy, and like a wicked sort of contagion, some of his wolf had to have been transferred to her.

Her unspoken protests over this tumbled and roared as her mind jumped from idea to idea. As crazy as it seemed, she thought she felt the beating of his heart inside her chest—much slower than hers and equally as irregular.

Her muscles began to contract, causing her to stumble. Squeezed nerve endings erupted with high-pitched whines. Soft grunts and groans escaped through her open mouth, loud in the relative quiet of the area of the park she'd chosen for her hiding place.

"No one in their right mind comes here."

Cameron Mitchell had agreed with that assessment last night, and he would know.

Reaching the narrow pathway between the houses of the rich and famous, Abby sighed with relief. No more crowds. Not one hint of a car in the distance. The trees here slowed the shed of the moon's silver rain, though not quite enough to stall the inevitable for long, for any wolf.

Will you find me before you shift, Cameron?

She would let him find her.

An angry sound rent the darkness. It took seconds to understand that she had uttered a strangled cry.

The dark atmosphere of the park engulfed her as she slowed her pace. Cameron's unmistakable presence closed in from behind and she nearly called out for him to turn around, and to beware. This area had been okay in the past, but felt wrong tonight. Totally, inescapably *wrong*.

She felt wrong.

The first snap of overstretched ligaments in her shoulders struck without warning. Searing shivers of pain moved through her like messages being passed across old-fashioned telephone wires, temporarily sidelining any attempt to move on.

With both hands on the old block wall, Abby felt an icy dab of moonlight on the back of her neck. Robbed of breath, she sank to her knees. Kneeling in the grass with her head lowered, she awaited the inevitable. "Find me, damn you, if that's what I deserve."

Strong hands yanked her upright. Tossed against the wall, hitting it so hard the last bit of air in her lungs rushed out, Abby felt a warm body press close. The angry touch she had expected didn't come. Neither did the questions she would have asked in his place. Gentle fingers brushed the hair back from her face. Familiar breath wafted across her lips with an impossible lightness in the midst of a rolling dark.

"I'm here," he said.

His voice. *His* body. She would have known him anywhere, in any circumstance, with her eyes closed.

Cameron had shoved her out of the light. Her heart matched his heart's amped-up beat as he massaged her underlying fear with his tone.

"Abby. Listen. You don't need to be afraid of me. I won't hurt you. I haven't come here to harm you."

"I…know."

Her vocal cords weren't working properly. Abby faced the beautiful Were with her eyes half-closed.

"Did you hear me, Abby?"

"Yes."

"Do you believe me? Can you talk?"

"In a minute. Need some air."

"I'm not sure we have a minute, if what you said is

true about the people in the bar. There are things I have to know, like what you think."

Reckoning time had arrived for her, along with a familiar fleeting thought that if Sam knew about this meeting with Cameron, as well as the last one, her life would be over.

But Cameron was here beside her. Cameron was a cop, not a monster.

She dared to voice the truth.

"I don't understand it. Never have understood," she said, looking at the naked skin of Cameron's chest. "I just know you, and others like you."

"Are you saying that you're able to recognize Otherness?"

She nodded.

"And that you know what we are? What I am?"

She nodded again.

"Okay." He spoke slower, gripped her tighter. "What about those people back at the bar? Are they after people like me? Is that what you were trying to tell me?"

"Hunters come there each month to party. You didn't know? Didn't you smell the odor of death on them? They are a universal killing machine."

Tension spread to his voice. "You used the term *werewolf hunters*."

"That's what they are. Hunters, intent on your kind."

"If there are such things, it would mean other people are aware of our existence."

"Plenty of them," she said.

Cameron Mitchell paused before speaking again. "What do they do with that knowledge, Abby? How much do they know? Do they see what you see?"

Out of a million questions, Abby picked one to address. "They see nothing I don't point out. They count on me to tell them about Weres."

"What?"

"I'm the one with the connection to your kind. I find you, and then I tell the hunters where to look."

Echoes of her confession tightened her stomach now that she had glimpsed more details about the so-called enemy, and this one in particular. He was so damn fine. His eyes were bright in the shadows.

Just then, as the night pressed in, and Cameron Mitchell along with it, Abby became fully aware of her bareness, and the fact that Cameron hadn't mentioned that.

They were temporarily hidden from the moonlight, crammed into the space where two walls merged, and yet the moon lit everything beyond their tiny puddle of shadow. Abby breathed in that light and spit it back out. A warning signal buried inside her mind suggested that the light was trying to reach her, and that if she moved back into it, moonlight would change everything.

Maybe, though, she just empathetically sensed Cameron's imminent transformation. His muscles were twitching. His body temp rang in at about a million degrees.

She had no option for avoiding his penetrating gaze, and sensed his ability to see right down into her soul. She struggled to block him from finding out about her secret longing for his kind, hoping he couldn't taste that secret the way she tasted his.

"It's not safe here," she warned.

There were so many ways to take this warning, which had been meant as much for herself as for him. The prickle of fear plaguing her announced that something was amiss, and that by encountering more moonlight straight-on, a bad thing might happen to her. She'd spent years dreading whatever that bad thing might be, never willing to find out. That's why she had avoided full moons, and why she needed to avoid this one tonight. The secrets she withheld had already gained in stature and weight, growing larger with each new breath.

She felt wolfish standing next to Cameron, but had always felt a little bit like that. Did she actually want to be a wolf, like Cameron? Is that what she wanted, down deep? Was she capable of it?

"Explain, Abby, why you..." Cameron began.

"I can't. That's the truth. I don't know what's happening to me, or how I know what you are. I'm not sure I want to know."

She kept her eyes locked to his. "How did this happen to you? *What* happened to you?"

"I was bitten in a fight."

"You weren't like this before? Weren't always a wolf?"

He shook his head. "The bite broke the bones in my arm and tore vessels to shreds."

"Did you get help? Did anyone help you?" She was desperate for answers that would prove him an ally, and no future adversary.

"I didn't believe in werewolves, Abby. I didn't know they existed. But I saw this guy's teeth, and his claws, and knew it wasn't Halloween. Because of the blood loss, I was taken to the hospital, where a suspicious doctor patched me up and then told me to go home. I now believe that doctor might have been something other than fully human and that for my own good he subtly advised me to get away from that hospital."

Abby didn't want to hear more, but was fascinated by his story. He'd been bitten. He'd had this happen to him. It wasn't his fault. Cameron had been a good guy in a rotten situation. This kind of thing hadn't been addressed by Sam Stark, either, whose theory was that once bitten, the man became a mindless monster.

"Is being a wolf bad?" she managed to ask. "How bad?"

"I'm here," he said. "I deal daily with a situation that might have had a worse outcome."

Her shaking had gotten worse, and Abby couldn't make it stop. Cameron Mitchell's body against hers didn't prevent more tremors from attacking, or keep the light-headedness away. Her chest felt tight. Her ribs ached. The waistband of her jeans inhibited all prospects of the deep breaths she needed to fill her lungs.

"Get…them…off me," she said, her voice hoarse.

The Were's face was close. She wanted him to kiss her, turn her into a wolf, take her away from all this. Anything to stop the plague of questions.

"What, Abby? Get what off you?"

"Clothes. Pants. *Please.*" Abby forced those words out, wriggling in Cameron's grip, wondering if his continued nearness might push her toward the answers she had been avoiding.

This Were had affected her in a new way. Meeting him again tonight served to emphasize and amplify her connection to him.

"Abby, I don't understand."

"Back off!"

He didn't oblige. Instead, he drew closer to her, placing his hands on the wall beside her to form a cage of formidable muscle and bone. One of those arms had been ripped apart by a bad wolf's teeth and claws. He had recovered, with serious consequences.

For a second—a fleeting tick of time that might have gone on forever for all she knew—Abby closed her eyes and rested her face against his chest, giving in to the impulse to be with him, and become like him if she had to.

Then she rocked back, hitting her head on the wall, gasping in surprise. Her ears filled with a roar—the roar of the return of the forbidden longing to possess Cameron Mitchell and be possessed in return. The longing to tear at him, devour him, mate with him over and over, no matter what the rest of the world might think.

Her eyelids fluttered from the strain of holding herself back. Her lips parted. "Help me."

Cameron's fingertip, sharp with an exposed claw, forced her chin upward. Sick with the sight of that claw, Abby nevertheless looked into his eyes. In silence they rode out the buzz of an electrical charge sealing the bond that firmly united them. The harshness of their breathing was the only noise in an otherwise quiet night.

Then Cameron kissed her.

He kissed her as if he needed to hurt her and love her simultaneously, and as if he'd pull the secrets out of her one by one.

He kissed her, letting her know that he alone had the power to face those secrets head-on and understand. It was a wet, smoldering kiss, utterly demanding and without letup. An angry action, almost painful, but also beautifully satisfying.

His mouth merged with hers, directed hers, taking and giving back, nipping, sucking, licking. He kissed her as if he'd eat her alive, consume her completely, and as though nothing less might do. Because nothing less would.

But the moment had been stolen, and was in the end merely a fleeting escape from everything else. When her lover stepped back, taking her with him, moonlight covered Abby's head and shoulders like a mantle of silver cloth. Light also covered him, and each angle of his exquisite face, highlighting the shadows beneath his eyes.

Chills swept over Abby's feverish skin. Those same chills covered Cameron's smooth bronzed flesh.

"Little wolf," he repeated. "No mistake."

Those were the only words Cameron got out before the luminous gold eyes became the only recognizable feature in a moving mass of muscle and sinew, and the man who was about to morph into something else entirely acted on her last request by slicing her jeans to shreds.

The woman beside him stared with an expression of terror and curiosity. No fidgeting. No running away. Nothing but the slightest sagging of her legs before she caught herself.

She stood there, not only naked from the waist up, but thanks to his claws, mostly naked from the waist down. Her breasts glistened with a fine sheen of sweat, lifting with each breath she took. Cameron wanted his mouth on her, on those breasts. His wolf gave an expectant shudder.

Her pants had been reduced to lengths of denim fringe attached to a waistband sitting low across her narrow hips. He remembered the pleasures of her concave belly and the jutting angle of her bones. Abby was lean and hard, defiant and brave, but not unyielding.

He could have her there. Take her right then. On the ground or against a tree, he could bury himself in her blistering depths, and she'd allow it, want it, want him. And that was a miracle.

A wink of silver caught his eye, tearing his attention away from Abby's perfection and temporarily holding his human shape together. The knife she had carried the night before was strapped low on her calf, its hilt gleaming faintly with an almost demonic glow. He had learned quickly about the destructive properties of silver. Without a shape-shift or the presence of a full moon, he still loathed to touch that particular metal. Seeing such a weapon tied to Abby's leg seemed like one small barrier between them.

She had to feel the chill of that silver blade. Abby, whether or not she knew it, was a wolf as yet unformed. Everything pointed to that fact. Already, without the pants, she breathed easier. The tight elastic bandage encasing one of her thighs and smelling like antiseptic and old blood didn't seem to bother her.

Wolfish growls echoed inside Cameron's chest as he contemplated his need to possess her. That had to be all right. His recognition of Abby's unborn wolf had to have been what cemented them together so completely. The moon had given them a blessing.

Little wolf...

Abby's secret reacted to his coming-out party. Though her body didn't shift, wolf light shone in her eyes as she dealt with a system that wanted to change, but didn't yet know how to go about it. Wolf was the source of her exquisite heat and her craving for freedom. It was the reason she desired him.

Have I done this to you?

Have I kicked your secret into the present, making the world a more dangerous place for you to be?

Though she shook, she continued to meet his eyes, perhaps unable to turn away from what she was seeing up close.

"Abby."

He shoved her back against the wall, freezing his human form with the utmost willpower, and tore aside her underwear. He was inside her before her next rattled breath, delving into her with his hands on her bare thighs and a knee between her legs.

His jeans brushed across her hips with a swish of fabric on bareness. The wall scratched her back. But that first thrust wasn't deep enough. He hadn't yet reached what he wanted to find.

Supporting her with his weight, he lifted one of her legs, breathing the magnitude of his desire into her mouth, receiving a mutual silent cry of need from Abby.

"It's still not enough. Can't you see this, Abby?"

She must have understood, because she wrapped that

sleek leg around him in a replay of the night before. She opened for him, biting his cheek when his mouth retreated for the slightest intake of air.

Her hips began to move, angling forward to meet each plunge he made with a cock so hard, it hurt. As his fervor to reach her sweet spot increased, sounds of pleasure bubbled up from her throat.

"Take me in, Abby. That's it. Let me in."

The only way he could stop this was if someone beat him off her. Within the petals of her hot, damp sex, he found an alarming sense of peace. A place for him. A homecoming.

Sure he'd lost his mind, Cameron stroked her heat over and over until she gave in that final, significant way, surrendering to the bond, to the connection, to this and to him.

The ecstasy made him howl with his lips crushed to hers. Breathing into her and taking in her breath in return, he reached the core of Abby Stark. They came in unison with explosive, shuddering orgasms that rocked them both and left him reeling.

Locked in Abby's embrace, buried deep inside her body, Cameron felt his wolf rear up. Riding the high of exquisite ecstasy, his wolf hurtled toward the surface where it refused to fade back, and could no longer be contained.

"Okay," he said to Abby. "Okay. This is me."

He had only time to set her on her feet, and loathed the coolness of the air that circulated between them, before the fire in his chest again spread upward into his shoulders, and trails of sparks tripped overstretched fibers.

Ligaments began to stretch in the usual order of neck, shoulders, chest, hips, legs, making sounds like elastic snapping against hot, wet flesh. Pain exploded in an abominable flash as his shoulders realigned and both knees buckled.

His stomach heaved up a roar. His spine cracked. Acute

distress accompanied this morph, because the joining of man and wolf probably wasn't supposed to exist in nature, and pain was nature's way of rebelling.

Who the hell knew why such a thing had ever taken place, or been allowed in the grand scheme of things from the start?

"This is me, Abby," Cameron repeated as his face began to burn with a pain reminiscent of being poked in both eyes. Cheekbones cracked and rearranged. His neck thickened with a chorus of vertebral chatter. Leg muscles elongated. Expanding chest muscles pulled at his rib cage.

Although the shift had gotten slightly faster with each passing moon, it took minutes more for the rest of his bones to settle into their new shape. When they did, he glanced down to see random patches of light brown hair sprouting on his chest and arms.

Hell and damnation, he would never get used to this.

He was a man, redefined. Not an animal on all fours with a fur coat, but a man-wolf combination with the man's mind intact—upright on two legs, with more muscle and acute senses than anything else on the planet.

His jeans were too tight, but he didn't discard them. The thickness of his skin felt strange. Body parts that hadn't already been hard for Abby now hardened. The hair on his head lengthened, and swept across his broadening shoulders. Inside his mouth were teeth that made claws seem like child's play, and bloodied his lips.

Cameron straightened up to his full new height and let loose of a long, low howl. Feeling imminently alive, he tuned in to his surroundings and the woman standing in front of him who, it turned out, wasn't really completely human at all. This was a female out of her element who had allowed him a glimpse into intimacy and real physical closeness, things he had lacked for so damn long.

And she, Abby, with a little wolf trapped inside her body, gave a responding growl when his shudders ceased.

Panic.

Thrill.

She stood there, watching. She hadn't moved.

Her eyes were wide and watery, her face paler than pale. More questions lay in her expression, the answers to them lost without his human voice. He had left that voice behind.

And…

She. Stood. There.

Anxiety rolled off Abby in great cresting waves. She held her breath. She didn't blink. He had the distinct feeling that she blamed him for her present predicament and her unearthly desires, without realizing that she must have possessed a wolf all along. Possibly this blame game had been why she had run from him tonight.

I don't know how this happened, Abby. I swear.

Admittedly, and without knowing for sure, he might have unwittingly unlocked her wolf with sex, but he hadn't been the one who spliced wolf into her DNA in the first place. *Someone else has done that.*

No ring of teeth marks showed on her flawless flesh, and yet something in her bloodstream dictated her new direction. He knew that part of her realized this, but how much?

Like recognizing like, Abby. That's what this is.

It's the source of our connection. The root of our desires.

He detected no scent of wolf saliva that might suggest a recent bite from a rogue, and which would have urged a wolf to blossom with the first full moon. Minus those bite and scratch marks, a family member must have put her wolf there. Given that fact, eventually the wolf bits would have been tripped, whether or not he had met her.

So, with no bites, what did that leave? Genetics?

Hell, he wasn't sure that inheriting the virus was possible. If it could be passed along that way, and he hadn't done this to her, why did he feel so damn guilty facing her now?

He howled again, releasing the awful tension of the moment.

How can you not have a clue about your own background?

Who are your parents? What are they?

He couldn't apologize for something they both had wanted. A transition in reverse was out of the realm of possibility, since a reversal was always tougher, and left him quite ill. However, he considered it because Abby acted as if she had been broadsided by witnessing his shape-shift.

This seemed unreasonable. Surely someone would have told her what to expect if they knew what she kept hidden inside?

Unless no one else knew.

When she moaned, Cameron's heart went out to her. He couldn't put his arms around her in a shape like this. He could not touch her.

The dark beast that had taken him over noticed a disturbance in the surroundings. A flare of anger raged through him for the distraction. His beast's intuition battered at him as if it truly was a separate entity and knew something the man didn't.

He whipped his head around to scan the dark.

What's wrong with this picture?

What is out there?

The answer came like a flash of unwelcome headlights.

Visitor.

Chapter 10

There was no time to stare, shout or break down into a mass of trembling emotion. As soon as Abby had heard the first snap of Cameron's bones, torrents of pain arrived, nearly breaking her in two and bringing in pain's wake an unbelievable few moments of understanding.

When his bones realigned, Abby felt as though each and every bone in her body reacted simultaneously.

When his shoulders widened and his chest expanded, tearing apart his bronzed flesh and pushing torn muscles and everything else in his system way beyond their limits, her body responded with a pounding, pulsating agony so forceful and complete she could not even scream.

The terrible agony went on and on until she barely controlled the need to hurl. But the excruciating pain did have an end. When it eased and the feelings of sickness passed, a full-blown werewolf stood beside her—huge, daunting, scary as heck.

Cameron, the wolf.

Fright careened through her. Abby looked down at her body, expecting the worst. But she had not changed. Miraculously, though her insides had felt tortured, she looked the same as she always did.

Chills arrived in droves. With them came an immediate amendment of that last thought. She wasn't the same, and would never be the same again. No one having experienced the slightest bit of what a Were's morph felt like could imagine a werewolf enjoyed it. Only a true monster would look forward to the effects of a full moon on a mostly human system.

Abby looked up, and into the werewolf's eyes. They were Cameron Mitchell's gold eyes. The light of intelligence shone from them. Colorful and dilated, they remained expressive and sympathetic that she had witnessed what he had become.

God. This was the creature Sam hunted, and what her scouting had helped Sam and his team to capture in the past. These kind, concerned eyes could have been similar to what lay in those other werewolf faces.

"How could I have known?" she whispered. "Why doesn't anyone know the truth about you?"

Cameron hadn't lost himself to the beast he shared a body with. Hints of him were there in the shape of the jaw, his height and the grace of every slight movement, including the tilt of his head. Cameron was a true hybrid—half and half. Not in the least bit crazed. No mindless monster.

Abby suddenly wanted to take it all back—all the scouting and lectures forced upon her, the brainwashing and the part she had played in Sam's schemes. It was, of course, too late.

Cameron's head turned toward the trees.

"I'm sorry," Abby said.

He glanced at her.

"So very sorry."

His attention moved. His muscles undulated.

"Who is it?" Her question came out faint. Any new-comer might be the wrong one. Someone approached, and with her senses still reeling, she wasn't sure if it was a wolf or a man. It could very well be Sam, or another member of his team out there.

"They will kill you." She choked out those words through a constricted throat. "Do you have any idea what kind of damage a silver bullet can do to a wolf? Just one bullet? Well, they have an endless supply."

All Weres had to know about the destructive proper-ties of silver. Cameron had known about her knife. She had to get him away from this spot, and somehow give Sam the slip.

Ducking under Cameron's arms, reluctant to lose the comfort and terror of his heat, she said, "We're sitting ducks here, ripe for the plucking." She feared that moving wouldn't increase their odds of survival by much.

"Got to move, wolf."

Daring to leave him, she crept along the base of the wall beside her like a burglar, skirting the moonlight, hating the moonlight. Reaching for her knife, she found the hilt too hot for her gloveless fingers to handle, and guessed that the effects of Cameron's shift still lingered inside her body.

Every few feet she traveled away from him hurt as badly as the tearing of his flesh had. Being separated from him made her feel as if she were dying inch by inch, because he was the closest thing to getting the answers she had always needed about herself. At that moment, she felt like a part of him, torn from the whole, and no longer fully human.

Of course, he wasn't going to let her go. She counted on that.

Without knowing what lay behind and what those hunt-ers actually intended to do to him, Cameron's desire to protect her overruled thoughts of his own health. Quickly catching up, he pulled her back to him easily with his greater size and bulk.

"We can't stand still. They will find us here," Abby warned.

The werewolf shook his head.

"Sam's been wrong in assuming anything. How many innocent Weres has his team killed, along with the bad? How many police officers and emergency-room doctors and construction workers did he take down, whose only problems were falling prey to the moon?"

She barely got the next part out. "I know there are bad wolves. I've read about the human-and-wolf carnage in and around the city. But I didn't know about you, and those who might be like you. You have to believe that. Sam probably doesn't know, either, and truthfully, I'm not sure he'd care to find out."

Soundlessly, Cameron crossed in front of her, waiting to make sure she'd follow. Abby's nerves buzzed faintly with his closeness. In a place inside her, deep down below the surface, her need for him remained strong.

"They will separate and spread out," she said.

At least she knew something about the hunters' routine.

"They'll hope to encircle their prey in the same way a wolf pack might. It isn't only the wolves in this park that are giving off an ominous vibe. It's what has come to find them."

And they'll find you, my beautiful wolf.

I can't have that. I won't allow that to happen.

Close on Cameron's heels, Abby followed. He walked fast, leading the way as if he knew where to go to outdistance the gathering storm. As a cop who had routinely patrolled this park, he probably did have a good idea about hiding places. Abby hoped so, anyway, until he paused to sniff the air.

The hair on the nape of her neck stood up. Inhaling, Abby smelled it, too—a body, close by.

"Officer Mitchell."

An unrecognizable male voice broke the silence, the suddenness of it making Cameron's ears ring.

"I wondered if you might need assistance?"

Stiffening, Cameron lunged to stand in front of Abby. His heart pounded. He raised his hands, ten claws fully extended.

The man who had spoken remained in the shadows of a large tree to their right, just a dark spot in a moonlit landscape.

"There's always trouble brewing," that man went on. "We cleared most of the parks of this kind of nonsense last year, but this one just keeps ticking."

"Who are you?" Abby pushed past Cameron.

"A friend."

"To Cameron, or to me?"

"That depends."

"Prove it," she challenged.

"Gladly, if you can first assure me you're not affiliated with the other people out here tonight."

Cameron glanced back and forth from the shadows to Abby, whose face remained bloodless.

"Well?" the man said.

"I don't owe you anything," she replied. "Not even an introduction."

"I thought so. Mitchell, I suggest you let Miss Stark go, and come with me."

Cameron went rigid with a buildup of anger and resentment for the whole damn night and what was going on. But he lowered his hands. The scent of the new guy told him who this was. Detective Matt Wilson. From the bar.

"If I get closer, I'll lose anonymity," Wilson said. "That

might be a very dangerous state around you, Miss Stark. So, you're either going to let Mitchell go on his merry way, with me, or be the cause of what might happen to all of us if we wait here for your associates to find us. Are you willing to take that chance?"

Cameron growled his frustration with this line of reasoning. The detective didn't seem to be aware of what Abby might be going through, and that Cameron didn't have it in him to leave her to face a possible first confrontation with her wolf alone.

No one deserved that.

But she hadn't shifted yet. Possibly Abby truly had only an inkling about what was going on inside her, but maybe not a full-fledged inkling. Although the moon was the brightest he had ever seen it, her body had withstood the urge to blend.

"I have friends nearby," Detective Wilson explained. "Unfortunately, Miss Stark has friends, too, and they are closing in. It's likely they won't harm her. You, Mitchell, are a prime target. Hell, I can see the bull's-eye painted on your back from here, and I'm wondering if Miss Stark helped to put it there."

Cameron took a step toward the shadows, his chest rumbling with sounds he did not utter.

"Time is short," Detective Wilson said to him. "It's your choice. But I'd remind you that I can help, and am willing to do so."

Abby moved. Cameron wasn't entirely certain that she'd be able to get anywhere on her own, or if the people she had alluded to as hunters would resist shooting first, before identifying themselves, and hit Abby by mistake, going after anything that moved. She'd been injured out here once already.

"Go," she said soberly, facing him. "I'll be okay."

He contemplated visiting the shadows to shed the wolf's

outline and regain the use of his voice, but as he turned, familiar sounds rushed in, along with Abby's sudden breath of astonishment.

The detective Cameron had met at the bar that night cleared the shadows as he began to transform. The shift happened incredibly fast, in seconds, and as though the detective had fluid body parts well used to rearranging. A formidable werewolf with dark brown fur stood on the edge of the grass, eyes flashing, teeth bared. Wilson hadn't been kidding around. The situation had turned deadly serious.

But then Wilson did a strangely human thing. He tossed his leather jacket to Abby and gestured for her to cover herself up.

"Shit," he heard Abby say as she backed up without taking her eye off the newcomer. "Another good one."

"Get out of here," Abby warned, glancing around. "Now."

God, yes, there were two werewolves facing her. The new wolf on the block didn't seem like a mindless criminal, either. He knew Cameron.

"I don't hunt," she said, needing to get that off her chest. "I don't like it when anyone else does, except that someone has to clean up this hole of a park and others like it."

She backed up several more steps, knowing she'd have to sprint in the opposite direction when she wanted to follow these wolves.

She was shaky, sure, but she'd recover and find a way to deal with Sam and the team if they found her. Somehow, she had to try to tell Sam about these two, and the possibility of others like them. But it would be a big giveaway if she did that now. It would let Sam know how close she'd gotten to the enemy. Sam wasn't partial to new slants on understanding. He'd punish her for breaking the rules.

Nevertheless, a lesson had been learned here, and it was a big one. Two out of two werewolves in one night turning out to be decent individuals were odds that went against everything Sam had preached. And though she had never bought it all, she had not anticipated this kind of turnaround.

Despite the decent shakeup, a quick comeback on her part was an absolute necessity. "I won't tell them. They won't hurt me because they need me. Now get lost."

Beneath the intensity of Cameron's wolf-eyed gaze, Abby felt like hanging her head. "Okay. So you know about me now. I tried to warn you. I tried to get you away from Sam. It's the best I could do, since I didn't actually want to get away from you at all."

I don't want to go back.

Don't want to face what happens tonight.

Did the beautiful man who was also a man-wolf combination hear her thoughts and understand? He hadn't moved. His attention didn't waver until the other wolf growled a warning that made him visibly uncomfortable. Like the new guy, Cameron bared his teeth.

Abby had to tear herself away. Danger rode the night, and she'd played a part in that. The chances of getting out of the park without meeting up with a hunter were dismal, yet she knew the park a lot better than the new guys Sam had brought here to indulge in tonight's full moon gaming.

With a hand to her forehead, Abby saluted the big, fully transformed werewolves. Spinning on both heels, she took off in the direction of the bar, swallowing the guilt of having been brainwashed by her father all this time, and hating being separated from the one wolf who had been about to show her something important about herself.

"How will I find you again?" she muttered as she ran. "Will I find you again after this, or will it be too dangerous?"

The werewolves didn't follow her. Moonlight did, though she tracked to the west to avoid it. One eerie howl in the distance, a sound that echoed in the park, seemed a response to her softly spoken questions.

"Maybe you will find me," she said.

Darting along on the pathway close to the walls, half-naked and wearing a stranger's leather coat, she hoped the hunters wouldn't stumble upon her. They had to have heard that howl.

She started to run. But as bad luck would have it, she didn't get far.

Chapter 11

Cameron raced alongside Wilson, considering the direction the brown wolf had taken, setting that path in mental databanks all cops possessed. He ached to turn around, didn't like leaving Abby at the mercy of whatever lay behind in the dark.

Detective Werewolf seemed to know exactly where he was headed. The massive park spanned blocks to their right, lit by nothing but moonlight. Taking out streetlights and park lights was a good deal for criminals wishing to hide dark deeds, and the city crews just couldn't keep up with new bulbs.

Vigilante. Abby had used that word when they'd first met, and Cameron supposed that's exactly what he had become. But who was better suited for going after werewolves that were up to no good than one of the same species? Who else had the strength to confront them?

He'd tried his damnedest to keep other cops on the outskirts of this park. What had happened to Stegman hadn't been pretty. He would always remember that, and that a Were's ability to speed the healing process made them almost indestructible in the long run, and more willing to face down an adversary. Add a little mental instability to the criminal werewolf soup, and the result was a pack with the ability to be every cop's worst dream.

So, what about Matt Wilson, his current guide? It was obvious that the detective not only knew his way around this area, but also knew about the hunters. Wilson hadn't seemed surprised when Cameron had told him to watch his back in the bar.

Wilson knew about Abby. He had to. If a new wolf like himself perceived the wolf in her, a more complex version of Were must have easily picked up on the thing huddled inside her.

Who the hell was this Wilson guy, anyway? It was a damn shame that furred-up werewolves couldn't ask questions.

I'm sorry, Abby had said. Because she found Weres for the hunters.

He and Wilson ran, over the grass and between the trees. The detective's T-shirt had been a good choice. Black and stretchy, it handled the pile-up of Were muscle while providing good camouflage. His own white shirt had to be like a flash of neon out here to onlookers. Unbuttoned, the shirt flapped open, hitting his sides as he ran and allowing him room to breathe.

Breathing was good.

Though the detective had said there was a target painted on Cameron's back, losing the shirt didn't seem like such a good idea. He had no idea where they'd end up, or what might happen when they got there. But he longed to be free of all restrictions. His wolf liked to let it all hang out.

Wilson proved himself to be fast on his feet. Cameron worked to keep up as the brown Were sprinted over unused pathways without bothering to give Cameron a glance, probably confident in his leadership skills.

Should he trust this guy?

Could he trust anybody with a secret that needed constant protection?

The route Wilson chose ran north after skirting the winding alleys of brick and block walls. He didn't head for the streets. Instead, after barreling through a narrow maze of high walls, Wilson finally veered toward one of those walls, leaped up onto it with the agility of an orangutan, and waited there, outlined by moonlight that showed off his massive size and mounds of flexing muscle.

With a running jump, Cameron followed.

They walked along the top of that wall for a short distance before Wilson gestured to him and dropped into a yard on the other side. Landing beside the brown wolf in a crouch, with his hands on the ground and his head lifted, Cameron saw a small stucco outbuilding close by, lit by yellow lamplight.

Wilson loped toward that building as though the word *home* had been etched there in invisible ink. But the place had a strange flavor to it, and a thick, fragrant scent pervaded the night.

Other than having been exposed to the wolves of the criminal pack, Cameron had never come across anything like the feel of this place. The small building in front of him and the area surrounding it housed more than one wolf, for sure. Had Matt Wilson from Miami Metro's Homicide division brought him to the home turf of a werewolf pack?

His head spun with shocked thoughts of how many more Weres there could possibly be in Miami.

The question now was whether this pack would turn out to be friends, or foes.

* * *

"Hold it right there."

Sam Stark, dressed in black from his cap to his boots, slid in front of Abby. His prematurely gray hair glinted in the moonlight as he spun her around.

Abby hated what Sam might be thinking.

"What the hell are you doing here, Abby?"

"I got caught."

Lying would be the only way out of this. She'd have to save the information dump and the chastisement of his actions for later. The trick at the moment would be getting Sam to believe her invented tale, so that he'd leave her alone.

"Got too close," she said. That much was true.

Sam brought her closer with a sharp snap of one arm. "Too close to what?"

"Them." The weakness in her voice had to be a side effect of oxygen debt. She was winded.

Sam's tone lowered. "One of the monsters did this to you? Out here?" His scrutiny became feral. "It didn't…"

"It only shredded my pants. I ditched the shirt because it had their filthy claw marks all over it."

Her shudders were real, and convincing.

Sam's right hand grasped the front of the leather jacket. "What's this?"

"One of the cops tossed it to me." *Also the truth.*

After looking around, Sam's attention returned with the intensity of a hungry hawk. "What cop? Where is he?"

"I didn't get his name. He helped me, and chased them off. I think he went for backup."

"Shit, Abby. We don't need cops out here tonight. You know that."

When Sam moved his hand, the jacket creaked with the sound of soft, worn leather and emitted a familiar musky, masculine scent Abby preferred not to inhale too deeply.

"What did he see, girl? That cop?"

"Nothing, other than me running away and looking like this. I told him some jerks tore my clothes to humiliate me, and that I escaped."

She had seen the expression Sam now wore a hundred times or more. His wide face creased. Pale blue eyes narrowed. "Why were you out here?"

Words failed her. When confronted with the full force of her father's moody inquisition, the lies seemed flimsy in explaining her presence in the park on the night Sam's hunters prowled. She had never come along, and this point was bound to be a stickler for Sam.

"Maybe you met that cop from the wake at the bar, the one pestering you? You didn't come back in. Did he follow you?"

"No one followed me. I made sure of that."

Sam wasn't going for it.

"I didn't go through the park, Sam. Wolves were skimming the street, not far off the boulevard."

That got his attention. Sam's expression changed to reflect his displeasure over that information. His cell phone came out of a pocket quickly. He punched a button and barked one word. "West."

To Abby he issued a second command. "Get back. Close things up. Take a shower and make sure you don't have one single visible mark on you. Stay inside. I'll deal with you later."

Taking off with his gun drawn, he said over his shoulder, "You should have known better than to come out tonight. Damn it, girl, haven't I taught you anything?"

Then he was gone.

Abby thought seriously about sitting down, right there behind Sam's disappearing back, and without a care as to who else roamed beneath the treacherous moonlight. She

held back the urge to shout "Yeah. Thanks for the concern, Dad."

She wasn't really sure what he had meant with the cryptic warnings, other than to suggest that if she had been bitten or scratched, she might become one of the creatures
Sam despised. That's the way Cameron had been infected.

Well, it was too damn late for worrying about that.

Or…possibly Sam had meant that after all this time of
tension between father and daughter, he'd finally have a
justifiable reason to be rid of her if she again ignored a direct order. He hadn't even tried to hide his anger.

Thank heavens he hadn't noticed the bandage on her
thigh.

A potent impulse came to think of better things. Only
one came to mind: an image of a golden-bronze werewolf with eyes like fire—a picture etched in her mind
and seared into her system. She had seen Cameron shape-
shift. She had observed it all, felt it all…Cameron's features twisting in pain. His body suffering greatly. Chills
returned with the memory of the sound of his realigning
bones.

In spite of that terrible event and the weakness in her
knees, and after witnessing two Weres emerging from the
shadows in full wolfed-up glory, Abby stood where Sam
had left her, scanning the dark. With her heart tapping out
a ferocious rhythm and her limbs restless, she looked up
at last, into the light.

"Damn it, Sam." The words came slowly, and with effort. "You're a fool, and you know nothing."

Two people rose from creaking wicker chairs when Matt
Wilson reached the porch attached to the building he obviously knew well. One of those people—male, tall, with
the chiseled features of a Viking and blond hair that fell to

his shoulders—cautioned the woman beside him to hold back with a slight lift of one hand.

Cameron's gaze moved to the woman. Small, and light of bone, her hair was the first thing he noticed. It was very dark brown, almost black, and hung halfway to her waist in a sleek mass that picked up the moonlight when she turned her head. Her eyes were big, her skin olive. She was dressed in black.

Cameron caught the scent. Both of these people were Weres.

"Wilson. We've been waiting," the fair-haired man said.

Wilson leaped onto the porch, taking the steps three at a time. As soon as he landed beside the two others, his reversal began, the shift as smooth as if Wilson were made of swirling liquid instead of muscle and bone. The cracks and snaps of muscle and sinew didn't startle the other two people, because neither of them was human.

Cameron cringed as Wilson's face reverted to its angular human features. When Wilson rolled his shoulders, ridding himself of a last bit of stiffness, the detective said, "They're out again tonight."

The other man nodded without taking his attention from Cameron. "And who is this?"

"His name's Mitchell. Cop."

The fair-haired Were nodded. "Is Mitchell the first name, or the last?"

Wilson waved Cameron forward. "He can answer that one himself in a minute."

Yeah, he might be able to talk in a few seconds, if he was Wilson. And just who were these people?

He didn't relish changing shape in front of strangers. He had a hard enough time dealing with the pain of a reversal on his own.

Wilson, apparently possessing the ability to read minds,

said, "Excuse us, Mitchell. You probably need some space. Come with me and you'll get it."

The detective led the way around the side of the building, which looked to be some kind of watch station or a decent-size guard gate for a mansion that may or may not be hidden in the distance. That's the impression Cameron got, anyway. It seemed to him that the two Weres on the porch were keeping track of things and awaiting Wilson's word on…what? Things that lay beyond the relative security of that eight-foot wall? Information on the hunters? Picking up stray Weres in the moonlight?

Though he was stunned by the fact that there were more creatures like him, and not at all sure about where Wilson had brought him, Cameron supposed that any Were in the area that had been around awhile sporting a fur coat had to know about the hunters, which proved that as a new wolf, he had a lot of catching up to do.

"You coming?" Wilson said over his shoulder.

These Weres appeared to be friendly enough. At least they hadn't tossed him back over the wall. Yet. Surely, though, as wolves, they'd want to get off that porch and into the moonlight. They would seek the light that seeped into them with its seductive silvery call.

Maybe they took turns.

"Mitchell. This way."

Cameron temporarily gave up the attempt to see through things and ended up beside Matt Wilson in a small yard. A solid roof of crossed beams and tile shingles lay to his right, as a temporary respite from the light.

Cameron's body shivered in reaction to the enclosed space, which put him immediately on guard.

"It's private," Wilson explained from under that roof, seeming once again to have mind-reading tendencies. "There are other places, but for now this is safer. I thought you might like to be near the cottage. The area is protected around here. Trust me on that, if nothing else. Sam Stark and his hunters don't have a clue about what goes on behind this particular wall, and wouldn't like what they found if they nosed around where they were unwelcome."

After turning to go, Wilson paused. "She's one of them, you know. Always has been." Then he disappeared around a corner, leaving Cameron to think this over without the addition of strange, prying eyes.

He saw clearly that Wilson possessed information he needed. In order to get it, he had to be able to talk. In order to take Wilson up on the offer of hospitality, he'd have to stay for a while.

Gritting his canines, Cameron's lids fluttered closed. Without Wilson's presence, the walled area seemed as remote as another universe. Still, shifting in close proximity to the others felt like the ultimate perversion. Like sharing something too personal. Like doing something truly unnatural in a natural world. And it was a lot like exposing himself, naked, in a crowd.

The wolf's hypersensitivity immediately noted the dimensions of the space and where the exits were located. Wolf knew how many inches from the light he needed to be in order to refuse the moon's call, and didn't like what Cameron was going to do.

But it really was necessary.

With a violent intake of breath, Cameron shed the negatives of the situation and willed himself inward. Straining with every ounce of willpower he possessed, he pulled his muscles into a state of overstrung tightness.

Patches of fur began to suck inward through his pores, tickling nerve endings before getting serious about pain. His shoulder muscles fired up and started to sting. More fire spread along the back of his neck, spilling onto his upper back and chest. Each bone of his spine became a hot, glowing coal as it began the compression process.

Limbs quaked with a series of rocking convulsions until standing upright became difficult. Breath was cut off as a rush of sickness rose up from his twisted, churning gut, only to get stuck in his seizing throat.

Flinging his arms wide to shake off the wolf, Cameron slowly began to feel more like himself, but the beat of the wolf's heart, amped by strain, continued for minutes, hard and steady and fast. He was uncertain, and out of his element.

He turned his thoughts to benign normal things. Unwolfish things. The feel of his crisp uniform at work. His face in the mirror. The comfort of his home, and the cleansing gift of a long, cool shower. The meditative images began to work. His heartbeat finally calmed, descending on a sliding scale until he remembered something else: a pair of emerald-green eyes meeting his, and piling fire on top of fire.

Abby.

He saw her as if she were there. Her pale body in the moonlight. The long legs and bare chest. The puckered nipples he hadn't gotten to sample, and the feel of the hot triangle of fur between her legs that had seduced him into forgetting himself and his agenda.

Near the finale of this absurd transformation, his body craved hers with an intensity so far out of bounds as to be totally uncontrollable.

Abby.

She made him feel beastly.

Damn it, he had to lose those thoughts about her. In order to process what was going on, he had to be able to think straight, and memories of Abby Stark didn't help. From these three Weres, he'd find out about werewolves and their deal with the moon. Finally, he would get to ask about what had really happened to him and how to move forward.

With a last-ditch battle between breath and willpower, Cameron finally tamed the beast. Popping sounds ceased. Pain eased back to a more neutral and acceptable territory. His face bones melted back to normal with one last sting.

But his craving for Abby Stark didn't dissipate when the wolf did. That craving got a whole lot worse.

Pressing the hair back from his face, then rubbing his forehead with clawless fingers, Cameron waited nervously in the new surroundings. An almost nonexistent breeze ruffled through his hair. He heard the scrape of chairs on wooden floorboards. Somewhere out there, pretty far away, a howl went up. Was it a sound of wildness? Joy? Hatred? Happiness or despair? Could hybrid humans ever be truly happy with their lot?

Although his mouth opened to return the call, his vocal cords didn't respond. The wolf had been suppressed for the time being.

With a glance at the cottage, and at the walls beyond it, Cameron spoke out loud. "Don't blow this." But he remained motionless, drawn by a perceived whisper in the dark. At least, he thought it was a whisper. *Hers.*

Of course, he reasoned, it was entirely possible the sound wasn't hers at all, and only the echo of madness, closing in.

Chapter 12

"Shit."

One cuss word just didn't do the trick. Three repetitions hardly made a dent in releasing some of Abby's anxiousness.

She had to circumvent the hunters, avoid a replay with Sam and ignore her father's direct order to return to the bar. In order to accomplish all that, she'd become the rebel she had always hid for the sake of peace in shared Stark space. The time had long passed for the real Abby to make an appearance, revealing who she was and what she wanted to do. That Abby wanted to find a werewolf...for something other than its pelt.

"I know you're out there. Can you hear me?"

Her remark was a déjà-vu moment from twenty-four hours before, and her tie to Cameron would not lie down and die. Messy emotions had been building inside her for some time, she supposed, but her meeting with Cameron had brought them to a head.

Had finding Cameron Mitchell been an accident?

"Head back to the bar? Not on your life." She was adamant about that. So, where to go? Where to start the search for her new identity and all that came with it? No way could she just stop and shout for Cameron Mitchell to come and get her, after telling him she'd be okay. Not with danger close at hand. Hunters were all over this park. More than one wolf trespassed here, too, some of them cop killers.

She knew that Cameron hadn't gone far. Her body told her this. The night vibrated with his presence as if he'd left a trail of energy behind.

Another thing was clear. Sam had to be stopped from killing good Weres along with the bad. Probably the hunting business needed to cease completely, since determining which wolf was which would be a risky endeavor without interrogations.

Sam had to stop his dreadful games, and she had to make this happen. She might be Sam's daughter, and might have dreaded that relationship for more years than she could count, but she had learned a thing or two from the tough old buzzard—like when to trust her gut.

She lifted her head, hearing the unmistakable sound of gunshot in the distance. If Sam had succeeded in bagging a wolf so soon, there was no telling who that wolf might be.

Was it going to be possible to convince Sam of anything? Had he ever been capable of love, empathy or real kindness?

If Sam had loved her mother, no evidence of that love remained. There were no photographs of her mom, no sign in the house that Sonja Stark had ever lived above the bar with her husband and daughter. Sam never spoke of his wife. Abby knew nothing about the woman who died before her fifth birthday, except for sudden whiffs of scent, so like part of a memory or a dream, which now and then filled the hallway Sonja Stark must have walked through. A rosy, feminine perfume that had been a treasured comfort in times of sadness.

The crack of another shot brought her around full circle, and shook Abby from motionlessness.

Not Cameron. They couldn't have found him. She wouldn't let them hurt him.

Gathering to run, Abby glanced sideways, sure she heard someone approaching.

"Wolf, where are you? Can you hear me?" Her whisper was accompanied by a full body sway.

When a howl echoed somewhere far off in the distance, Abby's heart revved. "Is that you? Wait. Watch out."

Sprinting over the grass bordering the busy boulevard with her shredded jeans flapping, Abby formed a wish for the brown wolf's loaned leather jacket, much too heavy for summer-night attire, to prove a magical talisman that would lead her to her lover.

"Leaving so soon?"

The female's voice, husky and low on the register, made Cameron turn back toward the building.

"You're free to do whatever you like, of course," the dark-haired woman he'd seen on the porch said. "But we were hoping you'd talk to us first."

"I'm Cameron Mitchell." They had asked for his first name, and he'd give them that. "And you are?"

"Delmonico."

The name brought Cameron to attention. "Officer Delmonico?"

She raised an eyebrow. "That fits me, and also my father before me."

"Jesus," Cameron muttered.

"No. Just Dana to my friends."

He couldn't even smile at the remark. Nearly every cop

on the force knew about this officer, at least in terms of her service regarding Miami's criminal factor.

"Do Weres make up the whole damn police department?" he asked.

Delmonico shook her head. "Only a few."

"How did I not know that?"

"How hard did you look?"

"Not very hard at all. But I've heard of you."

"I didn't do it." Delmonico threw both hands in the air and smiled.

Damn if he didn't smile, too.

"You helped to clean up that central park last year," Cameron said, "taking down Chavez and the warehouse housing a brutal fight ring."

She appeared not to want to take any credit for that incident, and said simply, "I did my job, and what had to be done. Like we all do."

"You've been Were for a long time?"

Moonlight beyond the roof's edge shone in her dark hair when Delmonico shook her head. "No. My initiation came after that night, from a bite by another bad guy."

"I'm sorry," Cameron said, meaning it.

"And you, Mitchell? What's your story?"

"I sustained an injury a few months ago on the job that landed me here. It took some time to recover from that injury. I'm not sure I'm truly over it yet."

"Yeah, recovery is a bitch, and then some," Delmonico agreed. "But here we are. And there are more of us than meets the eye. Come along and meet Dylan."

"The guy with the long hair?"

"The werewolf who saved my ass."

Cameron put up a hand to stall Delmonico, and spoke without offering a prologue. "Why do I feel her as if she's nearby, and as if she has become part of me?"

He dropped the raised hand. "Sorry. That probably

makes no sense at all, and you owe me nothing since we've just met."

Delmonico gave him a sideways glance and waited, as he had asked. "She?"

The explanation flowed out of him. Pieces of it, anyway. "I met her last night and can't rid myself of the memory, the feel and the scent of her, no matter how hard I try. She's not here, and yet it's as though she's right around the corner."

Delmonico faced him fully. "Wolf?"

"Maybe. Yes, I think so. I believe she doesn't know about that. Hell, I could be wrong. I'm not used to my new self yet, or the sensations that go along with this new gig. I shouldn't try to read others when I'm this messed up."

"Imprinting, Mitchell." Showing no sign that his questions might be rude or unintelligible Delmonico merely inclined her head and continued. "I know about that. It happened to me."

"Imprinting? What does that mean?"

"When two Weres have a meeting of the eyes that rings as being significant to each, the soul somehow becomes involved. It's as though there's a straight line connecting the eyes to what's inside of us."

"But what does it mean?" Cameron repeated.

"It means that you're married, that you're linked with that female until death do you part."

Cameron swallowed hard and tried to sound light. "As simple as that, huh?"

"Oh, it's not simple at all. When two Weres find each other—the right Weres, at the right time—biology takes a backseat to some kind of mystical wolf voodoo."

Cameron stared, confused, as Delmonico went on.

"There aren't any divorces in the Were world, so that until-death-do-you-part bit really means what it sounds like. If you've imprinted with another Were, you're bonded until one or both of you die."

Did he nod his head as if he understood? Cameron wasn't sure. He had to soak all of this in. "What if one Were doesn't want to be bonded to the other one?"

"Is that the case here, with you?"

"I have no idea who she really is at this point. She certainly doesn't know me."

"But you feel her when she's not here."

"Yes."

"You're obsessed with her?"

"Hell, yes. Obsessed."

"She doesn't have any idea what you are? What you have become?"

Cameron thought about that. Abby did know about him. He had changed his shape in front of her, showing her a werewolf up close, sharing his secret. He had perceived the wolf inside her and had felt its attention turn his way. Is that why he trusted her with his secret?

From the first moment, he and Abby had been all over each other, craved each other, and that kind of special attraction actually had a name in the world of the Weres. They must have *imprinted*.

And that meant Abby really was a Were.

"She knows," he said to Delmonico.

"Voilà, and congratulations on finding your true mate. I'm told it doesn't happen all the time, and that some wolves never do get to experience what it's like."

She disclosed those things earnestly, leaving Cameron with the impression that Dana Delmonico really had experienced imprinting for herself. His thoughts turned to the Were with the long hair sitting close to Dana on the front porch of this place when he had arrived, and what an odd couple those two made, with their opposite size and coloring.

"Wolf voodoo," he muttered to himself. "No getting around it."

Delmonico pivoted on her small, bare feet. "It's hell at first, being changed and torn from everything you thought made up your neat little life. But you're not alone, Mitchell. Remember that. I'm sure Wilson brought you here so that you'd know the truth, and for coping skills you'll need in the future."

"How did Wilson know I'm new at this wolf business?"

"You wouldn't have followed him here, otherwise."

He got that. He'd been easily swayed by the offer. So, what else was there for him to do except follow this other fellow officer, this she-wolf, and dare to meet the rest of his fate head-on?

"Come on," Delmonico said, turning back to the cottage.

"Right behind you," Cameron replied.

Chapter 13

Long after the crack of gunshot, the echo lingered, leaving a high-pitched ringing in Abby's ears.

She hadn't stopped running, and had no real idea where to go, other than forward. Her surroundings had started to blur. She'd lost any real sense of other dangers, having concentrated so hard on finding some small trace of the werewolves she sought.

Her current mind-set was dangerous. There had been at least three hunters in the bar with Sam earlier tonight, and maybe more than that. One hunter for each park quadrant, with herself hoping to elude those guys by sprinting through the middle.

She doubted those hunters would recognize her in the dark, especially dressed like this. None of them knew her. Sam always kept his business associates and their identities to himself, as part of the deal.

None of his associates stayed in the apartments with Sam and herself. She had served them in the bar that night, but would those hyped-up hunters be able to tell the difference between a furred-up werewolf and a woman out here on a mission? Her last injury, sustained somewhere around where she was right now, ached as the skin around it stretched with each stride.

She'd been wounded by a gunshot, but refused to believe that Sam's finger had been on the trigger, even after all was said and done. He hadn't brought it up, and Sam Stark wasn't the kind of man to let anything significant go by.

Tonight, there were two sides to worry about. Hunters and werewolves. At the moment, she preferred to meet up with the latter.

Why did werewolves like this park, anyway? Whatever the answer was made them frequent visitors. Did the grass contain some mysterious nutrient they absorbed through their feet? Was the air charged with positive ions, or did they merely crave the open spaces difficult to find in any busy metropolitan city, except for the relatively few acres of public park?

Had those shots she'd heard been in their honor?

Two shots.

Refusing to consider that the Weres who'd left her minutes ago had been the aim of those bullets, she wondered who else had heard the gunfire. No police sirens blared. Nobody shouted or came from the street to inquire, because everyone around here had heard the old adage about curiosity killing the cat.

Actually, curiosity didn't often kill anything, other than boredom. Thugs, criminals, gangbangers and werewolves that had dived into the deep end of the mentally deficient gene pool did.

Cameron Mitchell, possessing a dark secret that would likely get him killed if exposed, walked these few acres like some sort of supernatural guardian—keeping the peace, as she had always longed to do, only on the right side of the peacekeeping fence.

Cameron carried a badge, and would be sexy in uniform. On the streets, with supernatural instincts, he'd be a force to be reckoned with.

She ran on, unable to recall ever having been able to move so fast. Her bare feet were assaulted by twigs and other normally inconsequential debris as she cut across one edge of the mostly deserted space with her eyes and senses wide open.

Perceiving an anomaly in the silence, Abby finally slowed. Someone with quick reflexes grabbed her from behind and slammed her to the ground, knocking the air out of her.

"I told you to go home," Sam growled, leaning over her with one knee on her chest and a steady hand on her shoulder.

"So you followed me to make sure I did?"

She had never openly defied her father in this way, and that fact registered in his angry, questioning expression.

"I gave you an order, for your own safety."

"I didn't want to go back home. The action is out here."

"Those actions have nothing to do with you, Abby."

"They have everything to do with me. You'd never find the wolves without my help and direction. I'm part of this."

"Am I supposed to be grateful, and cut you some slack? You've already had one mishap out here because of poor judgment. Will you go for two by meeting up with something far worse than a couple of loiterers out to cause trouble?"

Sam snarled the words with an attempt to keep his temper under control, but his fingers dug deeply into her shoulder.

"Are you saying you'd care if I got hurt, Sam?"

Her father's eyes bored into hers. Abby saw nothing of herself in them or his expression.

"What's wrong with you tonight, Abby? What are you doing? You'll get yourself killed."

Sam's questions and the angry tone behind them stirred emotions inside Abby that she had decided not to repress. Her own anger ignited.

"Would you mourn me, Sam, if I died, or move on as if I'd never existed? Oh, wait. You'd have to work hard to find targets for your crew if I wasn't around to point the way to the Weres."

Sam's grip loosened enough for Abby to sit up, but she hadn't finished with him. As he studied her, she said, "Tell me about my mother, and if you ever loved her."

Then, with the mention of her mother and the change that came over Sam's face, Abby started to shake uncontrollably.

Matt Wilson stood on the cottage's porch with his shoulder against a vertical beam. His badge gleamed in the soft glow of overhead light.

Delmonico jumped two steps and gestured for Cameron to join her. She made no mention of their private conversation, and Cameron silently thanked her for that.

"You must be Dylan," he said to the Were Delmonico now stood beside. "Are you the host here? Is this your pack?"

A grin lit Dylan's handsome face. "I'd like to see anyone try to lord over Dana. Or Matt, for that matter. No, I'm not their Alpha. But we are a pack."

"Alpha." Cameron repeated the word, setting its meaning in his databanks. He found the term *pack* only slightly less intimidating.

"This is my home away from home," Dylan continued, "and my father's estate."

"I didn't mean to intrude," Cameron said.

"Any friend of Matt's is a potential friend of mine. And Dana has already given you high praise."

Cameron looked to Delmonico, who hadn't said anything on this side of the building. "How's that?"

"You're still alive," Wilson said. "That's Dana's version of an open-arm welcome."

A beat of time passed before Dylan laughed and Wilson joined him. But they cut the laughter short when they noticed Cameron's sober expression, caused by a suspicion that they hadn't actually been kidding.

"Sorry." Wilson moved toward the steps. "I'm sure you have questions. I know we do."

Cameron looked out at the dark. "I've been watching the park."

Dylan said, "We've seen you, and thought you might like to know that we do the same."

"You know what happened to me?"

"We recognize what you are, just like you recognize us," Dylan replied. "Maybe you'll tell us about what happened to you sometime."

Dylan's allusion to the possibility of Cameron being invited back here brought unexpected relief. There would be time to ask more questions.

"You were all part of the big cleanup last year in the park?" He addressed this to all three Weres.

"We did what we could." That was Wilson, more or less repeating Dana Delmonico's words.

Cameron shifted his focus to the high walls surrounding the estate. "Do the bad guys make it this far?"

"They try sometimes, but never manage to get in," Dylan said.

"What about the hunters?"

"Ah, the hunters." Dylan's gaze joined Cameron's on the walls. "They need a watchful eye, as well. Their numbers have been growing lately, in direct proportion to black-market demands for a sampling of our skin."

Cameron winced.

"You didn't know about that?" Dylan asked.

Cameron shook his head, not quite able to wrap his mind around the meaning, and deciding it would be better if he didn't try.

"They're part of a growing contingent of people who know about us," Dylan explained. "They hate criminal violence, just as we do, only they pick our species to chase down, and don't know a bad werewolf from a hole in the ground. So, they justify the killings in another way. Dollars. You, Officer Mitchell, are potentially worth more to Sam Stark and his associates than you are to the Miami PD as a cop on this beat."

Stark. Sam Stark. That was the name Dylan had spoken. Stark was also Abby's last name. He faced Matt Wilson with concern. "You said she's one of them. How did you know that?"

Wilson didn't pretend to be ignorant of the person Cameron had asked about. "Abby Stark is the Big Kahuna's daughter. If not actually killing wolves personally, she helps hunters in other ways that count."

Abby had confessed as much to him, so Cameron already knew about this, but not the full extent of her interaction with the people she called hunters. Or that her father led them.

"She told me she finds wolves for those guys. She told me that tonight after warning me about the people in the bar. The hunters in the bar. *Shit*. The hunters in her father's bar."

Wilson trained his eyes on Cameron's face. "Did you give her that kiss from me, I wonder? Did she show you her blade?"

These Weres knew a lot more about Abby than he did, it seemed, but not everything. Not the really big thing.

"Yes, well, it makes one hell of a problem for a lot of us, along with the bad guys out there," Dylan said, waving at the wall. "Although hunters leave little evidence of their kills, too many other dead things are turning up. Pretty soon someone will widen the search and investigate issues that shouldn't concern them. Like who else patrols the parks and cleans up potential messes before law enforcement officials hear about them."

Sure, Cameron thought. With Weres in the police department and possibly elsewhere in the system, those Weres had advanced notice of hazardous issues and could tidily cover things up.

"She will stop." As soon as he issued that statement, Cameron recognized the truth of it. "Abby will stop helping the hunters."

"Why do you think so?" Wilson asked.

"Because," Dana Delmonico said to the group in a low voice all the more noticeable for the quietness in it, "Abby Stark is one of us."

That information virtually shut down the conversation until Dylan recovered sufficiently enough to address Delmonico's remark.

"Sam Stark's daughter is Were?"

"Maybe not fully, or not yet," Cameron heard himself say. "Nevertheless, she now realizes she's not like everyone else around her, and more like me. It can't be long until she comes into her own. Her body wanted to change tonight, but she fought hard against it."

Wilson slapped the wooden post beside him and said seriously, "Well, if that isn't some kind of cosmic justice, I don't know what is."

Dylan required further confirmation. "You know this how?"

"By way of that kiss Wilson mentioned. Plus a whole host of other things."

"You're not mistaken?"

Cameron shrugged. "I'm pretty sure there's no way to be mistaken about that. I might be new to this whole *species* thing, but I've already learned that a wolf recognizes other wolves."

Dylan tossed Delmonico a thoughtful expression. Cameron observed how their eyes connected, and he relived the strike of the connection he and Abby had shared. Dylan and Dana Delmonico were indeed a couple. Seeing them, he fought a nearly overwhelming desire to go after Abby right then.

"This complicates matters," Dylan said.

"And places her in jeopardy," Delmonico added. "Imagine being the daughter of a major player in the wolf-hunting business, while becoming a wolf herself."

Cameron suppressed the impulse to shout that he had to be on his way. Instead, in a managed calm-cop tone, and with a straight face, he said, "I need to get her out of there before her father finds out."

Chapter 14

"Shut up," Sam Stark said. "Shut your damn mouth. What the hell is wrong with you?"

With a groan of frustration, Abby shoved Sam's hand away. She was bathed in moonlight, and had to escape. The light sank into her skin and down into her bones, icing muscle and marrow, producing sharp prickles of apprehension that bordered on pain.

"I guess that answers my question pretty clearly, Sam."

Folding her knees, Abby flipped over and used her hands to steady herself, though steadying herself completely wasn't in the picture. The shaking got rapidly worse, and Sam, who might have guessed the quakes were merely the effects of their heated confrontation, got to his feet without offering to help her up.

"You don't know anything of the kind," he said. "And you suppose that now is the time and place to have any discussion about family?"

"It's as good a place as any."

Abby's fingers curled against her palms, her nails drawing thin lines of blood, the scent dispersing in the air, and in the moonlight, like dust motes caught in sunbeams.

She could not get to her feet. She felt weak and unnaturally winded.

"Get up," Sam commanded. "It's dangerous to stay here."

"I'll move when you tell me one thing I've asked you for."

"Now you'll bargain with me, Abby? It isn't my health that's at risk by remaining in one place looking the way you look."

The shakes had gone internal, rocking Abby's stomach and chest. She closed her eyes and tried to rally. Whatever had taken hold of her tonight threatened to turn her inside out. Was she sick? Flu? Summer cold? Some sort of virus? Was it nerves revving for battle?

A series of terrible images sprang to mind.

Cameron, in the moonlight. The way his pulsating body had exploded into masses of rippling muscle and his skin had danced like water over stone. His beautiful features, drawn with the pain of a transition he had worked so hard to hold off for her sake.

Real fear crept into her heart for the first time. But heaven help her, the only person who seemed to truly care about what happened to her wasn't human.

Awareness of the bond connecting her to Cameron across the distance separating them made her muscles start to mimic his, twitching and contracting as the moonlight began to change inner sensation from ice to fire.

She looked at her hands and extended her fingers, recalling how Cameron's skin also had burned up in the moonlight.

Something was happening to her. She had to get away.

Sam yanked her up by the back of the leather jacket and

shoved her up against a tree. She wanted to fight back, needed to assert herself. The leafy canopy overhead offered a temporary respite from the light, but breathing seemed an impossible task.

"You're ill," Sam said.

"You think?"

"And you're half-naked under that jacket."

Abby glared at her father.

"You know the way home. I'll let the others know you're moving toward the street," Sam said. "Keep out of the way, Abby. Maintain a distance from the team."

"Or what? Maybe they'll screw up and put me out of my misery before I get there?"

Sam slapped her across the cheek so hard Abby's head turned. Her father had never struck her, had never actually paid that much attention to her, other than to shout. Talking about her mother had been an obvious touchy spot for him. Abby's new show of defiance had to be icing on the cake.

The slap that burned her face served to awaken more of the dark sickness rolling around inside her, inspiring that darkness to gather and rise up against such violence. When Sam turned away, Abby drew her blade. As he reached for his cell phone, she went after skin…her own skin.

Pushing back the sleeve of the leather coat, she sliced open her left forearm, severing enough small vessels to bring up a small river of blood. Sam might not notice, but *they* would smell the blood. If werewolves roamed this park tonight, they'd come running. Weres would either try to hack Sam to pieces, or lure Sam to go after them, leaving her alone, allowing her a few precious moments to herself.

The blood also might do something else, her frantic mind insisted. It would let Cameron Mitchell know of the immediacy of the danger here. If he scented her distress, he'd be forewarned about the seriousness of the hunters and take care to circumvent the trouble.

That's what Abby hoped as she stood on trembling legs that wouldn't hold her up for much longer, and with her blood pattering as softly as summer rain to the ground by her feet.

"Mitchell?"

The voice calling to him seemed blurred by a great distance. Cameron turned his head, stunned to find that he had dropped into a crouch, and that his heart pounded as if he'd been running.

He looked up.

"I guess it's true, then." The voice belonged to his new host, Dylan. "Abby Stark has wolf in her."

Puzzled about how he'd gotten into this position, Cameron kept very still. "What just happened?"

"You recognize her scent," Dylan replied. "I smell it, too. Wilson?"

Wilson shook his shaggy-haired head. "I sense the change in the air, but can't pinpoint the source like you do."

"Blood? Is that what's in the wind?" Cameron's body reacted with a jerk as he finally got the gist of what Dylan had proposed. "It's Abby's blood? Good God."

He sprang to his feet and started for the steps. Delmonico stopped him from descending by barring his way.

"It could be a trick," she warned. "Very likely it is. That woman might be wolf without knowing it, but she's also been one of those hunters for a long time. She would know how blood would affect you, especially her blood if you've bonded."

Wilson concurred. "And if she didn't do this to lure you front and center, someone else might have provided that invitation for her."

Cameron stiffened, horrified by that thought. "You think those hunters might cut her up in order to draw wolves out of hiding? They'd be cruel enough to do that?"

Dylan stepped forward until he was shoulder to shoulder with Cameron, and offered just two simple, incredibly strong words. "It worked."

Cameron glanced from Delmonico's practiced, blank-cop face to Dylan's. They were right, of course. His body strained to move. Independent of his mind, his system wouldn't be appeased for long by rational thought. Each breath he took in filled with Abby's scent. Each breath brought back the memory of feeling her bare skin against his skin and her lips crushed beneath his in an endless kiss. And those hunters might injure her in order to get a rise out of wolves in the area, and a rise out of him?

Well, it worked, all right. He was a breath away from shoving Delmonico aside. His legs were gearing up for a sprint.

"Talk to us," Delmonico said.

"It doesn't matter who did this to Abby, or the reason. Besides, how do we know what this is, for sure? What if it's a call for help? What if this is Abby's personal message to me, an SOS? I can't risk ignoring that, can I? I'll have to find her in either case."

He sounded breathless, and hardened his tone. "Thank you for the introductions. I'm grateful. I needed to find you, so I hope we'll meet again."

Sidestepping Dylan, Cameron leaped from the porch. Moonlight was waiting for him. Knocked backward by the suddenness of the start of his shift, Cameron clenched his teeth and stretched out his arms. "Bring it on, damn it!"

As his body ripped apart at the seams and his face began to morph, he let out a roar that shook the ground. But he didn't wait. He could not let more time go by with Abby in trouble.

Halfway through his wolfish transformation, he shook off the immensity of the pain. With his head pounding and his chest torn in two, he headed for the wall that had sealed him in with an offer of safety, and maybe even the companionship he had desperately sought. When he reached that wall, Cameron launched himself upward.

Claws scraped the brick in a sound like fingernails on a blackboard as he found purchase in the grooves in the mortar. Growls erupted from his throat, one after the other, as he hauled himself up—menacing sounds heralding his intent to do harm to anyone or anything that might have harmed his mate, and to anyone stupid enough to get in his way.

On the top of the wall he stood for a few seconds, strange sensations pinging through him that paralleled some wild, distant past. Wolves running. Wolves howling from mountaintops. Wind ruffling through fur.

Landing on both feet with a heavy thud on the opposite side of the wall, Cameron knew he had crossed into life-threatening territory. But he faced those kinds of things on a daily basis as a cop, and only one thing mattered tonight. Abby.

He did not believe she would intentionally cause him harm. She had warned him clearly enough. She had confessed about the part she had played in the deadly game of hunting werewolves.

If he had been mistaken about her...

If the other reason for shedding her blood turned out to be the case, and this was a particularly sadistic trap, he'd get his wolf on in the worst way possible, and do some damage of his own.

Seconds into his sprint, Cameron realized he wasn't alone. The aggressive growl he'd let loose was answered by each of the werewolves beside him. Three of them, all furred up and terribly intimidating as their muscles stretched and their pelts ruffled with each churning stride.

Not your problem, he would have shouted if he possessed a human voice. Then again, it had been their problem for a lot longer than it had been his. Hunters had been on their radar for a while. These wolves knew infinitely more about werewolves than he did, and the iron-rich scent of Abby's blood had disrupted the meeting, keeping him from finding out a few important things.

He inhaled. A real ocean breeze, rare this far from the beach, diluted the bloody scent somewhat, though he found it easy enough to follow.

Cameron growled again, and this time the gruff vocalization felt good, because in spite of the situation, he had companions from whom he didn't have to hide. These wolves knew the score.

His companions might have gone after a sighting of the hunters tonight, anyway, whether or not he had shown up in their backyard pining for a female they considered an enemy. But right now, he had become one of them. One *with* them.

Dana Delmonico as a wolf was dark, streamlined and larger than her human shape, though not by much. Her mate, Dylan, now running by her side, presented as a huge, impressively daunting figure, scary as hell in the moonlight, with fur as light as his hair. But then, Dylan had been nearly as formidable in his human skin, with those angular features and pale eyes.

Dylan, whoever he really was, possessed unnameable qualities that separated him from the other two Weres somewhat and lent him a regal air. Delmonico's mate was no blue-collar worker in his day job, Cameron was willing to bet. Maybe he didn't have to work, if the mansion behind the walls meant family money.

With so much wolf around, keeping his mind on the matter at hand took concentrated effort. Cameron's wolf liked being surrounded by others like him. The wolf in him reveled in running with this pack, as if he finally had a place, and belonged.

He snapped his teeth and sniffed the air, better able to separate scents in wolf form.

Blood. Getting stronger.

No mistake. It was hers.

His heart beat faster. His chest heaved and his veins pulsed. Abby had to be close, yet caution was needed or his new friends would be picked off *en masse*. And then what? What did hunters get for bagging a werewolf? Bragging rights? Underground bounty?

Abby, where are you?

When Delmonico gave a muted yip, Cameron looked to her. She had circled to his left and slowed, pointing at the ground. He raced to the spot, breathing hard through his mouth like the rest of the Weres.

Delmonico had found a small pool of liquid, very dark, nearly black, on the grass by the base of a tree. Abby's blood. He didn't need DNA testing in the lab to know this.

His insides twisted. A sound tore through him that he couldn't suppress. Half groan, half growl, it caused the other wolves to drop to their haunches. In predatory positions, all three Weres tensed, waiting for whatever was to come in complete silence.

That event turned out to be a bullet with Cameron's name on it.

Chapter 15

One hunter passed to Abby's left, creeping slowly over the grass as soundlessly as the prey he chased. This was a big guy she had served in the bar earlier that night—a bulky, middle-aged man with a recognizable attitude and the buzz cut of an ex-military man. He held a silenced rifle with a large scope, and carried the weapon easily, as if it weighed nothing.

He glanced at her only once before continuing west, following Sam's directions. This guy hadn't fired the other shots, or she wouldn't have heard them. She had led them astray with her lie to Sam about meeting up with a couple of stray werewolves near the boulevard. This bought her some time.

She hadn't been one for offering up prayers, but did so now, asking for Cameron to have been nowhere near those two earlier rounds of gunfire. She had to see him again, a meeting that couldn't be risked tonight. Although she had cut her arm open, being cut off from Cameron hurt her more deeply, and in a place so far down inside her as to be inconsolable.

Her self-inflicted wound throbbed mercilessly all the way to her shoulder and made her head feel light. Damn, though, if she'd give in to the urge to sit right down and bleed to death while Sam and his team rummaged through the place where she had met her own werewolf.

She craved Cameron now, more than ever. Their bond hadn't weakened one bit.

"Cameron. Change in plans. Stay away." Although her voice carried, the hunter she'd seen didn't return or respond to the noise.

Abby made a tally. She now knew where two hunters were. More of them had to be out there in the dark, and if they believed Sam, they'd all be heading in the wrong direction. That was another small point in her favor.

She gritted her teeth to keep from shouting about not knowing where to go from here. If she couldn't find Cameron and couldn't go back to Sam's house, what did that leave?

The other strange wolf she and Cameron had met up with had lent her his jacket, and it had been saturated with her blood, virtually ruined. For a good cause. Hopefully that Were would appreciate that.

She kept a hand clamped to her wound, hoping to stanch the bleeding. Through the lacy branches overhead, moonlight called to her like some kind of Siren from a horror movie, raising the hairs at the nape of her neck and causing a pulsing pressure behind her rib cage. Her bones ached. Her head hurt.

Thinking about closing her eyes, Abby stumbled forward in an unintentional move that planted her dead center in the silvery moonlight.

What the hell?

Temporarily blinded by the sudden brightness, other

senses took over. The sound of a low drumbeat began at the base of her spine, starting out slow and then rapidly increased in tempo. A surge of fire rolled through her, breaking up the chills.

The heat quickly became unbearable. Her shakes worsened the pain. The damn moonlight was doing this to her. The same moon she had always mistrusted had the power to manipulate the degree of her suffering, and desired to do so. Payback for all the nasty thoughts she had sent its way.

Holding back a slew of curses, Abby glanced up to assess her situation.

"What do you want from me, moon?"

The moon's answer was a whip of internal fire that flung Abby's head back. Fire covered her face, took over her lungs, covered her skin. Her only option was to withstand it.

Overheating from the inside, she tore open the jacket. Baring her chest felt better, slightly cooler, slightly right, even though so much about this was ultimately absurd.

Light cascaded over her face and neck, over her breasts and chest, its touch strangely personal. Moonlight slid like liquid over the coat and toward her wrists.

Another eerie impulse made her lift her fingers from the wound on her forearm and extend that arm away from her body. She watched the light envelop the bloody gap in her flesh, and heard an ungodly sizzling sound.

Jolts of electricity flung her sideways. She searched for the source of the storm but there was none because this lightning was inside her, crashing and diving from one corner of her body to the other, taking out everything in its path, leaving a trail of charred destruction.

Sickened, Abby leaned over to heave. Off balance, she teetered and nearly went down, but recovered in time to haul herself upright. Her skin glistened with sweat. Strands of her long hair stuck to the damp sides of her face. And she could do nothing about it. Further actions, such as ducking for cover, were impossible.

The point of this wasn't lost on her. She had been standing like this in the light when she met Cameron. She had hated the light even then, and the moon had taken this opportunity to return that hatred. The time for ignorance had ended. Her body was betraying her in a way she had to come to terms with. The damn moon had become a seducer, whispering its intent.

"What are you offering?" Abby challenged. "It had better be good."

And then she got it. Grunting with the effort of staying calm when she wanted to scream, Abby looked down at her arm—the wounded one—and found its ragged edges starting to pull together. Her injury was sealing itself up, in the manner of invisible fingers simply tugging on a zipper. She was witnessing a miracle. A damn bloody miracle.

Panic struck. Her heart skipped a beat. She shifted her weight from foot to foot, blinking fast, breath coming in gasps. There could only be one way this kind of spontaneous healing might happen, surely, if, in fact, it could.

The moon's ultimate revenge was to make her a werewolf.

Cameron couldn't open his eyes. The world had gone temporarily black, and had taken him with it. He fought to get his wits back.

"All cops know better than to walk right into a fight standing up," a voice scolded, but Cameron detected an ounce of concern tying those words together.

"Breathe, Mitchell," a female voice directed. "Dylan's going to remove the bullet, and you can't curse out loud."

Remove the bullet?

"Do you hear me?" she asked.

He nodded, or thought he did, because the next thing

Cameron knew, a heavy weight came down on his chest so hard that the world started to spin. Pain followed in an excruciating wave.

"Damn," a male voice said. "It's silver."

The female spoke again. "Is he too new to withstand it?"

"I'm not sure."

"They will be coming for him if they think he's been hit. We can't leave him."

"Dana, you've got a big heart that's aching for trouble."

"Yeah? Well, let's get him out of here and talk about that later."

A third voice, deeper than the other two, chimed in. "I'll lead them on a chase."

"Where?"

"Right to the street."

"Too bad we can't have others waiting there. I know a lot of folks who'd love to get their claws on these guys," the female said.

"There were other shots."

"The pack knows better than to be here."

"Then some other poor suckers might have eaten a bullet or two."

"We can't save them all, Dana. Nor do we want to. Right?"

"I'll provide the chase," the female said. "He will need both of you to carry him."

"And if I object to your running around on your own with bullets flying in all directions?"

"How well do you know me, Dylan?"

"Well enough, I suppose, my lovely wolf. Well enough. But honestly, I'll never get used to it."

"So get going," she directed, "or Abby Stark won't be the only one bleeding to death out here."

"I'm guessing you won't let that happen, either?"

"Protect and serve, Dylan. That's the gig."

"All right. Wilson, fur up, and let's get this guy out of here before I really get mad at these hunters and do something I might regret."

"So that you know," the deeper voice of Matt Wilson said, "if you do that regretful thing, I'll be right beside you."

Something hard slammed into Abby before she could react, and her only thought was of being sick to death of getting caught unaware…by anybody. But this new hit turned out to be a combination of scent and feeling, not an actual physical blow.

With a newfound agility fueled by a massive adrenaline dump, she whirled to face the next challenge, which turned out to be a naked woman who smelled like a Were.

Half-hidden by shadows, the woman visitor sniffed the air and said, "Hello, Abby," as if only Abby's scent might confirm recognition.

"Where is he?" Abby asked, her senses sharp enough to smell not only wolf but Cameron's heady scent.

"He's been hurt," the female replied.

"Take me to him."

"Can't. Sorry."

"Is it serious? Will he be okay?" Abby's heart beat furiously in her chest. The rise of that dark thing inside her that the moon had drawn closer to the surface made her vision sharpen.

"I don't know if he'll be all right," the she-wolf replied. "I think so. Hope so. Your father has done his homework with the silver ammunition. Did he do that to you?"

Abby waved her arm, still red and raw, but no longer bleeding. "No. But he might have if I'd handed him the blade."

"Then what was the point of all that blood?"

"The point was keeping Cameron away from here."

"You didn't stop to consider that it might have the opposite effect?"

"I told him what to expect out here tonight. I've been afraid he'd return for me." Abby put a hand to her chest to try to slow her racing heart. "I meant to warn him, and to draw other wolves out of hiding to take the heat from the hunters."

She had to take a breath in order to speak again. "I'm to blame for his injury. Please, whoever you are, take me to Cameron."

"I can't, you being who you are, and all."

"Do you know what I am?"

"I do. Mitchell was right on the mark about that. I can smell the wolf in you, though it isn't fully visible. I can see it in that wound on your arm. What will you do when your father finds out that he's been harboring a Were?"

"You said Cameron was right. Does that mean he knows about me?"

"Oh yes. He knows."

Abby glanced up at the moon. "How could he, when I didn't?"

The Were chick didn't answer that one. Maybe no one could have.

"I haven't shifted," Abby said. "Maybe I won't. Maybe I can't."

"And maybe it's just a matter of time, though it is curious that you're not shifting right now. Can I see your arms? Both arms?"

"Why?"

"I want to see if there's a mark."

"I haven't been bitten. At least, I don't remember being bitten."

"Then that alone helps to explain a few things."

"What things? I don't understand what you mean."

"But you've perhaps known for a while that you're not like the rest of the people you live with?"

Abby waved that away. "Don't all young people feel the same?"

"Possibly. Yet you've hunted us, alongside your father. I don't think many young people do that sort of thing."

"I did so for a reason."

"Do you know what that reason is?"

"I'm fairly sure I found out tonight," Abby said. "I think I might have been looking for help. In the past, I wanted to aid others who were being targeted by Weres, but now I have to believe I also might have been looking for someone to fill in the blanks in my own strange existence."

"Then you're in for a wild ride from here on out, because no one I know will believe that you can be trusted."

"I can live with that. I'll have to. Is it doable, though? Being a…"

"Not for everyone," the Were replied, following her train of thought. "And not by yourself. Certainly not in the middle of a mind-set that brings people in to hunt the very thing you'll soon turn into."

The conversation made Abby dizzy. Worry added to her restlessness. "Will Cameron be okay? Will you just tell me that much?"

"I honestly don't know. The bullet has been removed, but it will leave an insidious trail of poison in the body, as you probably know."

"It was a silver bullet? No. Oh no." Abby's ears stung with the news that it had been Cameron the hunters had shot.

Her pulse thundered. Her thoughts began to spin out of control. Cameron's scent, clinging to this Were woman, invaded every cell in her body with specific directives to find him at all cost.

"Why? Why does silver affect you like that?" she asked.

"You mean *us*?" the woman corrected.

Abby slid her knife from its sheath. "I used this on my arm and I'm still standing."

"Could be your wound wasn't deep enough to leave real damage."

"Yet it was deep enough to draw Cameron from wherever he'd gone."

Alerted by a noise other than her revved heartbeat, Abby glanced over her shoulder. She hadn't finished with this Were, and there was going to be an interruption.

"You have to go. They're coming," she said to the Were female anxiously.

When she looked to the shadows, that Were had already gone.

Abby closed her eyes and opened her senses further. Scent came on strong, and with it the amended vision. What appeared to be the noticeable heat signature of two humans, seen as a series of wavy red lines, came into view. The hunters had gotten close to Weres in spite of that lie to Sam about the direction he needed to take to find his wolves.

Make that three hunters.

No, four of them.

Why had they returned?

She had to take her own advice and get out of there. She wasn't like those hunters. She had no love of blood or pelts. She had never been like them because she wasn't human, and maybe hadn't ever been. That fact explained why she had perceived wolves so easily all this time, and also why she had been instantaneously attracted to Cameron Mitchell.

I'm not human.

Some part of her might have always feared that.

Spinning on her toes, Abby made a dash for the long length of grassy area beside her. She had made so many mistakes, it might be tough to fix them. Plus, she had a lot of catching up to do. At the moment, she would lead her father's team away from the Were woman who had helped Cameron and knew where he was.

At the very least, she could do that one small thing before circling back to pick up that she-wolf's trail…and following it to her lover.

Chapter 16

"Bite on this."

Cameron obeyed the direction and clamped his teeth down on something warm. Thick gel, the consistency of honey, squirted into his mouth. He choked, coughed, and someone's hand on his chin made sure he didn't spit the foul-tasting stuff out.

Were people trying to poison him? The nasty stuff slid down his throat, coating his tongue and tonsils along the way.

"That's it, Mitchell. Take your time. Ride this out. We can heal quickly, almost miraculously, if we do the right things."

Was this Abby? Had she found him? No. It wasn't her scent. Not her voice.

"Take shallow breaths until the pain subsides," the voice advised. "Your body will absorb the silver, and there's nothing we can do about that, but it didn't stay long inside you. We got that sucker out almost immediately—one perk of having sharp claws."

This was a male voice, and recognizable as someone he had recently met. Who, though?

As a breath-robbing stab of pain shot through Cameron, he squeezed his eyes shut.

"We'll have to do something about those guys eventually, but they've actually done us a few favors in the past by ridding the area of some tough characters."

"They've saved us time and effort," another voice chimed in. "What they lack in style, those hunters make up for in attitude."

"And…silver…bullets," Cameron muttered as the touch of the foreign hand left his face.

"Well, I think he'll live," someone observed.

"He will be one sick puppy, though. Thankfully, we have Mrs. Landau to take charge of the medical stuff."

Landau. The name rang a distant bell, but threads of Cameron's wits were separating, and chasing them down appeared to be out of the question since he couldn't move his arms or legs.

Bullet…

Numbness…

Jesus. Had he been paralyzed?

"You're safe," the first voice soothed. "It looks like you will heal, though not today or tomorrow. When we're injured in wolf form, the body automatically tries to deal with the problem. Since we're so much stronger when the moon is full, you can probably thank your stars this didn't occur on any other night."

Cameron's thoughts raced. Five years as a cop, and he'd never been shot. Others on the force hadn't been as fortunate. But he had to get up, couldn't wait for a few days to pass in a state of injured inertia. Too many questions remained unanswered. What had happened to Abby? Where had she gone? She couldn't be left out there to manage a first shift on her own.

Warm hands pressed on his chest, easing him back before it had even registered that he'd tried to rise.

"Not so fast, wolf. Ease up. You do want to get better, right?"

Yes, he did want that. He wanted it desperately. But…

"Dana went after Abby. She will bring back news."

Cameron only had the energy to sputter one word. "Wolf."

"Not tonight," one of the people present said. "Abby Stark didn't shift tonight. Not yet, anyway."

Then she might be safe, Cameron thought. The hunters wouldn't target a human. Abby would know better than to remain in the area, and understand how to take care of herself. She had lived among those bastards for a long time.

He had to either believe that, or go mad.

No, he had to get up and find her. The impulse to do so was too strong to ignore.

"Whoa, big boy." A female scent floated to him over the sour smell of whatever this bunch had used to stanch his wound. "I'd stay put if I were you."

"Dana?" a male immediately responded, and by the tone, Cameron put a name to this male voice. *Dylan.* Dylan and Dana Delmonico were a pair. He remembered the way they had looked at each other, and the flare of his longing for Abby worsened.

"I spoke with her," Delmonico said.

"That was extremely risky, Dana."

"It seemed necessary. She was looking for our new friend here. I think I put her mind at ease."

"Don't think so." Wilson's voice, lower than the rest, was quieter, and calm. "I'll bet Miss Stark is frantic by now. She has to realize what she is, without shifting. And she's dead center in the middle of Sam Stark's personal battle with the rest of us."

Delmonico took issue with that suggestion. "She's

strong and capable. Though her father might be a monster, it's obvious that Abby wants something else."

Cameron felt all eyes turn to him without having to open his eyes and look.

"So," Wilson said. "It's like that, is it?"

"Yep," Delmonico replied. "A pair."

"Will we have to sit on Mitchell to keep him down, or will he see the reasoning behind the need to heal first?"

"I'm thinking chains might help," Delmonico said.

Cameron cracked his eyes open to find Delmonico smiling down at him. Yes, damn it, he felt sick. He hurt worse than almost anything he recalled, except for one event—the terrible, life-altering few days of his body's rewiring from a human system to a far more complex one. He had barely made it past that. At one time he had prayed to die, to get the ordeal over with.

Nothing on the planet was worse than having a pair of razor-sharp canines sinking so deeply into muscle the force shattered bone. A bite with the ability to change cells and DNA, and turn the soul of one creature into another type of being that it wasn't meant to be. What kind of world would allow for that? He had to ask that question and demand an answer.

"In the meantime, he'll be anxious," Wilson said. "And he'll miss a few days at work. I'm guessing he'll get some slack because of last night's incident and being considered a hero within the department for a few more hours. We can come up with an excuse for his absence, and call it in."

"And he'll need some rest, without company and noise," another female said. "You all have things to do."

"Indeed we do," Dylan replied soberly.

"Right," Wilson and Dana said, one after the other.

Cameron felt them leave. The temperature of wherever they had put him dropped noticeably. But one body remained, the feel of its presence similar to standing near a light that had been burning for quite a while.

"I don't suppose you'll listen to any advice," the unknown female said softly.

Cameron opened his eyes again to return the narrowed gaze of a gray-haired woman with a kind, concerned face. How right she was, he thought. Despite the savageness of the pain racking him, and feeling like death warmed over, rest was the farthest thing from his mind.

Abby now supposed that being good at stealth had to be a characteristic indicative of her animal side. She kept running, making sure the hunters were on her tail, close enough to see her movement, yet far enough away for them to be uncertain about what they had their sights on. She wondered if they'd shoot anyway.

She ached with the effort of ignoring the pull of the moonlight. Hunting had taken on a whole new meaning beneath it. But someone close to her had been shot, and either Sam had pulled the trigger, or one of the other men was vying for the privilege.

Cameron had been hurt, the female wolf had told her. She had no idea why that she-wolf had bothered to pass along the information. Possibly out of sympathy for another creature who wasn't completely one thing or another, and who hadn't yet reached her potential either way.

Had Abby Stark been a wolf playing at being human all this time, with only small hints about being different as a starting point on the road to enlightenment? Hell, where was the certainty about that now? Where were the claws, the fur, the teeth, if moonlight ruled her, as Cameron had insinuated?

How would any of that amount to being a chip off the old guy's block?

Maybe she had been exposed to a wolf bite once upon

a time, and Sam hadn't told her. Truth be told, she'd always been different from Sam. In terms of inherited family traits, that left her mother as a role model in absentia. For a long time, she had imagined herself to be like her mother. Now look. Chances were good she carried the blood of some other species in her veins, and hadn't a clue as to how it had gotten there.

A bite she didn't remember had to be it. Or a scratch she had failed to locate. It all went back further than her tryst with Cameron. It had to.

"Cursed," Abby said, figuring she'd have to dig deeper into family matters and mythology in order to find out about herself and how this might have happened.

Perhaps a person could become wolflike without really being one because of so much time dealing with them. Maybe too much sympathy did the trick. What had that wolf said moments ago? That the fact of having no bite marks explained some things. Did that mean a ring of scar tissue made from a wolf's teeth would have proved a point she wasn't aware of?

"Don't know shit."

Clearly she had to get help with a few important details, such as what would happen to her now, and what to expect. Like how to get around Sam in fairly close quarters, in order to pick up her things, when she despised him more than ever.

Moving out of her apartment was the first step to separate herself from the hunters, and yet was that an option if she wanted to keep tabs on the game? What better way to find out what went on, and about Sam's plans, than being an insider?

Could she face Sam knowing he might have shot Cameron?

She was livid about the way things had turned out, and wasn't sure she'd be able to pretend things were okay, even to use Sam for information she might in the future share with the wolves.

Help was needed, now, tonight, so that she'd gain some bearings. The she-wolf she had met had to lead her to Cameron, or to others like her.

And how would a wolf pack react to having a hunter in their midst, even if that hunter wasn't completely human any longer?

She ran faster, putting more distance between herself and the hunters. The park stank of wolf presence. She stank of sweat and blood and the metallic edge of too much uncertainty. One of these warring factions—man and wolf— would eventually kill her.

Caught up in this insane dilemma, Abby let her mind wander. Suddenly her steps faltered. She smelled something strange and looked up in time to see a heavy net of knotted rope descending from above to swallow her up.

Chapter 17

Fighting like a tiger to get free of the heavy net encapsulating her, Abby struggled and pushed against the rope, kicking and tearing at what held her in a crouched position.

"No use burning off more energy," Sam said. "You tripped the wire."

She didn't stop struggling.

"What are you doing here, anyway, Abby, when I told you to go home? See how that little rebellion panned out?"

"Is this how you catch them, Sam, before you shoot at close range? You drop a net?"

Irritation deepened Sam's voice. "Actually, we prefer to catch some wolves alive."

She didn't know that, and was horrified by the thought.

"You don't need to know any more than you already do," Sam said. "That part isn't your business. The question I have is about what the hell you're still doing out here, and who it might benefit?"

Abby looked up at her father through the holes in the net. Her heart raced. She was tired of being out of breath.

"Something has happened to you, Abby." Sam stood over her imperiously. "Mind telling me what that is?"

"Mind getting this thing off me first?"

Sam made a motion with his hand to stay the hunter on his right and said, "Consider it penance for being foolish twice in one night."

Abby swallowed hard, disliking Sam more than ever.

"It's heavy, Sam."

"So are your recent transgressions."

"My transgressions? I'm only running around in a park where you make a habit of killing things."

Sam went quiet. Abby's heart stuttered.

Then Sam spoke to the other hunter. "You go on. I'll deal with my daughter."

With those directions, Abby's mind moved on to one relatively new thread in particular—the werewolves that hunters caught in nets, and how Sam disposed of them after they'd been trapped. She wondered what it felt like for innocent Weres to look up at the instruments of their death without being able to do anything about it because they couldn't even state their case without a human voice.

All those beautiful pelts, not all of which came from criminals.

Her mind skipped to Cameron, whose skin hadn't been completely covered by the fur these hunters coveted when he had shifted. She wondered why he didn't have a full pelt, and what hunters might do to a catch like Cameron, with no pelt money coming. Throw him back? Kill him, anyway?

How did Sam dispose of his kills so neatly, and so close to thousands of people?

"Let me up," she said as calmly as she could manage. "Before I start shouting and scare everyone."

Sam stepped closer, towering over her, his stance as imposing as the rifle in his left hand. "What's wrong with you?"

"I told you I'm sick."

"That's not the whole story."

"Isn't it enough?"

"You're in the way, Abby. I'll take you back and lock you in. We'll talk about this tomorrow."

"I want to talk now."

Sam didn't free her. He continued to stare down at her with a curious expression etched into the lines of his rugged face.

"I really am sick," she said.

Sam's response hit like a hot poker to her soul. "Your mother wasn't stable, but I thought you'd missed that gene. I've watched you for signs of imbalance all these years, and don't like what I see tonight."

Abby's eyes met his. She felt the darkness of dread coming on. "What did you say?"

"You've been teetering lately, been off the norm and not willing to listen. You've been wandering in places where you don't belong, just like she did."

Abby blanched, and felt the blood drain from her face. "The first time you mention my mother, and it's to cough up a thing like that? *Off the norm*, Sam? What does that mean?"

His face came closer. The scrutiny was intense. "Let's hope you're not too much like her, after all. Because…"

"Because what?"

"We'd have to do something about that."

It was an ominous reply with no follow-up or further explanation, and it left a hole in Abby's heart. She stopped breathing long enough for her lungs to burn. Flames of the flash fire she'd experienced both in the moonlight and in Cameron's arms began to rip their way through her chest.

Her limbs felt heavy. Dizziness returned with a brief whirl of vertigo.

But Sam had nothing more to offer, no insight to guide her toward understanding, other than allowing her a flat-out inner acknowledgment of having been right in the previous assumption that Sam had not loved her mother.

We'd have to do something about that...

Angry enough over this to want to shout out what Sam could do with his hunters, and where to stick them, Abby nonetheless felt tears welling in her eyes—hot, salty tears. Her mother had always been a sacred thought, a long-held love and a thing apart. Sam, after all this time of prolonged silence, wanted to defile that image.

She'd been tough, or had tried to be, living among Sam and his varying band of hunters. But at her core, deep down inside, lay a spot that resisted toughness and needed to be filled with light and love.

An angry growl rose from within her that Sam might not have heard. Another noise got his attention. Someone shouted in the distance, and Sam's face solidified into an expression that Abby classified as feral.

He sent her a pitiful look. "You think those things over, and I'll be back." He took off, leaving her entangled in the rope without pausing to witness the pop of a claw, as narrow and as sharp as any knife's point, ripping through the tip of the finger Abby raised to flip him off with.

So, it was true. This was proof, at last.

"No mistake."

More growls bubbled up from her throat to combine with Abby's startled exclamation over the ungodly appearance of the claw. The growl was echoed someplace close by. Choking back a reaction, Abby turned her head toward rustling sounds heading her way, her sight clouded by a haze of unspilled tears.

"Cameron?" she called out hopefully as two werewolves, the biggest she had ever seen, rushed forward, fully furred up, their pelts thick and spiky, their eyes glowing like hot coals.

It wasn't Cameron, though. Of course it couldn't be, because he'd been shot. He'd been hurt.

"Who the hell are you?" she demanded as they slashed the rope with their claws and bit through the knots with their teeth, shredding the net in a few quick, crazy minutes.

She thought seriously about screaming when they reached for her. Loud noise would bring Sam and a hunter or two running. But she'd recently found three wolves to help break the spell she'd been under. Three wolves out of three hadn't made a move to harm her in any way.

And these two, completely different for all she knew, had their paws on her arms, and were staring at the claw she still held raised.

"Not human," Abby said in a voice reflecting full knowledge of that fact. "And in need of help."

In hindsight, as they pulled her to her feet, she might have asked, "Good guys, or bad guys?" first, before declaring herself one of them. Their grip was rough and tight, one wolf per arm. On her feet again, they hustled her away, heading for the shadows, loping east, away from the direction Sam had taken when he'd left her alone and vulnerable in the middle of a virtual minefield of werewolves.

As she now saw it, good guy or bad, one outcome looked pretty much like another.

As soon as the woman with the kind voice had exited the room, Cameron got to his feet, fighting for a decent breath in a system that had betrayed him by keeping that breath from him.

He was in a room—a bedroom lit by one tiny lamp and thin ribbons of moonlight streaming through louvered slats in an open window. The room came furnished with an oversize bed, two small tables, a large wooden bureau with a mirror above it and an upholstered chair.

He was alone in the strange room, and couldn't stand up straight. He had been shot, they'd said, by a silver bullet. It hurt to think about that.

As he looked to the closed door, Cameron wondered if whoever owned this place would need to lock a stranger in, or if he'd be free to roam around. They had told him his recovery might take a while, but time was of the essence. Abby was out there somewhere, alone. She might be searching for him, and he couldn't breathe or move his feet.

"Where am I?"

Since the voices he'd heard here had been friendly, possibly they had brought him to the cottage behind Landau walls where earlier tonight he had met Wilson's friends. In that case, and if the door was locked, he might be able to use the window for his escape.

He hadn't been out of it long. The moonlight streaming in meant that it was still dark. Hopefully, it was the same night.

He made his way toward the window by placing one hand over the other and working his way around the bed. But even then, he had to take breaks.

"No good to you like this," he said to the image of Abby that ruled every thought he had, pictured in an ongoing, continual loop. Abby as he'd first seen her, magnificently defiant and brave. Abby, naked and in his arms. Abby at the bar, looking pale and frightened. Abby, with moonlight on her bare skin and a pleading look in her eyes.

Sick or not, he wanted her so badly he was willing to forgo a little healing in order to reach her. He had to reach her. It had become clear that as Dana Delmonico had said, he and Abby were a couple. They had imprinted man to woman, wolf to wolf, soul to soul. Theirs was a trinity of connections. A triple threat to the heart. And his heart hurt without her.

"Abby," he whispered as he pushed off the bed and grabbed hold of the sill. "I will find you. Never doubt that."

Inwardly, he added, *It might take a little time.*

"Silver be damned." Needing air, Cameron reached for the shutters. He looked out of the window to find the ground a full three stories below. That ground was populated with more Weres than he could imagine existing in one place, even in anyone's worst nightmares.

Abby didn't know if she was being saved, freed or captured. As the wolves led her through the dark, deserted grounds of the eastern border of the park, they hadn't slowed or glanced behind them. If these wolves were connected to Cameron's friends, surely they'd use more caution and be attentive to the hunters prowling the moonlight. But no, they marched in the open, not seeming to care.

Fear began to spread through her, snarling and deep. Where was Cameron? She swore she felt him thinking about her. He wasn't very far from here. Maybe if she tuned in, she'd find him.

She could use her knife on at least one of these wolves if they turned out to be from the wrong side of the tracks, and if they'd free up her arms. The silver knife throbbed against her bare leg, its hilt touching newly sensitive skin. She hadn't been able to reach it while trapped in that damn net.

Something with a whooshing sound went by. Abby ducked, pulling one of the wolves down with her, listening to a second silenced shot ring out.

The wolf on her right fell to one knee. Blood and splintered bone fragments spurting from the wound made it roar. The other wolf let go of her and ran, leaving Abby to the mercy of Sam's sudden approach, and behind him, the hunter that had earlier been by his side.

Sam's boot came down hard on the wounded werewolf's chest, and held firm as the beast writhed. "Dose it quickly," he barked to the other guy. "And call it in."

Abby's ankle lay beneath the wolf's heavy leg. It took her a minute to free herself as Sam grinned down at her.

"I knew you'd be of use," he said.

Standing up straight, Abby faced him defiantly. She had werewolf blood all over her, and a downed wolf by her feet.

"In fact," Sam said, "you've turned out to be exactly the kind of bait we've needed to hurry things along."

Her voice shook with anger. "Bait? Are you saying you left me in that net on purpose to attract your prey?"

"Not entirely, but your punishment had an added benefit."

"Sam," she said, her voice low. "Do you think so little of me?"

"Of course not, *daughter*. Do you think I'm totally without feeling? We didn't leave you there. We circled around and kept watch. Those monsters couldn't have harmed you. We wouldn't have let them."

"How certain you are, Sam. But what if they hadn't meant to harm me at all? What if they were trying to get me away from you?"

Sam waved that suggestion away as nonsense with a drift of his hand. "That's what I meant by being off balance, Abby. Can you hear yourself?"

The hunter Sam had led to this spot knelt by the werewolf. From his back pocket, he withdrew a syringe.

"What's that?" Abby demanded.

"Something to ease his pain."

"Temporarily, or forever?"

Sam's hand on her elbow made her shiver. Her father led her aside and said calmly, "Haven't I given you nearly everything you've wanted? Did I ask for much in return?"

Actually, Abby immediately thought, he had given her

something. Cameron. Due to Sam's games, she and Cameron had met. What grateful daughter wouldn't stop to appreciate that particular twist of fate?

Should she tell Sam right that minute, exacting her own sort of revenge, how like the beast on the ground she was, or soon would be in the future? Although the claw had retracted, she felt it there beneath her fingernail, ready to spring.

Inside her, wildness existed, and had grown stronger. For all she knew, she had more in common with the beast on the ground than with Sam Stark, who would "take care of that" for her if he knew about the wolf connection.

"I think you owe me an explanation," she said, "for so many things."

"I told you we'd have discussions later. Right now, I have business to tend to. You can see that."

"Where will you take…" She'd almost said *it*, with regard to the beast, but only because she wasn't sure of the werewolf's gender. There hadn't been time to find out what their intentions had been, or where the two wolves had been taking her.

What if they had been Cameron's friends?

Bad wolves or not, a wave of sadness engulfed Abby. Too many possibilities for blame and for shame brought a rush of anger to the surface. Getting away from Sam seemed like an impossible task.

"What now?" She eyed Sam fiercely with her hands balled into fists behind her back.

"You mean since you can't be trusted to leave the park where you'd be safe, and will continue to get in the way of a damn good outing?"

"Yeah, that's what I meant."

"You'll have to tag along."

"I don't feel much like being used as bait."

"Then consider it a favor for your dear old dad."

She heard the hunter using a phone to call for help in moving the werewolf they had shot. Closing her eyes, inhaling the smell of wolf blood, Abby had to rein herself and her anger in...at least until her father turned his back.

Chapter 18

The door behind Cameron opened. Turning to look at who stood in the doorway took far too many seconds of the time ticking away in his head.

"Going somewhere?" Wilson asked, wearing only his jeans. No black T-shirt, no shoes, belt or badge. His hair was mussed, as if he had just changed back to this shape in honor of this visit.

"She's out there," Cameron replied. "And she's in trouble."

"How can you be sure?"

Cameron looked at Wilson directly. "Do you have a mate?"

Wilson nodded.

"Then your question makes no sense."

"Problem is, my friend, that you aren't ready to go out there, into a night full of hunters and God knows what else."

"Then maybe you'll bring her here," Cameron said. "Help her like you've helped me."

"Funny. We were just about to do that very thing."

Cameron waited out a few beats of silence before saying, "Who are those guys in the yard?"

"They're my pack."

"Do they mind if I see them?"

"I'm not sure they'll show you their faces yet, but they're ready to run up against a hunter or two."

"Because you asked them to?"

"Nope. Due entirely to Dana's insistence."

"Delmonico."

"Dana seems to believe that your Abby needs protecting from the very people she's helped in the past."

Cameron did his best to nod his head. His muscles quaked. "What is it with silver?"

"It hurts like a son of a bitch, doesn't it?"

"Said from experience?"

"Shot in the forearm a few months ago."

Cameron took that in.

"We've gotten wind of wolf blood being spilled on the east side," Wilson said.

Cameron stiffened.

"Though that's not close, we have to check it out."

"Because you're cops?"

"Because it's in our best interest to do so as cops and Weres and decent beings, human or otherwise."

"I can go along. I can…"

"Stay here and heal up," Wilson interrupted, "so that you'll be ready to do your share some other night."

"I'm no good here."

"We will find her, Mitchell. Don't worry too much, or Dylan's mother will put you to sleep. She's in charge of this sick bay, you know, and she's fiercely protective of any wolf that lands in this room. She takes it as her own personal mission to set things right."

"I need to thank her, Wilson, and all of you."

"Oh, Mrs. Landau will be back any minute now. You can count on it. She's too formidable for the use of a first name. Trust me on that. And I didn't do anything you wouldn't have done in my place. None of us did."

Wilson had more to say. "I checked your files. I hope you don't mind."

"And?"

"The files told me that you have no immediate living relatives, since your parents died in a car accident a few years ago. You're a Florida native, and live alone in a place bordering a bad area, probably due to those huge paychecks we're handed each month."

"I could have told you all of that."

"Maybe having no family to worry about is what makes some people better cops and more willing to risk their health and lives for a cause," Wilson said. "It's true, then? You're alone in Miami?"

Cameron nodded. "More or less."

Wilson turned and said over his shoulder, "I'm here if you ever want to talk. I'll leave you now. Stay put and take the cure. You were a lucky bastard that the bullet didn't reach anything vital. We're pretty sure Sam Stark didn't take that shot, or you'd be hanging in his basement by a hook instead of enjoying that pretty bedspread beside you."

Wilson didn't smile. Cameron didn't, either. And then Matt Wilson closed the door behind him without waiting for Cameron to formulate how to better word his thanks.

Cameron leaned heavily on the windowsill. He watched Wilson leave the house and join six others on what Wilson had insinuated to be Dylan Landau's manicured front lawn. He had seen Wilson shift once before, and this transformation was equally as fast. One minute Wilson was there, and the next, he was a werewolf among six other werewolves of varying size and color, all of them tremendously big, strong and dangerous.

Sam Stark would wet his pants if any of these guys caught up with him. These Weres were a beautiful, intelligent, lethal pack comprised of cops and detectives and who knew what else. Cameron's wolf gave an internal bark of acceptance. His body shook with the desire to be out there with them.

Lucky?

Hell, yes, he was lucky. And he hoped, as he watched the silent, furred-up Weres jump the wall, that Abby would recognize a friend when she saw one. And that it wasn't too late for them to find her.

He growled his displeasure over the situation, and then growled again. Each rumble in his chest sent shocks of pain through him, but he would make it, and heal miraculously, someone here had said. He'd be out there before he knew it.

Just not right that minute, he thought as he rested his head on the wall.

Abby smelled wolves before she and Sam had covered three yards. Her body's response was to cough up an immediate growl that she slapped down with a chokehold on her throat.

What she didn't know was if these new wolves were on Cameron's side, or feral animals intent on doing harm wherever they could. They were precariously close to the boulevard, where lines of cars paraded in each direction, and people gathered near several popular nightclubs. All sorts of odors from the city vied for her attention, but wolf remained potent among them.

These wolves smelled like wet dogs.

They weren't like Cameron. Neither was their scent anything like the smells clinging to the leather jacket loaned to her by the big brown wolf Cameron had followed.

This started to make sense to her. She was now reasonably able to differentiate between types of wolves by scent alone. Plus, good guys probably wouldn't have trespassed so close to the tourists, and likely geared themselves toward minding their manners in public.

Bad guys were on the move.

Sam's cell phone vibrated. She heard it, felt that buzz as though the phone had been in her own pocket, though they had paused near a big palm tree that slightly diffused the moonlight.

Between the approach of rogue wolves and the light dappling her face, Abby felt the strangely familiar shock of separating skin. One claw again began to pop, easing its way through her fingertip. She had to squeeze her eyes shut against the immediacy of the pain, and to keep from shouting.

"Here," Sam said in a decibel above a whisper.

Abby threw him a look. Sam had no idea how sensitive a werewolf's hearing was. Any of them between the park and the street would have heard Sam's directional cue.

One did.

"Too late," she said as Sam whirled to face the oncoming werewolf—a beast with the corded musculature of a bodybuilder on steroids.

Sam now had a rifle. It came up quickly, and calmly, Abby thought as Sam took aim. But the werewolf didn't seem to notice Sam or the weapon. This monster had eyes only for her.

It came on intently, with its gaze fastened to her face— a huge sucker, a freak and much too large for a normal Were's range of fast moves.

Sam fired off two rounds in quick succession before the beast got close. The first bullet struck its left shoulder, the second its right knee. The monster kept coming, growling menacingly as it stumbled forward to reach for Abby.

"Damn freak," she heard Sam say before a third bullet hit the wolf between its eyes and the thing went down.

She'd been holding her breath. When Abby finally looked to Sam, it was to find his rifle pointed at her chest.

"Sam?" she said, only then noticing that all ten of her fingers sported lethal claws, and that her hands shook from the trauma of birthing them.

Sam stared at her in silence, in much the same way as the monster had stared.

So this is it.

Abby stood tall as she faced her father and somehow found the ability to speak. "I suppose this will need to be part of the discussion you've postponed?"

With her heart in her throat and her knuckles pulsing, Abby heard the well-oiled rifle trigger start to compress.

The wind whistled around her as if alive and urging her to move. Only it wasn't the wind. It was the slipstream of a werewolf barreling in at top speed.

Furred and fanged, the wolf rammed into Sam, knocking him back a few steps and dislodging his hold on the rifle. A second werewolf rushed in to pick up the weapon. That wolf's hands slowly rose to show off a set of threatening claws.

These werewolves didn't hurt Sam. Though he might have killed her tonight, right there where his team had taken down so many others, their concern seemed to center on her.

Abby remained upright, swaying as if Sam had fired the rifle, unable to process what had almost taken place.

Sam knew about her.

Sam had seen the claws.

Having been manhandled by numerous people tonight, she shook off the brown wolf's sudden grip on her arm, and looked into his eyes. The damn Were inclined his head to her after shifting his gaze to check out her hands and the claws scraping her thighs.

He truly wasn't going to hurt her. This werewolf smelled like the leather jacket she wanted to draw back and cuddle into.

Acknowledging that, Abby let him lead her a few feet away from Sam and what might have gone down if this wolf and his friend hadn't arrived in time.

The wolf's companion, a paler, larger version of werewolf with bright, intelligent eyes, waited with those eyes on Sam, who hadn't budged from the spot he'd been knocked back to. Sam's harsh, irregular breaths lent a horror-movie detail to the tense, overheated atmosphere. Sam Stark faced the werewolves he had been hunting, and they were granting him life.

She wondered if that would change anything for Sam. But he shook his head and spoke to her with a terrible slowness. "Just like her."

There wasn't time to wonder about that. Everyone present seemed to sense the approach of another hunter—an angry human, and very bad news.

With Sam's rifle in hand, the paler wolf took off. The brown wolf at her side gave her arm a tug. There wasn't any point of remaining to find out what Sam had meant by his remark. He had already proved himself an uninterested husband and a lousy father figure. Instinct warned that he actually would have shot her.

By leaving with the Weres, the meager tie with her father would be severed for good. His face, and the disgust on it, told her that.

Abby let the brown wolf lead her away. She didn't look back. Her wolf had announced itself with evidence of its true nature, and the old Abby Stark had to accept the consequences.

"I'm not human." She repeated her new mantra as she picked up her pace to match the werewolves' long strides, leaving everything she'd known until that moment behind. For good.

Chapter 19

Cameron lifted his head from the wall to sniff the balmy air coming through the open window. His heart gave one solid thump.

"I feel you out there, Abby."

He still hurt badly, but the edge of the pain had subsided. He could track the progress of the silver with his eyes closed or open. From the bandaged hole in his upper chest, tentacles of the substance spread outward in a design similar to a child's depiction of rays coming off the sun. Those tentacles had solidified. Some of them were visible through his skin.

Although the process had been halted somewhat by the bullet having been removed so quickly, added to whatever Mrs. Landau had done to help the matter, he felt each and every ache the spread of silver caused. On the positive side, he was alive and breathing, and able to perceive in the breeze coming from the window the signs of Abby's distress.

She was scared, and calling.

Cameron looked down at himself to estimate his energy level. His body heat had waned, due, he guessed, to the damage caused by the bullet. He was naked, but his pants hung on the back of the chair. With shaky hands, he reached for the jeans. He had to get to Abby. Their bond demanded action and her protection. As mates, she had become his responsibility, though he would have felt responsible for her, anyway. His illness equated to a temporary setback, that was all.

What might happen when the others found her?

Chances were slim this wolf pack would bring Abby here, exposing so much of their lives to a person they had long considered an enemy. Maybe they had another place in mind.

He stepped into his jeans carefully, smelling the small droplets of blood on the denim that had scattered from the wound in his chest, and ignoring the stains.

The reasoning process would not stop. He'd been a cop for too long, where suppositions and educated guesses often helped in solving cases. But he'd never have guessed what lay behind the Landau walls. Not many people knew about this compound, or what the Landau family did here, he'd be willing to bet. He had been privileged to garner an invitation, and lucky that members of this pack had been willing to help him in a time of duress.

Hell, he could have died out there tonight.

Dana Delmonico's words about Dylan Landau came back to him. *The werewolf who saved my ass.*

It seemed to him that the wolves in Landau's pack saved a lot of asses, so maybe one more rescue wouldn't break the hospitality bank.

He glanced to the door, figuring that someone might try to stop him before he reached the house's ground floor if he'd been listed on the roster as an invalid. Surely they'd try to stop him if his face reflected the way he felt at the moment.

The door was not an option.

Cameron winced as he looked to the window. Jumping from the sill was the only way out, though he wasn't sure he'd survive such a fall in his present state. Somewhere inside his head a hammer struck repeatedly at a steel plate, causing his ears to ring and his teeth to ache. His shaky limbs threatened to fail if he moved too fast in any direction. The last time he'd felt like this was *that* night, in the beginning, and the events that had kicked this wolf thing off.

Before that, he'd been just a guy, a cop dedicated to his job. Now, the night called to him. He somehow knew that Abby's first shift was imminent—if not tonight, then soon. And if that didn't happen on this night, she had to possess a special ability to ward off her wolf for as long as possible.

An ability like that would come in handy.

However, it all came back to how Abby had been infected by the wolf virus, how lethal the strain was and how long she had carried it inside her.

"Have to get to her," he said aloud through chattering teeth.

The whole imprinting thing was a royal pain in the behind.

"But it is what it is."

The shutters retracted fully with a scrape of wood on stucco. Cameron had to lift his dragging left leg onto the sill with both hands in order to climb up.

Someone had told him that being in wolf form might help the healing process, since the wolf was so much stronger than the human. He hoped to God that was right. Yet there was no telling what the shift itself might do to him in this condition.

The thought of his wounded chest expanding brought

up bile. The idea of his spine stretching made him grimace. But he wasn't of any use to his mate cooped up in some bedroom on a strange estate with his body out of commission. His thrashed body ached to get to Abby as much as it ached to lie down and recover. Odds were decent that he'd make it.

Perched on the window ledge, Cameron gauged the distance to the ground. Three stories seemed doable, maybe. He needed the wolf.

Moonlight found him, caught him in its luminous embrace. The light brought more cold and waves of chills before melting through his top layer of skin. Each layer the light descended lessened the cold. He grew warmer as it worked its way inside, and he offered the moon his face. The pounding in his head ceased abruptly as muscles began their dance. His spine cracked. All ten claws sprung at once.

Cameron stared at his hands as other features began to morph in slow motion. Inhaling moonlight, his chest broadened, pulling the bandaged bullet hole out of proportion. He growled with pain, and closed his eyes to try to gain a foothold on the objective at hand.

Find Abby.

Hearing the door to the room swing open behind him, Cameron turned to look. The gray-haired woman with the kind face stood on the threshold wearing a stern expression.

"I've yet to meet a young wolf with a single shred of common sense," she said.

Using what energy he had leftover from the shape-shift in progress, Cameron smiled at Dylan's mother, thinking the likeness between Dylan and Mrs. Landau a positive ID.

"Have to," he said in a grunt of apology for spoiling her healing work.

"I suppose you do," she returned.

Sliding sideways, he found a wrought-iron railing covered by the shingles of the overhanging roof, and from there he climbed down through the shadows with his claws digging into the wood. Racked with pain and sore from the inside out, he descended the floors like a monkey, without the need to jump.

Waves of pain doubled him over when he reached the grass. It was too much exertion, too soon. Hands on his knees, he shuddered through a few long breaths, still in the shadows of the house, and eyeing the line of moonlight just inches away from him. Then he brought his head up.

Someone watched him from the dark patch of grass near the front porch. The Were moved forward to the edge of the light coming from a window above its head. Cameron waited without straightening up.

"It's about time," Dana Delmonico said smartly. "I was beginning to wonder if you'd died up there."

It took a moment for him to reply. "Nope. Just evading the posse. Aren't you part of that posse?"

"Hell, Mitchell, I'm here to help your decrepit carcass over that big wall. And by the way, you look like hell."

The situation remained dire. Partly shifted, he did feel like hell. In spite of that, Cameron smiled fully with an emotion resembling honest-to-goodness appreciation for this woman.

"So what's stopping you?" he said, shoving himself upright. "Bring it on."

Abby had no idea where these Weres were taking her, though the direction was north. The only things bordering the park on the northern side were Cuban-generated businesses and rows of supermarket warehouses. Beyond those things lay a stretch of suburban homes considered by many people to be on the wrong side of the tracks.

She began to get worried. Heck, she'd been worried

from the get-go. The image of the way Sam had raised the rifle and aimed it at her heart played over and over in her mind. The words he'd used weighed heavily.

Just like her.

Right that moment, she understood his dilemma. She had claws.

But what about being his daughter? Did that count for so little?

Her mind flashed on who the two wolves guiding her through the night might be. Nice guys? Rescue mission? She hoped for both of those things, and that Cameron sent them.

Her arm still hurt, but the muscle around it had gone numb. The unwieldy claws she wasn't used to hadn't disappeared, and scratched at her thighs as she ran. Each new scratch made the two werewolves beside her growl, as if the scent of her blood incited them in some way that harkened back to wilder times than these, when the blood lure was upon them.

But really…no way could she imagine wilder times.

Unfolding events were nerve-racking, and yet she was alive, and according to the female wolf she'd met earlier, Cameron was alive, too. That's all that mattered at the moment. She had to hang on to the fact that someone waited for her, wanted her, called to her, in a world that had grown increasingly cold and lonely and dangerous.

It was too late to go back.

The wolves beside her had incredible strength and speed, contained enough to keep her alongside. When the warehouses came into view, they slowed, circled east and bounded through a series of dark, unpopulated streets and alleys where only people with nefarious businesses dared to show themselves after midnight.

No one saw them. At least, she didn't think so.

"Cameron," Abby whispered so the sound wouldn't echo off the walls of the warehouses, sending her thoughts along the connection binding them. "Cameron, can you hear me?"

They passed the buildings at light speed. The wolves didn't shift back and forth as they raced in and out of the shadows and the moonlight, proving they had some control over their shapes. Abby kept a tight hold herself, realizing she might slip further from humanness the longer she remained in the presence of these wolves.

Hindsight couldn't be avoided. She knew now, from the sensations flowing through her, that wolfishness had been coming on for some time. Capping this were her empathetic reactions to Cameron's shape-shift that had left her shaken and weak.

Possibly that event had kicked off the actual physical changes leading to the appearance of her claws. A case of wolf by osmosis, maybe, or by association.

The farther they got from the park, the sicker she felt. There was too much moonlight, and too much wolf to avoid the pain of the claws. Again Sam's words came to the fore, as if he had just spoken them. *Just like her.*

Her...

He had been speaking about her mother—meaning that her mother must also have been rebellious or immune to Sam's continuous demands. Maybe Sam had been a hunter back then, too, and her mother had disapproved.

How was she going to find any of this out now, when it was obvious she couldn't go home?

They entered suburban territory before her wolf guides finally slowed. Neither of these wolves breathed hard, though she had to struggle. They pulled up by the side of a small duplex with a stone fence, and went right up to the door. One of them put a muscled shoulder to the wood, and the door opened wide enough to show a dark room beyond.

She did not want to go in there. But both wolves waited beside the door until she did.

Chapter 20

Cameron huffed as he joined Delmonico on top of the wall. He watched her traverse the narrow ledge with a grace more indicative of a cat than a wolf. Her fur raised and rippled in the moonlight with her excitement. Blood had been spilled in the park beyond the safety of the Landau estate. Wolf blood. Delmonico smelled it, just as he did.

His shift continued in earnest.

Excruciating pain arrived in seconds. The sounds he made were blasphemous. Pondering how many times his body might be able to take this kind of torture, Cameron completed his transformation crouched on one knee.

Delmonico waited patiently. When she finally stood, she nodded her head and preceded him to the ground in an area he hadn't explored on what had to be the northern side of parkland. Delmonico didn't stop to show him a map or acknowledge the grunts of leftover pain he coughed up. She started out at a lope on well-honed legs conditioned to chase after things, assuming he'd keep up.

Damn if he wouldn't.

They moved in and out of the trees on the park's periphery. The hour had to be late. Few cars passed by on the road beyond their sightlines. Residents of this section of the city had long since tucked themselves in.

And then, before he knew it, they were out of the park, sprinting along white lines in the center of the road. Not long after that, Cameron began to recognize things. When his internal GPS placed him on the outskirts of his own neighborhood, his mind cleared despite the awful lingering sharpness of the pain radiating from behind the gauze taped to his chest.

His block. His street.

He glanced at Delmonico questioningly, but she kept running, right past his fence and up the steps of his front porch.

Cameron had scented wolf presence from halfway around the block. Dead center in the tangle of those smells laid the heady fragrance he had been searching for. Abby's lush scent mingled with the metallic tang of werewolf blood.

Abby was here.

He blew through the wolves manning the door, and into his living room, skidding to a stop on the polished wood floor. Excitement kept his wolf front and center until he beheld the familiar stubborn look of defiance on Abby's beautiful face.

Cameron waited for her invitation to approach. *I'm here, Abby. You're all right?*

She didn't reach for the knife strapped to her leg, and reluctantly met his eyes.

There it was: the snap of the meeting of their souls. The bond that tied them together with an undeniably intimate connection. Nothing else mattered—not his lousy condition, the presence of his wolf or the fact that others might be observing this reunion. He wanted to touch her, and didn't dare. Not yet.

When Abby finally spoke, her voice broke. "Sam tried to kill me."

Cameron continued to stare at her without being able to console. Touching her when looking the way he did might be another kind of blasphemy, and scare her to death.

She looked so damn hurt.

Closing his eyes, building a wall against the level of the pain sure to come, he began his shift reversal by willing his wolfishness inward. The power of his need to hold Abby, to be with Abby, drove his rugged exterior back to a more manageable shape. It wasn't easy. Not even close. But the wolf eventually drew back to expose a human configuration.

Crushing blows of pain hit him, returning from wherever the pain had been hiding with the wolf in charge. He immediately wanted to wolf-up again in order to withstand this kind of trauma, but held out against it. When he opened his eyes, he reached for her with smooth human hands.

Abby took a step back.

"It's what we are," he said, ignoring the quakes that still rocked him. "You and me, Abby. However it happened, and whatever comes next, we can face this. We have to. And we're not alone."

She looked tired, frail, gaunt, and no wonder. Sam had tried to kill her? Was it even possible to wish harm upon a beautiful soul like hers?

"I had no idea it was this bad," he said.

Abby's gaze dropped to his chest, to the bandage above his heart. She came forward tentatively, and rested her fingers lightly on his chest. "How badly does it hurt?"

"I don't think I'll be liking silver anytime soon, or any

other kind of flying bullets. I must have missed the class on ducking to avoid this kind of thing."

Abby's fingers presented no painful pressure. She spoke in a low voice. "They think silver is effective because it's like moonlight molded into metallic form. They believe that a substance mirroring moonlight injected deep into Were tissues can explode a wolf from the inside out, as if it's too much of a good thing. I never understood that. If it's like moonlight, which can heal as easily as it can transform, surely that's a good thing?"

"Or not," Delmonico said from the hallway, where she leaned against the wall with her arms crossed, naked as a jaybird and not the least bit self-conscious.

Abby's attention transferred to Dana. "I met you in the park."

"You did."

"You helped Cameron."

"The guys by the front door are responsible for that."

Abby looked to the door, then again at the bandage on Cameron's chest. "Silver is supposed to kill Weres when nothing else can."

"I'm not sure what is does exactly, or why," he said. "But it hurts like hell. I was damn lucky to have had experienced help on the spot. Whatever they did was its own form of supernatural."

Abby looked up at him from beneath long lashes in a way that gave him a thrill. "I can't go home," she said.

"You'll stay here."

"Sam will find us."

"He'd have one hell of a time trying."

"I can't stay."

Cameron waited for her to explain herself.

"I have to do something about them," she finally said.

"Them, Abby?"

"The hunters. Sam's hunters."

She faced Delmonico. "They think you're all monsters. They will never give up what they do out there. They will never stop."

"We know that," Delmonico said.

Abby rushed on. "Now that you know who they are and where they are, what will be done?"

"That's not up to me personally. Neither is it up to Mitchell."

"You don't want to stop them?"

"Didn't you want that? You scouted for them," Delmonico calmly tossed back.

"Always," Abby said. "I always wanted the violence to cease. But there are monsters, and they're killing innocent people. Sam's arguments were believable."

"And now?" Delmonico pressed.

"Now you're..." Abby didn't finish the statement, probably, Cameron supposed, because she didn't know how to. She had no idea how to process events that had unfolded so quickly in the span of a mere forty-eight hours.

When she found her voice again, Abby said sadly, "They will continue to go after Weres, good or bad."

Cameron said, "We can try to keep all the good guys away until we have a case to build against your father for something people actually know about. You do see the problem, Abby? Who believes in werewolves?"

Abby shifted her focus again to Cameron. "You patrol the park for that reason, to keep bad wolves in line?"

"Hell," he returned, running his fingers over his face to try to ease the ache inside his cheekbones. "I didn't know there were any good guys."

Abby shook her head. "Neither does Sam."

"What if he did?" Cameron asked. "Would it change anything?"

Abby had no answer for that question.

"How's the bar business? Prosperous enough that your

father wouldn't miss the money from a pelt or two?" Delmonico asked.

Deathly pale now, Abby closed her eyes.

"Maybe it's more that hunting is a sport?" Delmonico pressed.

"Power," Abby said with her eyes still shut. "It's about power, and who wields it."

"Guns kind of mess that theory up," Cameron said. "As far as hunting goes."

"So do men who can change into beasts and purposefully sever a human artery with one swipe of a claw," Abby said. "Beasts that can change a person's DNA by passing along a contagion that either kills or transforms."

The room fell silent for several seconds.

"There are bad guys in every corner of the planet," Delmonico finally said as she pushed off the wall. "Which is why some of us are in law enforcement, and also why we're having this conversation. Everyone here knows the kind of damage a bite or claw can inflict, and has vowed to prevent that whenever possible. Weres hate the ease with which a bad batch of virus can be passed along from one being to another as much as Sam Stark does. The true Lycans among us dread that contagion even more."

"Lycans?" Abby repeated.

Cameron might have been imagining it, but thought he saw interest cross Abby's peaked face.

Wilson entered the room before Delmonico addressed Abby's remark. Thankfully, Wilson wore pants. "You know," he said, "that's five more sentences than I've heard Dana say in as many months."

Abby stared at the newcomer.

Cameron spoke up. "Abby, meet Matt Wilson, werewolf detective with the Miami PD."

"Oh," she whispered, taking this in and swaying slightly. "I've ruined your coat."

"And your arm along with it," Wilson noted. "Shall we have a look at that cut?"

"It's not deep."

"Yet I can smell the silver in it from here." Wilson nodded to Cameron, asking for permission to close the distance. "Dylan, are you there?" he called over his shoulder.

Delmonico stepped forward. "Maybe it's not a good idea to expose Dylan right now, too."

"She's not going anywhere," Wilson said. "Are you, Miss Stark?"

"Actually, she probably is," the man with the blond hair corrected from the doorway. "Miss Stark might need some space when she hears a few things that her father neglected to tell her. When that's in the open, she can decide what she wants to do."

Dylan Landau turned his light eyes on Abby. "Isn't that right, Abby? You need to understand what's going on?"

She took Cameron completely by surprise when, instead of answering Dylan's question, Abby turned and fell into Cameron's open arms.

Abby refused to turn her head. Although Cameron's chest was partially covered in gauze, his skin felt as warm as she remembered, and she desperately needed warmth.

Careful not to disturb his wound or cause him more discomfort than she'd already seen etched in the lines on his face, she kept her cheek pressed to him, comforted by the sound of Cameron's heartbeat. The rest of the Weres gathered in the room allowed her some time without speaking, and for a while she enjoyed a false sense of being at peace. But that peace came with a hefty price tag soon to be exacted.

Cameron spoke first. "*Lycan*. Can someone please explain what that word actually means?"

Abby dreaded whatever the explanation would be.

Dylan Landau said, "*Lycan* is a term for being born Were, with no artificial injection of the wolf virus."

"Born, as in from birth?"

"From two pure-blooded parents," Dylan said.

"Are you one of those, Dylan?"

"I am, yes."

Lycan. Pureblood. Rare. Fifty thousand bucks per pelt. Those facts rushed through Abby's mind with the force of Sam's voice behind them.

"Are any of the rest of you Lycans?" Cameron asked.

"No," Wilson replied. "Dana and I were bitten, just as you were. We're relatively new to this side of things."

"Does that make a difference in the Were world? Being bitten versus being born a Lycan?"

"Oh yes," Wilson said.

"How?"

"Abilities. Senses. Reactions. Strength. The ease with which problems are dealt with. An internal encoding process and the proper system for passing the original genes along to family."

Abby made herself look at Dylan. The handsome being standing in front of her was the elusive catch that Sam had always hoped to find. He was a myth. One in a million.

Her stomach clenched. She swallowed a groan, lifted her head and said, "I might have been bitten when I was young, but can't recall the incident. Wouldn't I have changed before now if that was the case?"

Dylan nodded. "You would have changed with the first full moon after the virus had been introduced to your system. Moonlight at full strength is the catalyst that kicks the wolf into full bloom for all of us."

"For all Weres, yourself included?"

Dylan nodded. "Lycans can decide when to shape-shift after the initial wiring phase is over. After the first moon, most of us can change without moonlight."

Abby took this in. "You mentioned wiring."

"That first phase comes upon us at different times," Dylan said. "Some Lycans shift early, at puberty. Some of us take longer. We have no say in the matter of timing, but the end result is inevitable."

Abby felt like laughing hysterically. All this time, Sam had watched and waited through full moon after full moon, year after year, for a pure-blooded werewolf to show up, when Lycans possessed the ability to shape-shift without the moon. It was irony strong enough to kick Sam Stark in the groin. It was the reason Lycan pelts fetched astronomical prices. With the ability to shift at will, catching one off-guard would be tough. Maybe impossible.

She had been in the dark about so many things, and she hadn't been the only one.

She spoke again to Dylan. "So the fact that I haven't changed means…what? That I didn't have enough wolf virus inside me to process a full change in shape, yet enough to give me claws and an innate awareness of other Weres around me?"

Her heart began to pick up its pace in anticipation of more dreadful news soon to be delivered. The room seemed suddenly airless and way too small to contain both her new knowledge and her growing anxiousness. The walls closed in, as did Cameron's strong arms.

Dylan's voice remained calm. He said simply, and in the manner of having explained this to more than one person in his lifetime, "Your symptoms indicate that you are coming of age, Abby. A late bloomer isn't completely rare or all that unheard of. Maybe because of your circumstances and your fear of being the very thing you are, your body has held off on presenting your wolf to the world."

He had Abby's full attention now. The back of her neck prickled. Baby-fine hairs on her arms stood up, underscored by a roller coaster of chills.

"By circumstances, you mean living with a man who'd be willing to kill me if he found out," she said.

Dylan's eyes were on her.

No! she wanted to shout. *I'm not ready for what you're going to say. I may never be ready.*

She eyed the door and the hallway, thinking she'd run, planning her escape, but unable to move her feet.

After watching her closely to see how she'd react to his previous statement, Dylan delivered the blow she'd been anticipating.

"The truth, Abby," he said, "is that Sam Stark can't be your father. He can't be a blood relative at all, because Sam isn't Lycan, and you are."

Chapter 21

Sam isn't my father.

I am Lycan.

Growls of protest erupted from Abby's throat. Her ears throbbed with the blond Were's explanation for her current state.

Sam can't be a relative at all.

Not a relative. Not my father.

Her instantaneous relief over that became sidetracked by the question of how this wolf thing had happened. A quick shuffle of memories about Sam's reluctance to speak of her mother sat on top of the list, as did the fact that he had been willing to shoot her. Sam's finger had been on the trigger.

She had always wondered why he treated her like a servant most of the time, with little effort in the way of showing emotion or an aptitude for caring for his progeny. This was the answer. Sam had been merely tolerating her. They didn't share blood or genetics. She and Sam Stark had no true bond whatsoever.

Her wish had come true.

Reeling with the information presented to her, Abby zeroed in on the other words haunting her. Sam had told her that he'd been watching her for signs. Signs of being... *just like her.*

"Like my mother," she whispered.

According to Dylan's explanation, it took two Lycans to produce another one. Undiluted blood had to be passed down from one generation to the next. And that's what Dylan had suggested she was. *Lycan.*

This was earth-shattering news, and totally revealing if true. Here was an explanation for being drawn to Weres, and for all those years of feeling different.

Yet she had to be sure.

"There's no way a Were can be half-Lycan?" she asked.

"No way," Dylan replied. "Impossible."

"Then my mother," Abby said at length, "had to have married Sam after I was born. She had to have had a reason for being with Sam. What could possibly cause a werewolf hunter to take on a Were and her daughter, or vice versa? Why would my mother live with a killer with a vendetta against her race? If what you're saying is the truth, my father has to be someone else."

"It's possible that Sam didn't know about your mother. She might have kept it from him," Dylan said.

Abby shook her head. "Maybe at first, though not for long. Sam told me tonight that he had watched me for signs of being like her. This had to be what he meant. He had waited to see if I'd be a werewolf."

She felt foolish for not having seen that, for not putting things together sooner, and on her own. It all made a terrible kind of sense now, thanks to Dylan's explanation.

However, was it actually true?

Was it believable that Sam had waited for her wolf to show itself, and that possibly her mother hadn't actually died of pneumonia, as she had briefly been told?

"I suppose we'll never know the answers to your questions," Cameron said. "And after tonight, seeing Sam in person wouldn't be a good idea."

Abby refused to let her legs give out, or her stomach to turn over its contents. She was surrounded by Weres and infatuated with one of them for reasons just coming to light. Both she and Cameron Mitchell were werewolves. She had been a wolf since her birth. Hell, she'd been a wolf in her mother's womb.

Fight, or flight? This was too much information to process at once. *Shout? Argue? Run? Maybe a combination of all those options.*

And maybe not.

Modulating her quivering voice, Abby looked up at Cameron with a confession on her lips. "This is too much. Please, can we be alone?"

"You don't want to hear more?" Cameron asked. "Figure things out?"

"I need to hear everything, just not now. Not right this minute. I can't breathe. I need to think."

Cameron inclined his head to her, then to the others, without releasing her from the protective, possessive circle of his arms.

The cut on her arm had begun to sting again, as if she had just made it. Moonlight had entered her through the open gash, tugging at what lay inside. But if what Dylan said proved true, moonlight didn't have to rule all Weres. Lycans were exempt. Why then did moonlight thrash around inside her, mercilessly trying to change everything it came into contact with?

"If you need us," Dylan said to Cameron, "you know

where we are. If you need anything, you're welcome behind our walls."

When the Weres filed out, taking their extraordinary heat with them, the room seemed empty and cold. Until Abby met Cameron's gaze.

Then, wounded, sick, anxious and off balance in a world that had gone insane and swept her along with it, Abby, on tiptoe, pressed her lips greedily, hungrily, terrifyingly, to his, hoping to escape from reality for a little while.

Cameron, injured and unenlightened, returned her kiss with a groan of acceptance and a hunger of his own.

This will hurt you, her mind cried out to him. *This is my fault and I'm sorry.*

Did he hear her silent apology? Did his own wound grind him down?

He tore the leather coat from her shoulders and let it fall to the floor, his mouth never once leaving hers. She tasted the medicine he'd been treated with, as well as the fire of fever beneath it. As her hunger for him deepened, her wounded arm blazed with pain as if she had taken in some of Cameron's hurt, temporarily allowing him freedom from the pain he had suffered on her behalf.

This is what she needed, wanted.

Cameron's lips covered hers with a ferocious passion. His hands cupped her face, then slid to her bare neck, caressing, exploring, needing to touch every inch of her, reflecting her own desires to have all of him.

Wolf to wolf.

Their surroundings faded away, leaving only one noticeable thing: the smell of the place where they stood. She was in his house. Cameron lived here, slept here. His scent was everywhere, and she couldn't take in enough of it, feel enough of it or give enough back to him to make up for what had happened to them.

Going back was not an option, she reiterated, though

the future looked bleak, because she had lost her hold on humanity tonight.

I am like my mother.

And if that were true, she'd meet Cameron body to body and cell to cell without having to worry about a bite or a scratch changing her. She'd allow herself one more transgression before any more news came that might break her.

As Abby reached up to slip her fingers into Cameron's hair, she thought she heard her mother's voice echo in her own sultry moan of satisfaction. In reality, the sigh of pleasure came from her lips.

Cameron set aside his pain and reveled in having Abby in his arms. Her fingers wound through his hair before they flitted lightly across the back of his neck on the way to his bare shoulders. When she slid her hands under his arms, her fingers splayed. She clung to the muscles near the line of his spine, generating spasms of pure unadulterated greed in every corner of his body.

He had time for only one thought:

There were too many clothes in the way.

With his eyes shut and his mouth locked to hers, he clasped the fringe of what was left of her jeans, tugged and felt the waistband release. His palms skated over the delicate line of her lower back before dipping to the seductive curves of her buttocks beneath. His exploration made her lift her mouth from his. She didn't speak. Her breath was feverish.

He wanted this more than anything. More than life itself.

"No waiting for this?" he said, watching for a signal that she wanted it, too.

Abby shook her head, said, "No more waiting."

She was perfect, naked and willing. And she was a wolf. Cameron growled with delight and the extremes of his

pleasure. More words or questions would have been useless, meaningless, when their mouths, lips, hands and bodies said it all.

Impatiently, he took her to the hardwood floor. Sitting
upright, he pulled Abby on top of him. She knew instinc-
tively what to do.

She began to move her hips as though he was already
inside her, rubbing him senseless with her silky, savory
skin, luring him to her.

He stretched out on his back, keeping her in his lap,
where she sat with both hands on his chest. She was lean,
beautiful and mesmerizing. Her slender back arched. Her
breasts gleamed. The furred-up spot between her thighs
that was the gateway to possessing her completely taunted
him with a promise of what was to come.

Cameron followed the soft touch of her fingers across
skin made sensitive by the invasion of the silver bullet. Her
hands moved lightly, deftly, over the contours of his chest,
ribs and stomach. Randomly, she leaned over to kiss his
skin, and to deliver a moist lick of her tongue.

His body accepted whatever she wanted to do. Fate had
brought them together, and they were safe. Other than
fate, how else could being with her like this be explained?

He uttered a curse when her silky hair tickled his shoulder. He let loose another oath when she bit down hard on
a spot near his collarbone with her small human teeth.
As if that bite possessed some magical property Landau's
medicine lacked, the pain of the wound that had sidelined
him melted away, replaced by the sheer passion and excitement of the moment. He had never been so hard and
so ready. He had never loved anything or anyone so much.

Abby knew this, of course. She had to.

The sound of his zipper opening broke the silence. She
slithered down his body, dragging his pants along before

returning to position her damp, inflamed sex over his pulsing erection.

With his hands on her hips, Cameron lifted her slightly, far enough to ease her over him. He sighed as her scorching heat took him in.

She was not to be held back. Expertly, intuitively, she took over, moving quickly to take all of his hardness inside. Each inch she traveled left waves of incredible pleasure. As if sharing his pleasure, she threw her head back, exposing her long, bare neck. Raising himself, Cameron took that smooth, pale flesh between his teeth.

She liked this. Her lush lips parted, though she made no sound. Cameron held back a howl as each movement of her sleek body threatened to do him in. The pleasure was too intense, his reaction too quick, and too soon.

"Slow down, Abby. Please."

Sweeping her into his arms, Cameron got to his feet. She allowed this, but barely. His bedroom was down a short hallway that seemed to stretch for a mile. Cameron carried her there, insane over the way her bareness met with his, and the way her legs curled over his forearms.

In his room, he tossed her onto the mattress and glanced down at her with his wolf vision to see the expression she offered him in the darkened room. That expression was the epitome of a need so great it registered as violent.

Abby wanted this for reasons only she understood. He guessed one of those reasons to be the necessity for an outlet to release the surprising, life-altering events of two nights in a row in that damn park. She had to be jumbled up inside.

He'd give her that release and more, gladly. He would make her see how much he cared.

Kneeling beside her, perched above her plushness, he waited out the seconds ticking by. She didn't reach for him this time, but lay there, looking up at him with her arms spread wide and her legs slowly opening.

It was the invitation he needed.

He tore the silver knife and its sheath from her ankle and threw it away, then ran both hands up her legs, following with his eyes, drinking her in.

He found her sweet spot, the apex between her thighs, and pressed his warm palm there. She groaned softly, and gritted her teeth. When he inserted a finger, she arched off the bed. When he added another, she grabbed at the sheet, writhing beneath the intimacy of his touch.

He dropped to his knees and held her legs steady. One long lap of his tongue over her sex was all he could manage before his body threatened to burst.

"Not so slowly, then," he said, moving up beside her. He ached to get on with this. He wanted to hear her shout.

He entered her only far enough to bury the tip of his desire, and took a deep breath to settle himself. His heart raced, beating against the hole in his chest. Abby's blistering heat beat at him, inside and out. She was sultry, her every move naturally sensual. Her eyes were wide open and shining with a wildness she could hardly contain. She whispered his name softly, in the purr of a low growl...

And he sank into her with a plunge so deep it filled her to her core. Their hips ground together so tightly it seemed to him as though they were one in body and in spirit. He felt spasms rock her, and the rush of molten heat that met him as she wrapped herself around his length.

All of that sent him hurtling past the edge of control.

And then she wrapped her long legs around him, as she had before, in the dark, in that blasted park, encircling him with her fire, holding him captive. Trapped in her embrace, his only option was forward.

He eased back and entered her again, exerting himself

in the desire to reach what lay beyond that molten core, wanting to find Abby's wolf, needing to access her soul.

He drove himself inside her wet, waiting depths again and again, building a rhythm, each thrust coaxing her orgasm to unfurl. Over and over, deeper and deeper he went, wearing down her veneer of handling this until their bodies slammed together so hard the bed shook. Glass in the window beside them rattled, and still, Abby's eyes dared him to give her more.

"Someday, wolf to wolf, Abby, we'll go there."

Perhaps sensing his slight hesitation, Abby's long, lithe legs became a sleek, fleshy vise.

Okay.

All right.

Cameron drove into Abby one last time with an effort fueled by every need he'd ever had, all bundled into one motion. He didn't do this for himself. Not completely. This was a sharing. An example of how much he cared. He meant it as a promise for a future, offered to her on a rumpled bed, in his room, in his home, on his terms. He offered her this with his own soul tied up in a big red bow.

"For you, Abby."

Her hips stilled. Her legs loosened. Suddenly motionless, Abby gasped aloud. Inside, her climax rose, its progress tickling his erection. It hurled upward to meet him, and his body responded with a pause that gave her room to imagine what lay ahead.

She began to tremble. Strangely enough, so did he. Abby's shudders spurred him on.

He drove inside her with a final furious thrust that might have split a normal woman in two…and then he joined her in an orgasm that drowned out the world and everything in it.

As their bodies locked together, and they were unable

to breathe or twitch, their pitched voices mingled in a howl
of ecstasy that shook the rafters.

There were few hints of anything human in the sound.

Chapter 22

The world revolved in moving patterns of light and dark, taking all breathable air with it, leaving Abby with a sense of unreality. She blinked slowly, trying to catch hold of something permanent and unmoving with which to center herself, but only Cameron's body, lying across her naked one, kept her from spinning out of control.

He wasn't asleep. He might have been daydreaming of an inevitable physical rematch, just as she was, because his pulse hadn't slowed much. His resilient skin was slick with a fine film of sweat, as was hers. The sex had been strenuous. Possibly they should have paid more attention to Cameron's wounds.

Maybe he was silent now out of the need to recoup his strength. Or maybe this was Cameron being chivalrous in giving her time to recover, not realizing that their erotic antics hadn't taken anything from her, and had, in fact, been invigorating, even challenging, in ways she didn't fully understand.

One thing was certain. Cameron Mitchell was not only compelling but addictive. Better than food. Far beyond anything reasonable. He was the perfect rogue in bed, the seducer, the lover, the man, despite an injury that should have slowed him down. And all that beautifully sculpted muscle, so close and scented with their sexual drives, drove her crazy, still.

Cameron seemed too good to be true, and she had fallen for him, hard. She had to fight to keep her hands and her mouth off him, and purposefully deflect the desire to scan his formidable outline. And if she craved him so much, why did she imagine she'd learn more on her own, without him by her side?

Why was she going to leave him? Family secrets, that's why. She would be no good to anyone without knowing her background. What she really was, and who her mother was. First on that to-do list would be facing Sam, no matter how difficult and dangerous that might be.

Sam was out there, and only he had the answers to everyone's questions, especially hers. Sam, who had proved himself a complete bastard several times over, held the key to both her past and her future. She'd never be whole or at peace until she learned about those secrets.

If Sam had been willing to pull the trigger tonight, setting his sights on his adopted daughter, how had he lived with a Were for any period of time whatsoever as his wife?

Cameron rolled over onto his side, allowing her a full view of the length of his truly magnificent body. All perfect. All there in plain view, right up to the bandage taped to his chest. Behind that bandage lay some of Sam's brutal handiwork. But though Cameron had been shot with silver just hours ago, the injury hadn't prevented the culmination of their raging carnal desires, which showed just how strong Cameron really was.

Leaving him, even temporarily, would be the toughest thing she'd ever done.

"I want to know everything about you," she said softly, something she wanted nearly as much as round two of the extreme physical pleasure he gave her. Yet the rush of a newly discovered kind of blood in her arteries also gave Abby a feeling of being left behind on her own life story, and a sense of hollowness remained after being sated.

"Everything about you," she stressed, running a hand over his shoulder.

When he looked up, Abby averted her gaze.

Night flooded through the window next to the bed. The moon had dropped from its position high up, where it had lorded over its Were children, though strong light flowed over nearby rooftops and into Cameron's backyard. That light had now become part of her, and the key to a strange existence. At present, its pull remained deniable, but for how much longer?

She was a Lycan, and as such, her pelt would bring a fortune to anyone capturing it. She'd be hunted by the best teams Sam had with no letup, because Sam now knew for sure what she was. It seemed that he might have known all along what she had the potential to become. Was that why he had kept her around? Not out of any kind of familial loyalty, but to grow his own special million-dollar pelt?

Abby's stomach heaved up nothing but emptiness. Her involuntary convulsion made Cameron raise a hand to turn her head.

"Abby." His tone was serious. "We can't take it back. We can only move forward, making the best of what we have."

She had granted Cameron access to her body, and desperately needed him again—inside her, merging with her. Only with their intimacy had she forgotten the rest and briefly glimpsed her own real strength. Together, they equaled something truly special.

And yet she was about to leave that behind.

She was going to leave him to find the truth about herself.

"I know that," she said. "But I'm stuck, neither here, nor there. No longer fully human, yet unable to shift into the thing I could become."

"Never fully human to begin with," he pointed out.

"So your friend says."

"He'd be the one to know. You can sense Weres, but it seems reasonable for Lycans to be able to sense more, sense things beyond what the rest of us can. From what I understand, Lycan blood has been around for quite some time. Years. Centuries."

When Abby's eyes met his, her instinct was to let her body's needs take over. Stay with Cameron. Figure this out. The sparks in his eyes and in his touch made her inner fires sizzle and dance, yet as if she'd been the one shot with that silver bullet, Sam's secrets left their own dark hole of disturbed emptiness.

"I don't deserve you, or this," she said. "After what I've done to Weres."

"Don't, Abby. Don't even think things like that," he argued. "How were you to know?"

But she should have known better, Abby thought. And she'd be good to no one until she found herself.

"I have to go." She continued to caress his face. Sensing the protest building up inside him, she placed a finger over his lips to try to hold the arguments back. If he said something logical, she might give in, change her mind, leave those questions unanswered. If he kissed her again, she'd lose sight of her goal.

He took her hand in his and squeezed her fingers. Raising himself onto one elbow, he said, "I can't let you leave. It's my job to protect people, and the trouble out there stinks."

"People," Abby said, "is a term that doesn't describe either of us, really."

"You have claws, and not much else to help you face what's waiting, Abby. What good are the claws when those hunters have guns? A fight with teeth and nails is personal and face-to-face. What's the distance covered by a bullet shot from a gun or rifle? Where's the sport in that? Those hunters don't have to really see you. They won't look into your eyes and see the light of humanity in them."

"They also kill monsters." It was a weak protest, at best.

"They do, but their sense of sport has gotten out of hand."

"Yes. Way out of hand," Abby agreed. "But maybe we caused Sam to do this. My mother and I. Maybe something my mother did caused him to hate Weres so deeply."

"You didn't know your mother?"

"She died before I could."

Cameron nodded. "Are you thinking that Sam might have killed her?"

She stared at him. The prickles along her spine returned because, damn it, she hadn't thought that, hadn't allowed herself to consider the idea…until now, when it was out in the open, and spoken with the voice of a man who had been bitten by a werewolf and had his life changed forever.

Possibly she had been dreading that particular scenario.

Could Sam have killed her mother?

"Maybe," she said. "Maybe he had something to do with her death. I don't know."

These were terrible thoughts, horrendous suppositions. She had tried to find out about Sonja Stark so many times, and come up short. She'd hid her search, hoping someday Sam would toss her a bone.

"I won't rest until I find out," she said.

"I can help with that, Abby. The department has access to all sorts of information."

Again their gazes connected, causing a stir deep inside Abby. "You'd do that for me?"

"Yes."

"Because I'm like you? Because I have nowhere to turn, and don't understand what I am?"

"Because I want to know you better, too, and this seems like a good way to start."

Glancing to the window, Abby was able to draw in her first decent breath in a long night of turbulent events. "Thank you, Cameron."

He sat up to face her. "You don't want to stay here, with me?"

"I can't. Not now."

He took that in. "Dylan and the others will help. You heard them say so."

"How do we know they spoke the truth?"

"About you?"

"Yes. About me."

"Is there another explanation for your inability to shift, when your claws proved the point?"

"It doesn't feel right."

"This feels right." Cameron caught her elbow and, with a simple snap of his arm, brought her closer to him, level with him and down on her side, so that she had no option but to study his face. He said, "I'm not sure it would be like this if we weren't alike to some degree."

His statement brought her more sadness. Abby held her tears back by the sheer force of her dogged determination not to weaken any further.

"Then why did Sam marry a Lycan, someone so unlike him, and a creature he hunts with each full moon? What was that like for my mother?"

Cameron pulled her closer, close enough to render his face a bronze blur in the darkened room. He placed a kiss on her forehead, and another one on her cheek. His large hands cupped her face so that she had to stay motionless.

His lips brushed her mouth, then came back to linger. Not a real kiss—merely a breath and a touch and a reminder of the benefits of remaining with him. But she didn't really need a reminder of that, and moaned when his hands eased over her neck, her shoulders and arms. He found her right breast, and closed his hand over her fullness with a palm made of pure, radiant heat.

Unable to fight him, Abby shut her eyes. Just this once, and for one more time, she wanted to be Cameron's partner.

Her pulse quickened when he lightly rubbed his fingers over her. No one had ever touched her like this, as though each part of her nakedness was something to be treasured. Cameron wanted her. He might even love her.

Arching her spine, she pressed herself against him. His reaction was to roll her onto her back. Wanting his mouth on hers, Abby reached for him. But he shook his head, having other ideas about where to place his lips.

With a slow lap of his tongue over the raised bud of her nipple, he then closed his velvety lips over it, his tongue teasing and darting in an agonizingly delicious process.

It was too much pleasure for her, all at once, and in one night. Abby bucked off the bed. But one of Cameron's arms slid beneath her, holding her firmly as he followed his caresses with a soft suckle that electrified her into stillness.

And for her, this was…

Was…

Indescribable.

He continued to lick and nibble and bite, holding her captive with each new action until the rhythm of her rising orgasm beat at her insides, threatening to end this session way too soon. She was completely helpless against the oncoming tide.

Cameron halted that internal pressure by lifting his

head. "Not done," he said in a sexy, throaty tone of promise. "No need to rush. Go with me, Abby. Trust me. Let me have all of you tonight. Stay."

There was no way she could have replied. Again, the room was spinning. Cooler air breezed across the front of her dampened body as he moved backward, leaving a downward trail with his talented tongue. She felt his hand between her thighs, encouraging her legs to open. He rubbed her swollen sex in the same way he'd rubbed her breast, slowly, back and forth, adding pressure with each pass.

She threw her head back, anticipating what he might do next.

Clamping her teeth together to keep from screaming, she clutched at the sheet as Cameron again inserted one long, lean finger into her, parting her, testing her unnecessarily, readying the way for what she'd been waiting for. Her heart pounded. Her body throbbed as that finger brought more fire, more dampness, and a swift second rise of that distant drumbeat.

And then the finger withdrew, and Cameron's mouth replaced it. With a tender kiss and a quick dart of his hot tongue, he did that thing she had only heard of. He used his mouth to seduce her into an orgasm that burst with the light and fury of an exploding star.

She groaned, screamed, as the climax went on and on, and Cameron's mouth continued to give pleasure. But it wasn't over. He wasn't through.

Before her climax had ended, he was inside her, his cock as seductive as his mouth had been. He moved in and out of her, not gently or taking his time, but with the real power of purpose. Cameron Mitchell would have her, take her, possess her until she'd have to deny all others and lose the will to leave. He'd mark her as his and split her in two if he had to, in order to get his point across. There was no one of them without the other. This joining was conceived of wolf magic and mystery.

She came again in flashes of brilliant color and all-consuming flame, and then came once more after that. Her lover beat at her, tortured her with his strength and his prowess as a lover, not letting up until he could take it no longer.

And then, as his own heat burst inside her, he lovingly whispered her name.

Chapter 23

Through their rasping, spent breaths, Cameron heard the sound that outpaced his thundering heart, and thought he had to be mistaken.

No, there it was again, coming from the open window.

When he paused and stiffened, Abby looked up.

"Outside," he said, on his feet in seconds.

Sure that Abby had risen with him, he moved to the window and cautiously looked out. Though he saw nothing, he sensed danger with a certainty that chilled the back of his neck.

Abby stood beside him, naked and as beautiful in her wild, rumpled state as anything he had ever set eyes on.

"Smell?" he said, and she took in a long, deep breath of night air, and then backed away from the window.

"Not humans, Abby?"

She shook her head. "Wolf. More than one."

"I assume if they're friendly, they will come to the front door."

"I think we might have ruined your front door when we came in," she reminded him.

"Well, that's not good," he remarked thoughtfully. "Anyone might waltz in here like there's an open invitation."

Abby glanced to the hallway. "Or might have already."

Again, Cameron looked outside. "Being Were sometimes has its perks. At least we know when someone else is in the vicinity."

He knew the seriousness of having wolves in his neighborhood, and that this didn't bode well for someone. The three Weres he'd met that night had gone. As far as he knew, not many other people were aware of his address. No one that counted, anyway. He'd moved to a neighborhood far from the precinct on purpose, not keen to get cozy with his neighbors in case the wolf in him took a wrong turn. Also, he had a hunch that a lot of the rogue Weres doing damage in and around the park came from this area, and he'd hoped that with close proximity he'd be able to keep an eye on them.

"Stay here, Abby."

She gave him a questioning look.

"I mean it. Please stay here. I'm going out for a better look around."

"Kiss my behind," she said soberly, and he smiled.

"Gladly. But give me a minute."

Abby smiled back, and that smile lit up her face. She reached for her knife and found it missing.

"It's on the floor," he said, wondering how Abby could be Were and handle that damn knife so easily, supposing that being Lycan had a lot to do with it. There were a lot of questions to ask those other Weres the next time they met.

The next sound from outside came from behind the fenced yard next door. "Too close for comfort," he said.

"What are they after?"

"My guess is that they're onto our scent. Especially now

that we've…" He ended that sentence differently. "And that just won't do."

"I'll get out of here."

"Yep. Right now, and with me."

"The moon's still up," Abby noted.

"Even better. No need to take the time to get dressed."

Abby strapped her knife, in its leather sheath, onto her leg.

"You do realize you won't be able to hold that with claws?" Cameron said.

"Who said I'll have claws?"

"Hell, Abby, you are a freaking enigma. A lovely, freaking enigma."

"Time to move, wolf," she said over one bare shoulder as she raced from the room.

In reply, and with his eyes on that bare shoulder, Cameron growled.

Side by side, they left the house and moved into the street. Cameron figured there was only one place to lead a couple of bad wolves, when protecting Abby sat foremost on his mind, and hoped that going there wouldn't wear out his welcome. Like it or not, it seemed that the Landau pack was going to see a lot more of his sorry ass.

Tonight the Landau walls would be guarded. Quite possibly, their pack would have a presence in the park near enough to those walls to keep loafers well away from discovering a house full of Weres. If any of the purebloods there smelled like Abby, that compound would have to be very well protected.

Abby's scent was like candy. Like catnip. What better way to attract a wolf was there, than allowing it a whiff of her highly erotic she-wolf pheromones?

Cameron cursed the distraction that made another round of sex impossible. The light bouncing off rooftops hit him square in the face. It was party time. In this instance, though, he welcomed the magical voodoo intrinsic to that light. He'd be stronger, fiercer, faster, all furred up. He'd be better able to protect Abby, in lieu of carrying his day-time gig's weapon.

"Follow me" were the last words he got out before his shift began.

Cameron had never really seen Abby in full motion, other than in his bedroom. Yet here she was, running by his side, tense, determined and looking as though she could do some damage to whoever showed up to chase them.

She kept up, without the benefit of a partial fur coat to cloak her bareness. She was barefoot and naked, except for the strip of brown leather on one lower leg that was the sheath holding her knife. And she was very pale in the moonlight, with the colorlessness of a ghost.

He'd forgotten to ask her for more details about the hunters, such as if they prowled the park all night, or had set hours. If they stayed until sunrise, a direct route to the Landau compound for him and Abby would be out of the question. A werewolf seen running through the streets with a naked woman by his side would be equally as bad.

He'd have given anything right about now for his own cell phone and the gun he had locked up before heading out to the bar tonight for Stegman's wake—a gun that wouldn't have done much good against a nasty set of were-wolves bent on trouble.

Had that fight in the park been only last night? Hell, he felt as though he'd lived five lifetimes in forty-eight hours.

He grasped tightly to Abby's hand, careful with his claws, needing to touch her. She ran like the wind, breathing through the bruised mouth he had repeatedly ravaged.

His block and the several beyond it had plenty of houses. The pathway Cameron chose cut through the worst parts of the area, where buildings marked by graffiti and littered with debris were the norm.

When cars passed, he and Abby hid in the shadows. There were, he knew, about three miles between his house and the Landau compound by street—a big circular pattern and a long way under any circumstances. In the dark, under a big moon, and with the wolf's urge to both pleasure and protect Abby, reaching Laudau's walls seemed a particularly difficult feat.

"They're coming," Abby announced.

Inevitable, Cameron thought. *And a goddamn shame.* His strength had been compromised by not only the silver bullet that had mercifully missed his heart, but by his energy output since then. Weres might heal miraculously, and he certainly had beat the odds of enjoying a nice, long hospital stay, but he felt more sluggish than usual. The bullet hole in his chest burned all the way through to his shoulder blades.

He hated when others were right, and he'd had to nix a full recovery. The timing of this new attack sucked.

"Building on your right," Abby called out, already heading that way.

Why, Cameron again thought, didn't Abby Stark show the slightest bit of fear or distaste over his current wolfed-up state? Sure, she might be a werewolf internally, yet she continued to exhibit no outward signs of shifting. How did she control that? If it was a matter of willpower, hers had to be second to none.

They dived for cover from a passing car, beneath an overhanging roof beam, where they'd get a better idea of whom and what followed them. Seconds ticked by in silence before the assailants appeared. Two of them, as Abby had predicted, all muscled up and begging for trouble.

Abby's knife was in her hand, though that hand now trembled. Cameron felt the presence of her silver blade as strongly as if she had used it on him. The narrow piece of polished metal seemed to draw on the remaining slivers of silver in his system, so that his skin rippled and pulsed, and a wave of light-headedness struck. He made a sound that caused Abby to move the knife, and even that minor change made it easier for him to get air into his lungs.

When he breathed deeply, he caught a whiff of something foul. The potent odor of unwashed wolf. Bad guys, then, he confirmed, growling his displeasure over facing two hyped-up werewolves so near to the street.

Abby's hand wasn't the only part of her trembling now. Tremors rocked her stance. He heard her teeth snap shut, probably to keep them from chattering. But she didn't back down. Without a voice, appeasing her wasn't an option. They were backed into a corner and would have to make a stand.

"I'm ready," she said.

Swear to God, he loved Abby Stark for that vote of confidence.

Chapter 24

Abby had been around some fairly rough-and-tumble people in Sam's bar, and had often defended herself from unwanted advances, but none of those people had tried to kill her. Only Sam had been willing to pull a trigger.

And now this.

Being angry and upset, though, tended to give her a boost. Adrenaline pumped through her so hard her nerves sang. Brandishing the knife took both hands.

Her companion had bested bad wolves before, but he'd been injured too recently to predict a good outcome here. Another cop had died trying to keep the peace the night before when facing these bad wolves, and cops were trained to take down criminals. But cops weren't ready for mentally malnourished werewolves with a wicked agenda. Only Cameron, Sam and the rest of the hunters realized what this kind of trouble meant.

"They smell," she said as Cameron took one more step forward. Abby recognized the odor and the feel of their evil intent without waiting for them to prove it. These rogues had the watery black eyes of rabid dogs, and stank of smoke and grimy pavement.

They materialized in a tiny patch of moonlight and kept purposefully inside that light. Their everyday human shapes wouldn't rival the scary picture they presented, and for them, image was probably everything.

These werewolves were nothing like Cameron—weren't creatures of beauty and natural animal grace in their furred-up incarnations. Both of them were varying shades of brown, with short, shaggy fur that lacked sheen. She'd seen drunks with that kind of dullness to their skin, leached of color and energy due to too many years of nights on the town.

Their muzzles were grotesquely elongated, showing off mouthfuls of big yellow teeth. They panted with the effort of holding back their desire for a kill. One of them growled. Undeterred, Cameron growled back. When the larger wolf raised its paws menacingly, Abby raised the knife so that the silver caught the light.

Their eyes moved to her, and what she held.

Cameron stood a good head taller than the biggest wolf, and in Cameron's spectacular stance of defiance, he seemed to Abby like the prince of menace. His muscles rippled as if they were alive and capable of moving on their own. His hair hung in his eyes, giving him an air of untamed wildness. This tense demeanor spoke volumes. *Come and get it, if you dare.*

She'd have hit the road if she'd been his opposition. These two idiots had other ideas—one of those probably being that two jacked-up werewolves against one wounded animal and his small mate were damn good odds.

In unison, the werewolves sniffed the air, their attention shifting back and forth from Cameron to her, their eyes intent on the blade. Abby thought she saw confusion cross their misshapen features. What wolves were doing with a silver weapon had to be the question they were asking themselves before getting on with their attack.

The shudder of anticipation that ran through Cameron also ran through her, contagious and cold. Able now to hold the knife in one hand, Abby placed her other palm on Cameron's back, allowing his radical electrical charge to surge through her.

Her body responded immediately to that influx of power. Claws sprang from all ten of her fingers simultaneously with the tearing of sensitive skin and a single crack of pain. That first jolt caused another one, and like a game of dominoes, where one domino leaned into another and everything tipped over in a predisposed pattern, the dark thing she carried inside her that she'd ignored all these years rose to the surface with the all-consuming intensity of an impending sexual climax.

This new thing hurled itself upward and outward so fast that Abby didn't have time to acknowledge what might happen. Knocking internal organs out of its way, coating everything inside, in seconds the darkness spread through her, causing upheaval and pain so violent she wouldn't have imagined it possible to withstand the surge.

She dropped the knife and uttered a curse that tapered into a howl. She spoke to herself. *Do not close your eyes. You cannot afford to lose ground, or lose this battle.*

But she had to shut her eyes. The pain flooding her body was too great to withstand. It seemed too great to survive.

And in that instant, when the world went dark, the rogue werewolves sprang.

A sense of urgency beat at the air as Cameron heard Abby whisper his name. He could not turn his head, had to leave thoughts about her behind for now, if they were to stay alive.

That was the name of the game. Live, or die.

His opponents were large, but clumsy, and for that, Cameron was grateful. The smaller of the two snapped its jaws repeatedly as it came on with misplaced self-confidence. Its needle-sharp teeth caught Cameron in the hand as he reached for its neck, and the blood spurting from the wound hit the oncoming werewolf in the face. But not before Cameron began to squeeze the breath from his attacker.

The big wolf was on him in a flash, its mouth and claws seeming to come from all directions. This hulk had a powerful punch. Taking a blow to his shoulder, inches from his previous wound, forced Cameron to spin full circle. He dragged the smaller assailant with him in the turn with his hands still on the wolf's thick, matted neck. The two attackers' bodies collided with each other, knocking the bigger bastard off its feet.

Out of the corner of his eye, Cameron saw Abby move. She picked up the knife. He caught the glint of her bright eyes as she jumped on top of the downed werewolf and struck at it with her blade. But this wasn't Abby, wasn't exactly the woman who had been behind him the moment before. She hadn't fully shifted, but some kind of change had taken place.

I can't help.

Abby, hang on.

Pain sharp enough to make him nauseous stabbed at Cameron's chest as he forced the wolf he had hold of to its haunches. The furry bastard flailed, growled and spat. Its fur was soaked in Cameron's blood, and the scent made the wolf ready to do anything to eliminate the hand cutting off its air supply.

With a push of its heavy thighs, this rogue tried to propel itself upward. But Cameron had been ready, and had been trained to fight. Tightening his grip, gaining better access to the wolf's windpipe as the wolf struggled upward, Cameron squeezed. The wolf's eyes widened with surprise. It thrashed around before it finally gasped, shuddered and lost the fight. Cameron held on until the breathless bag of bones fell to the ground.

Satisfied to be rid of one fanged idiot, Cameron whirled to find Abby and the other rogue on the pavement. It took him more precious time to figure out what had happened.

Blood spewed from a small round hole in the werewolf's right shoulder, but that wouldn't have taken it down unless Abby had delivered a well-placed silver blow.

She glanced up at him from her crouched position with the light of success in her beautiful eyes…and a red-feathered dart protruding from her neck.

Abby! No!

Dropping down to support her with his bloody hands, Cameron's senses warned that the fight wasn't over yet. There was more scent on the wind, which meant more intruders.

Not wolves.

He should have foreseen this, in hindsight. Should have predicted it. They'd taken too much time here, time they didn't have.

Sam Stark strode into the moonlight, dressed in black and looking like the grim reaper. Two silent, fully armed hunters flanked him on either side.

"I suppose I should thank you for the assistance," Stark snarled soberly. "But I don't speak monster."

Cameron figured that he was supposed to believe that a very untimely ending had come, and almost bought into it. But if cops believed there was no way out of messes on a regular basis, no one would wear a uniform and a badge. Add werewolf into the mix, and…well…the unexpected was always around the corner.

The big plus here was that Sam Stark didn't know the first thing about him, or his identity. According to what

Abby had said, Sam didn't stop long enough to care about his targets.

It might not have made any difference if Stark recognized a cop when he saw one, or not. *Monster* was the word Sam had used, and that kind of name-calling said it all.

"Get up," Stark ordered.

Cameron stayed put, on his knees, holding Abby, whose eyes had fluttered shut. She'd been drugged. He pulled the dart from her neck and tossed it aside.

"Don't you hurt her," Stark snapped.

That's going to be your privilege? I'll bet you're hard just thinking about it.

"I have another dart loaded and aimed," one of the nameless hunters said.

Sam Stark gestured for the man to wait and said to Cameron, "Leave her, wolf, and get up."

And if I don't?

Dealing with werewolves was so much simpler, he thought. With one growl, Weres knew when danger was at hand. With humans, things were never so easy. Some people looked okay, but hid a rotten core that produced child-abusers and other types of hardened criminals. It sometimes took the escalation of a problem to see the truth. Sam Stark smelled of anger, and had taken on physical aspects reminiscent of the dark angel of death. The man appeared sane, yet was barking mad. Why? He had been willing to kill Abby not long ago. Did he hope to reserve the pleasure of seeing that through now?

Stark's ultracalm demeanor and iron scent suggested to Cameron that Abby had been right about Sam. For Sam, hunting wasn't merely a sport. It was much more than that, and the culmination of something he had been waiting for. Something bigger than bagging a werewolf or two for a bankroll.

As a cop, Cameron had seen this kind of attitude in

cases where a personal vendetta ruled a man's actions. Payback for an affront or an offense.

The man Abby had presumed to be her father was seriously messed up inside, and seeing Abby's claws clinched whatever issues Sam had going on.

He had to get Abby out of here. Out of Stark's reach.

He had to try.

Cameron got to his feet slowly, pulling Abby's limp, glistening body up with him. With a swiftness that made the hunters jump back, he swept her into his arms.

"Shoot it," Stark directed. "In the back if you have to."

Cameron heard the swishing sound of the hunter's black vest moving. He looked down a rifle barrel and growled.

The sound of hell breaking loose came soon after.

Chapter 25

Sirens, heading their way with great speed, rent the night with the eerie wail of distant gods keening. The suddenness of the sound made the hunter's finger hesitate on the trigger, and in those few seconds lay the difference between this life and the next.

Cameron took full advantage of the pause.

Turning on his heels with Abby in his arms for the third time since they had met, Cameron utilized the speed and dexterity of a wolf in full bloom, under what was left of a full moon, and heard the metallic ping of the dart strike the wall beside where he had been standing.

He took off, gripping Abby tightly enough to crush her bones, and without stopping to catch his breath or look behind. Cops were on their way, heading into the area fast. He heard Stark's hunters scramble for cover. They would be hard-pressed to explain the guns and the darts, the blood spatter on the ground and the whole idea behind the "hunter" scenario to the Miami PD.

Cameron wanted to kiss the officers answering this call. Maybe he would, if he and Abby got out of this in one piece.

Darkness swallowed him up when he reached the next street. There were no homes here, just rows of factory after factory, most of them either closed for the night or abandoned altogether. At the moment, and while making a getaway, Cameron couldn't have asked for anything better.

Abby didn't move or speak. She lay huddled against him as lifelessly as if her bones had melted. Her claws had disappeared as soon as she closed her eyes, yet as he carried her and felt the heat of her bare skin on his, Cameron sensed her life's spark. She was out of it, but alive, and a series of ongoing changes were taking place inside her.

Her body began to exude a new scent. Her skin had a different feel. He remembered the extraordinary flash of her eyes when she'd faced down the rogue, and recalled hearing her whisper when Sam appeared out of the blue, "I'm sorry."

Hell, Abby, I'm the one who is sorry.

One block. Two. Three blocks, and he'd covered all the miles between his residence and the side of the park he needed to find the hard way. Sirens in the distance had stopped, which meant cops had arrived at the scene he'd left behind. Chances were good that Stark and his cronies also had a head start on a getaway. They'd be flirting with disappointment and fuming over having lost some of tonight's booty.

Possibly, if the rogue Weres Sam chased every month had changed back to their human shapes after they fell, old Stark would have given his hunters their money back—if they had paid for their hunting privileges and weren't satisfied with the way events had unfolded.

How much had Stark promised? At the very least, those guys got to see a werewolf or two up close. Bad thing was, they had also seen the woman they knew as Stark's daughter, and had to be wondering what that was all about.

Pondering things brought up too many ways things could go. Any way he looked at it, Abby's situation marked a change for everyone.

He couldn't take her to her home, or back to his. His comfy little nest had been discovered by bad guys because it had been saturated with wolf scent. Between himself, Abby, Dylan, Delmonico and Wilson, it wouldn't be a safe haven again for quite a while. Only one place met the criteria now.

The corner of the park near the boulevard lay just ahead, slightly ominous now that so much had happened in and around the boundaries. Stark had to have run the opposite way with his specialized weapons of wolf destruction. No reek of guns or human sweat tainted the night.

Personally, he didn't give a flying fuck for Stark, a sentiment that was probably mutual. Stark had lost this round, but there were thirty days between this night's full moon and the next one—plenty of time for Sam to widen his search for Abby.

Cameron paused long enough to place a tender kiss on Abby's damp forehead before continuing on.

He circled around the farthest tip of the park, relieved to see the colored stucco and brick walls of the Miami mansions he'd been seeking. The night was dead quiet here and lacking signs of disturbance, but as soon as he approached the wall he needed to scale, an unfamiliar voice above it halted him.

"Glad you made it," a half-furred-up, red-haired female said, gesturing with her claws for him to wait while she went for help.

So, how many Weres did Landau have in this pack? Who was the red-haired she-wolf?

Two big males landed beside him and attempted to take

Abby from his quivering arms. *No, you don't*, he silently sent to them. *This treasure is all mine.*

"Knocked out, but she will come around," a hazy voice stated.

"When?" The familiarity of this second voice made Abby's heart kick.

"Give her some time for the healing you refused. She's safe here, so there's no need to rush."

This speaker, an older woman by the sound of her tone, radiated the confidence of a healer. Was she in a hospital for freaks? Had she died and gone to werewolf heaven?

"She moved."

"I think she hears us. Abby?"

She didn't want to answer. Wasn't ready to wake up.

"Abby." Cameron's voice was a welcoming lifeline dropped into utter darkness. "Abby, it's all right. We got out of there and are with friends."

She shook her head slowly on something silky and feather-soft. A pillow? Depleted energy left her with only the breath for one word. *"Sam."*

"Gone," Cameron said. "At least for now."

She managed to stammer, "G-got away?"

"We did. I think you were my good luck charm."

It was okay to relax and give in to the need for sleep. Cameron was there to watch over her. He wouldn't let anything happen.

Warm fingers rested on her forehead. "Sleep, my love. I'll be here when you wake up."

Should she thank him, kiss him or beat at him with her fists for making her understand why she had previously wallowed in darkness? Abby contemplated all of those things.

"Abby, can you hear me?"

She was too weak to reply, and kept her eyes closed.

"You know. You do know what you are," he whispered. "You can heal quickly if you want to."

"Like her…" Abby replied as the color behind her eyes lightened and she was cast adrift on the tide of fatigue. "Like my mother."

"I sincerely hope the invitation to come here included her," Cameron said to the Were in the doorway without having to look to see who it was.

"And if it didn't?" Dylan replied.

"Then I'm sorry, and owe you one."

"You know we can't let her go now that she has been here."

"I figured as much," Cameron admitted. "I'm fairly sure Abby won't want to go anywhere, anytime soon, though. She might even relish the break. This has been a long night for me, so I can't imagine what it's been like for her."

Dylan came closer to glance down at the bed. "I met Dana on a side street, under a full moon."

Cameron looked at him.

"She was in the middle of her first shape-shift and had no idea what was happening."

Cameron nodded. "She told me you saved her ass."

"She fell out of her patrol car, onto the street. What law-abiding citizen wouldn't have helped her, especially when she took off her clothes?"

Sensing Dylan's readiness to talk, Cameron turned to face him. "Yep," he agreed. "It's hard to avoid them when they start on their clothes."

When Dylan smiled, it was one of the most charming smiles Cameron had seen on a man.

"You bonded with Delmonico that night?" he asked.

"As if it was meant to be," Dylan confessed. "I looked into her eyes and…well, no one else would do after that. She had gotten under my skin."

"Amen to that." Cameron glanced again to Abby, who was now sound asleep. "Although I have no idea what Abby is, really."

Dylan sat down in the chair by the window Cameron had escaped from earlier that night. This time, Cameron thought, he had a reason to remain. That reason's silky auburn hair fanned out across a floral pillowcase. Her face looked unbelievably pale.

"Can you tell me about her, Dylan?"

Dylan nodded. "Abby is the product of a liaison between two Weres whose bloodlines date back to the Flood. Before the Flood, no record of our kind exists."

Cameron interrupted with a question in need of clarification. "*The* Flood? You're talking about the one of biblical notoriety?"

Dylan nodded. "Some say that it had to be either on the Ark, or around then, that Lycans came into existence. But more evidence points to the figures etched in the tombs of the pharaohs, long before that. There were numerous depictions of men with the heads of wolves."

Cameron had seen some of those pictures in books and in documentaries on Egypt. He inclined his head, meaning for Dylan to go on.

"Whatever our origins, like in most cultures, Lycan evolution is only as strong as the purity of its bloodlines. In order for the traits we possess to be contained and passed along, the mating of two pure-blooded Lycans is required."

"What about your mate? Delmonico?" Cameron asked.

"Dana was bitten by a drugged-up madman, which rendered her blood suspect. In this pack or any other one, her children would never be allowed."

"That's harsh."

"It's the only way to protect ourselves from what has happened all around us."

"You mean the furred-up asses killing people all over the place, and the sudden explosion in their numbers?"

Dylan nodded. "Our DNA is fragile. When a Were bites a human, the result is unpredictable. Bite a criminal, and you might end up with a supercharged criminal. The virus does nothing to fix a deviant mind, and, in fact, magnifies what's already there."

Dylan looked to the window as if seeing parts of the past few months in the rapidly lightening dark. "The pack we cleaned out of the park last year was masterminded by a wolf that handpicked his followers for his own cruel purposes. He bit the initial few, then started the ball rolling as if it were some kind of psychotic pyramid scheme."

"Damn," was all Cameron could say.

"Most of that pack was killed when the warehouse housing them burned to the ground. A few missed their date with the funeral pyre and are around somewhere, cloning themselves."

"Easy as a bite or scratch," Cameron said. "The police were there the night it all went down."

"They were on the periphery. Weres got there first."

Cameron blinked slowly. "Let me guess. There are even more Weres in the Miami PD than I know about after tonight?"

Dylan smiled.

"Are you one of those few, Dylan?"

"I'm an attorney." Dylan held up a hand. "And I'm aware of the jokes."

"What kind of attorney? One that specializes in werewolf issues?" Cameron said with more levity than he felt.

"Something like that. I'm in the DA's office."

Cameron blew out a breath. "District attorney. You're *that* Landau."

Cameron shrugged and said soberly, "Dana and I won't have children."

"Because it isn't allowed and you'll follow the rules?"

"Because it's important to others that we heed those rules."

Cameron smoothed a corner of the sheet covering Abby's slumbering body, contemplating the personal stuff Dylan had shared.

"You've imprinted with Delmonico," he finally said. "This, according to you, means that you'll be together forever, metaphysically speaking."

"Yes."

"And that's okay with you? Not having a family, I mean?"

"We'll make do, and it will be worth every minute."

Cameron believed Dylan. He honestly liked the guy. Dylan was maybe a bit too handsome for some people to automatically take seriously at first, but his quiet inner strength and palpable Lycan vibe made him a serious contender for the term *formidable*.

"I was bitten in a raid," Cameron said. "Like Delmonico was. And I believe you're telling me all of this about rules and DNA as a subtle lead-up to the fact that Abby is like you. She's a DNA-kissed Lycan who has imprinted with a bitten Were male."

"Thanks for making this easy," Dylan said.

"Nothing deviant about my brain," Cameron remarked.

Dylan gestured to the bed. "She's been stunted, but has started her change."

"That sounds ominous, Dylan."

"Do you remember what you went through after receiving that bite?"

"I'll never forget it."

"Hers might be worse."

"I'm not sure that's possible," Cameron said.

"What you went through is called a Blackout."

"Jesus. It has a name?" Cameron ran a hand through his hair and let out a long, slow breath.

Dylan continued. "It's what happens when the body rewires itself, reconfiguring into the new thing it will become."

"Aren't Lycans wired from the start?"

"The blood is in the veins, and the virus is in the blood, but for Lycans, it remains static until we come of age."

"Abby has to be twenty-three or four," Cameron said.

"She's late for her date with the moon, but that's not unheard of, given where she'd been living."

"She'll go through that Blackout thing now that the changes have started?"

"Yes. And for some reason, it can be a far worse ordeal for females to get through."

The hair at the nape of Cameron's neck stood up in anticipation of more bad news he was sure would come.

"There are relatively few female Lycans," Dylan explained. "Maybe that's because their systems are fragile, and maybe because their trip through puberty is rougher than ours and takes a toll with other kinds of blood loss. Whatever the reason, pure-blooded Lycan females are rare, and coveted."

Cameron got to his feet, suddenly very anxious about where this was going.

"Sit," Dylan suggested. "Please."

"I don't think I want to."

"It's okay, Cameron. You have imprinted with Abby, and no one can take that away from you."

Cameron eyed Dylan skeptically.

"What I'm trying to say is that I have a theory that might explain her circumstances and the reason she's here."

"I'd love to hear it."

"Someone might have been waiting for Abby to rewire," Dylan said. "Someone close to her."

"By someone, you mean the only person who might have known about her all along, and about what she is."

Dylan said, "Sam Stark."

Cameron's stomach would not calm down, nor could he make it. There was something so bleakly ominous in what Dylan had proposed, it took some time for him to wrap his mind around what Dylan's theory might be.

Good thing his own mind still worked like a steel trap.

"A hunter raises a wolf for what reason?" he asked, and the answer he immediately came up with made him sick. "His own private pelt factory? Something to torture? Hell, Dylan, you aren't suggesting that?"

He was getting sicker by the second.

Dylan held up a placating hand. "Sam Stark used Abby's innate ability to ferret out other Weres. You don't suppose he wondered how she could find those Weres, and why she was the only member of his team who could?"

"If we followed that thread, we'd have to believe that he actually has known about her all along."

"Oh, it's quite possible that he knew. Probable, in fact." Dylan reached into his back pocket and pulled out a folded piece of paper. He smoothed it out on the bedside table and handed it to Cameron.

"He has been feeding Abby silver, in small doses, for years. My mother sees things like that. It's why Abby has been able to keep the changes at bay, though they couldn't have been resisted much longer."

Cameron shifted his glance to Abby as Dylan pointed to the paper and went on.

"Here's an interesting fact about Abby's mother. I thought you might like to know the story."

Cameron did not want to pick up that paper. He told himself not to touch it. But in the end, he had to know what the hell Dylan Landau was talking about.

Chapter 26

Abby heard every word of this conversation between Cameron and Dylan. The information filled in a few blanks, but she wanted more than anything in the world to rip that paper out of Cameron's hands. He had read information that was important to her. Didn't they realize she had been groping for clues?

Screams never made it past her throat. Shouts would have been premature. Tonight, out there in the park, she had briefly contemplated the theory Dylan Landau had just proposed. Sam had been watching her, waiting for her wolf to make an appearance. Maybe he did so for the pelt that soon might cover her body. Maybe Sam had, in effect, been raising his own Lycan for lurid purposes. Or else he could have merely used her to ferret out werewolves for as long as she'd be able to.

How could those ideas be proved?

None of that helped to explain about her mother. Who Sonja Stark really was, and why a Lycan tolerated a man like Sam. That just didn't sit right with Abby.

Patience was no longer on her list of accessible personality traits. She had become increasingly impulsive lately. Her secret fears had been shared. She was no longer fully in control of her body because a wolf curled up inside her, getting ready for its birth. That wolf might be pissed over the transition taking so long.

Sam had fed her silver to delay the process.

Possibly that was why she could handle her knife.

Go on, wolf, she refrained from shouting. *Do what you need to do. I need to get on with this.*

She might not get her wish right now, though. Not yet. With her eyes shut tight, Abby knew the moon had waned and that finally the longest night in the history of time was finally coming to an end.

"Why didn't they charge Stark, Dylan?" Cameron broke the silence. "Who handled the case?"

"It was before my time in office," Dylan replied.

"How did you find this information?"

"It's the digital age, Cameron. My office takes full advantage of that."

"Here? At this hour?"

"Contrary to some of those jokes, attorneys do sometimes earn their paychecks by taking work home on a regular basis. I have a computer at the cottage that's tied to my office. All it took was striking a few keys on our secure database."

"Abby will want to see this stuff."

"Are you sure about that?"

More silence before Cameron said, "Hell, I'm not certain of anything."

Footsteps led away from the bed. Cameron's voice stopped them.

"Was yours bad, Dylan? Your Blackout?"

Seconds ticked by before Dylan said, "If I'd had a gun

with me at the time, I probably wouldn't be standing here today. You?"

"I had a gun, but didn't use it."

She heard a door open, and Cameron say, "Delmonico made it through the Blackout."

"Dana," Dylan said, "is one tough cookie."

"Did you help her?"

"I tried to take her mind off what loomed."

"How?"

"We made love like the animals we were, on every available surface."

"Nice image, but not the truth?"

"The truth is that some people are built to be tougher than others. Dana rode it out. It didn't take her long to cross over, and she survived. Who knows why? She's the daughter of a cop and has risen through the ranks as an officer on her own merit. She is merciless on crime, a respectable adversary to those on the wrong side of the law, and a genuinely nice person. Dana is one in a million, and thankfully all mine."

The door closed on Dylan Landau's last remark. More silence followed before Abby felt the depression of the mattress and a soothing voice said, "Well, if fornicating is what it takes to ease the pain of a Blackout phase, I'm all for it. How about you, Abby?"

When she said "Okay," Cameron said, "I knew you were awake."

She opened her eyes. "Have I been drugged?"

"Yes, by a dart in the neck from one of those hunters."

"Do I have you to thank for getting me out of there? You're becoming quite the white knight."

"Can you move?" Cameron asked.

"I feel like I've swallowed lead."

"You did, you know. We can't know for how long."

"Why didn't the silver kill me?"

"I don't know."

"What was in the dart?"

"Don't know that, either. Dylan's mother gave you something to combat the drug. So, what did you hear, Abby? How much?"

She said, "We're in Dylan's house?"

"His parents' house."

"And it's an oasis for people like us?"

"That appears to be the case."

Abby attempted to move her right arm, and succeeded in raising a hand to her temple, where the current ache was centered.

"What's on the paper?" she asked, observing how Cameron stared at it.

"Can it wait until morning, Abby?"

"No. It can't."

The intensity of his gaze told her he was trying to gauge her state of mind.

"I suppose you come from a happy family," she managed to say. "With a mother and father, and a brother or two. You had dinner on the table when you got home from school, and Sunday picnics by the water."

He remained sober. His brow creased. "The brother you mentioned died in combat in Iraq. There was only one Mitchell sibling."

"I'm sorry."

"Me, too."

"What about your parents?"

"They both died in a car accident two years ago."

Abby took a steadying breath. "Then you understand that the hole created by loss never goes away, and that the heartache of losing someone remains long after they're gone."

"I do understand that."

He waited for her to go on.

"I don't remember much about my mother," Abby said. "It's obvious now that I knew even less than I thought, since until tonight I believed Sam held the position of father."

"I suppose you're relieved to have that position reopened, given that Sam Stark has proved himself a murderous bastard."

"Sam didn't need one specific night to prove that to me."

"Did he hurt you, Abby, in the past?"

"Besides tonight's damn dart, he hurt me only in ways that he and I appreciated. Psychological stuff, mainly."

"Why did you stay there with him, around him?"

"I stayed because of her memory. Because my mother had walked through those rooms where I walked, and because I hoped that Sam would one day tell me about her. Also, and in part, I stayed to keep tabs on Sam."

"For what purpose?"

"I suppose for reasons that would have seen him behind bars someday if he went too far with his games."

"You mean the hunting games that led him to you and to me?"

Abby moved her hand to her neck, where tiny pulses of pain jabbed. "You were out there patrolling because you also were aware of what roamed that park. One of those creatures bit you, setting your own search in motion, so you hunted them, too. For a while I believed Sam's hunting club had a beneficial purpose. Until…"

"Until you met me."

"Yes." Her lashes covered her eyes. "Until I met you, and my deepest fears about Sam's lust for Were genocide was confirmed."

The intensity of Cameron's gaze demanded that she look up.

"Landau's pack gathers here, Abby. It's a real pack, and I wasn't even sure what they meant until I saw them in action. You've met some of them and have seen what they're like. I don't know if they've lost their own good people to hunters and bad guys, or not, but they do watch what's going on. I wasn't alone out there. Sam isn't alone in the hunt for criminals who can change shape. The difference is that Landau's pack knows the difference between a good wolf and bad wolf."

Abby turned her head away from him, and said, "Something fierce fuels Sam's hatred of your species. That's what usually spurs hatred on, isn't it?"

"*Our* species," Cameron corrected gently.

She turned back. Her voice sounded faint. "One pelt? Sam could have done this, raised and tolerated my presence all those years, for the dollar equivalent of a fancy car?"

"You heard everything Dylan said?"

"I didn't hear nearly enough to begin to fill the emptiness I have inside."

Cameron's tender smile lifted her spirits, but he hadn't answered her question about what was on that paper. His sigh told her how torn he was about giving her what she wanted, and that he planned on withholding the information for her own good.

"What's on that paper, Cameron? Tell me about my mother."

He didn't look away. Instead, he said in a low, gravelly voice, "Sam killed her, Abby. Supposedly in self-defense."

Cameron observed how Abby's face whitened further and kept the paper out of her reach. He felt sick with worry. Abby looked like death warmed over, and he didn't know what to do about it, or how to comfort her after a blow like the one he'd given her.

Bad news took time to process, but this was a torment. Used to death and accidents in his day job, the death of his own parents had taken him a long time to come to terms with. Sometimes he imagined them in their cozy home, awaiting his next visit, and the sore spot caused by reality of their absence opened up all over again.

An accident was one thing. How did anyone accept a killing so close to home? The paper Dylan had handed him stated that Sam Stark had indeed killed his wife, and that the courts had let him off with a judgment of having been justified in doing so.

The single sheet didn't list details of the case, though details were going to be necessary in order to balance Abby's mental state. Looking at her now, Cameron feared what the future might bring.

"What?" she said through bloodless lips. "What did you say?"

"We will get answers and find out what happened. In the meantime..."

"Screw the meantime. I need to get up."

She tried to sit up, but was too weak to make it past her elbows. Abby wasn't going anywhere, and Cameron wanted to kiss Dylan's mother for giving her a draft to help her stay put. This is exactly where he wanted her at the moment—right next to him. Safe.

"It's early to turn the table on that judgment," he said.

Abby's big eyes were fever bright. "These Weres told me my mother was a wolf. You've seen what Sam does to wolves. Can you imagine him living under the same roof with one?"

"So you'll what? Take matters into your own hands and go after him? Do you suppose Sam will sit down and explain things to you when confronted about this information, when his message tonight was loud and clear as to what he thinks of your relationship?"

"I'll make him explain."

"Or die trying?"

She went quiet, probably dissolving into thought.

"It can wait until we have the facts, Abby," Cameron said. "I will help you get them."

She averted her eyes.

"In any case, you've been drugged by those damn hunters and won't make it past the door in your present condition."

She closed her beautiful eyes. He thought he saw the gleam of a tear moisten her lashes.

"Sleep. Rest," he said.

Strangely enough, those were the same instructions he had been given when he lay in that same bed. Had he taken them to heart? No. And if he had heeded outside advice, his lover might not be here with him now.

"You're tough," he said. "But toughness isn't everything. You'll need a plan when dealing with the devil."

Maybe Abby resembled Dana Delmonico in some ways, he decided. She had lived side by side with her mother's killer for years. No matter what circumstances of this case turned up, Abby wasn't going to let them go. Neither would he have been able to in her place.

He rested a hand on her warm, damp forehead, and stroked strands of hair away from her ashen cheeks. He wasn't sure what he murmured to her, but kept it up until her breathing eventually changed from ragged to even.

Desiring more closeness, and to keep her in his sight, Cameron stretched out on the bed beside her, on his side to keep her in full view. He lay with his head on one arm, and the other above her head, where her auburn hair fanned out across the pillow.

"I will help, Abby. You're not alone. I'll stand beside you," he whispered to her. "That's a promise."

As the sun started to rise and the sky outside the window turned pink with the dawn of a new day, Cameron finally closed his eyes.

When he woke up, the space next to him was empty.

Abby was gone.

Chapter 27

She had no way to explain to anyone around her how bad this news had been. Sam had known all along what had gone down, and hadn't once mentioned anything about it to her.

But that wasn't the only reason she'd have to kill him.

The phrase *late bloomer* echoed in her mind. Someone had mentioned that in regard to her Were status. In her favor, she'd have another month until forced to contend with the claws and whatever else would come her way. Thirty days lay ahead until the rise of another full moon that might bring a phase called the Blackout. Until that time, she'd be just another…what? *Girl?*

Pain had a monopoly on her system, both inside and out. She almost wished for the all-consuming trauma of her body's first transition to have something to focus on besides the awful images of Sam facing down her mother. Of Sam pulling the trigger, or slicing through female flesh with a silver blade. The pictures kept coming, each one worse than the one before. Self-defense. Sonja versus Sam.

This next meeting with him was going to be personal, and between Sam and herself. Involving anyone else was out of the question. Cameron had suffered already on her behalf. The kindness shown to her in the house she had left behind seemed extreme under the circumstances, and yet had proved to be another example of how far Sam's understanding of the Were world had gone astray.

From the lawn, she glanced over her shoulder at the home that had offered her its hospitality, curious about being allowed to leave. Landau's place didn't fit the bill of being a house at all, really, for someone used to the cramped space of a tiny studio apartment above a bar. This house looked more like a transplanted Southern plantation.

Three stories of whitewashed wood accented with aged brick rose gracefully from a wide expanse of lawn. Numerous windows flanked by black shutters dotted every floor. Some of those windows had Weres behind them who might be looking out.

She had to hurry.

Skirting a long porch that spanned the side of the building, expecting siren to go off at any moment, Abby followed the foundation toward the back of the house. Rimming the lawn, off in the distance, sat the wall delineating this compound from the public spaces beyond, marking it as private property.

Werewolves lived here, creatures who now believed her to be one of them. They had witnessed the kind of damage Sam inflicted on his adversaries and therefore might believe she had lost her taste for humans with oversize chips on their shoulders.

And they'd be right.

Would she be allowed to return here, to the house with black shutters, where things seemed so calm and peaceful on the surface, if she survived her upcoming confrontation?

Survival was paramount.

Cameron would be waiting.

Sam had more than proved himself lethal. He outweighed her by miles and had had years to hone his skills. Sam was hard muscle, anger and festering defiance packed into compact layers of human skin. As for her claim to fame, well, there was her moderate skill at wielding a knife, plus a full set of claws when she needed them.

Though she had found her knife on the bureau in the room where she'd been tended, and felt its familiar weight again strapped to her leg beneath some clothes that had been left for her, it was of minor consequence against Sam's professional arsenal. Nevertheless, her anger had to match his.

"We're not so unlike, Sam. We both have darkness inside."

Her darkness dictated her next move. The circumstances behind her mother's death dictated it. Waking up next to the world's sexiest Were went a long way toward dictating what had to be done. Sam killed randomly. Any one of the Weres she had met tonight could be next. And Sam had seen Cameron. It didn't hurt to remember that Sam had been ready to kill her.

All of that was of little consequence, though, when compared to the fact that Sam had killed her mother. Her Lycan mother, she'd been told by the Weres she had just left behind.

The dichotomies of Sam's beliefs were astounding, and filled with gaps. In those gaps lay the answers to the questions plaguing her. She had to make Sam talk about it. He'd have to confess to what he had done, in person, to Sonja Stark's daughter. She'd never be whole until this happened. A chance at a life free of the uncertainty in her past was the dream.

Someone had to face Sam.

"Someone has to stop him."

She had a vested interest in the outcome. Cameron couldn't help her now. No one could truly deal with another person's demons. Those demons had to be faced, confronted and dissolved in order to live, love, grow and breathe. She had a lot of inner issues, but not enough of them to share with white werewolf knights or pure-blooded wolves.

She reached the wall unhindered by shouts or Weres halting her progress. No guards were in evidence. She heard no growling dogs, and didn't locate a single alarm box or length of hotwire. None of this compound's occupants actually needed protection, and no one here was likely to want a hasty exit.

She didn't want to leave. Already, her heart protested by doubling its beats. Her lover was here, warm and sleepy.

"Cameron."

She couldn't look back.

He couldn't help her now.

Scaling the wall wasn't easy or without its consequences, yet she managed. On top, she had a bird's-eye view of the park, and eyed it with distaste. Although the rising sun would have cleared away the prowling monsters and hunters alike, scents piled up, most of them from the start of a normal business day somewhere off in the land of Miami's ignorant hordes. Inside those scents lay the ones she had left behind and longed never to lose. The smell of Cameron's taut, golden skin and his silky, mussed hair. Those were the fragrances that had done her in.

"Don't you dare look back."

Her next thought seemed odd after all that had gone on. She was going to miss work on the part-time day job, and would probably be fired. A lot of stray dogs might he happy about that, but there was irony here, too, on so many levels. Animal control…from an animal.

She drew in air from a pink-and-blue sky. Offering her face to the early sunrays, Abby allowed herself one last indulgence—a whisper to her soulmate that he might or might not hear.

"I'm sorry, wolf. I know you mean well. You'll have to believe me on that."

Then she jumped down from the wall.

"She's gone," Cameron said, passing Dylan on the stairs he'd decided to use this time, instead of heading for the window.

Dylan reached out a hand that stopped Cameron's momentum. "Maybe she has to do this on her own."

Cameron gave the Lycan a cursory glance. "You know where she'd be going, and what she'll find there, given what was on that paper."

"I can make a wild guess about it. But what if she doesn't want to be rescued?"

"Screw that. What chance does she stand?"

"She knows Sam Stark better than anyone."

"I'll bet that went through her mind last night when he was about to pull the trigger."

"Cameron, you know how it is. You have to understand it. You're a cop. Some things might be too personal for company or interference."

Cameron's jaw tensed. His chest ached dully behind a fresh bandage. "If wolves imprint for life, what happens when one half of that duo dies? Do love, longing and hurt ever leave the half left behind?"

"I don't know," Dylan admitted. "I am able to put myself in your place, and I can imagine what it would be like to worry about your lover."

"Then you understand why I have to find Abby and do what I can to keep her safe."

Dylan's hand dropped away. "Things used to be easy," he said, "once upon a time."

"Yeah," Cameron said soberly. "I'll second that."

Dylan shoved a hand in his pocket and came up with a set of keys. He tossed them to Cameron. "Garage. Silver sedan. Dana can drop me at the office." He rummaged in another pocket and came up with a cell phone. "Take this. Make a call if you need help."

Cameron turned so fast he didn't get a thank-you out.

The stairs winding through the Landau house took him straight to the front door, which stood open as if it had felt him coming. He didn't meet anyone else on the porch, lawn or the driveway leading to what he supposed had to be a distant gate.

The grounds were so large he had no idea of the location of the cottage where he had first met members of the Landaus' pack. He wondered who the hell the elder Landau and Alpha of this pack might be if his son was the DA, and a place like this was affordable. Cameron found it hard to imagine a more formidable Lycan than the one he'd already met.

The garage doors also stood open. All four of them. Six cars occupied the space, most of them black. The silver sedan, its color a possible insider joke for those with wolf bloodlines, turned out to be a Mercedes.

Cameron wished he had his inconspicuous Ford, and his gun. He'd be willing to bet that Sam Stark kept a weapon or two on hand at all times, and the thought of those weapons worried him.

"Stupid move, Abby," he shouted as he folded himself inside the car. "Sam has to have seen this coming."

Shouting made him feel slightly better about wearing borrowed clothes in a borrowed car after spending too much time in someone else's house. His parents had taught their kids not to abuse a welcome, and he'd passed that point by a mile.

"A Mercedes, for fuck's sake."

The engine roared, and quickly settled to a purr. He eased the transmission into gear, stepped on the gas pedal and headed out, feeling as though eyes watched his exit from all angles, and wishing a car this expensive had the capabilities of a time machine.

Abby didn't bother to hide her approach to the bar. What good would sneaking in have done?

The stairs to the two apartments lay on the side of the building, next to a vacant lot. She climbed slowly, going over and over this meeting in her mind until she wanted to scream.

There was a possibility Sam wouldn't let her get one word out, and that he'd been expecting her. If he'd taken the time to really know her, he'd be assured of her visit and be waiting by the door. But then Sam had never cared to get to know her better.

The hallway leading to the apartments was quiet. There were only two doors here—one hers, one Sam's.

She felt for her knife and tugged the blade from its leather sheath. The weapon felt both comfortable and foreign in her hand, but her grip was steady. The shakes had miraculously disappeared.

Six steps. Seven. Ten, and she stood in front of Sam's lair, waiting for, what? The door to burst open? A shotgun to blast through the wood?

Neither thing happened as she sucked in a breath and reached for the knob.

"I suppose you spent the night with *them*," Sam said from the end of the hallway, hidden in the dark. "I can smell the wet fur from here."

"You know what I am," Abby said without turning around. "So it seems I'm the only one here who was surprised."

Sam's gruffness showed in his voice. "She told me you might resist the call of the moon, and that hate had powerful side effects that might keep you in line. I fed you plenty of hate."

"And silver. By *her*, you mean my mother?"

"The creature that birthed you."

"And whom you married."

"I didn't have any other choice."

"Was that why you killed her?"

She heard Sam grind his teeth together.

"And yes, you fed me hate by the bushel—for Weres, and for me, and for never being good enough to earn your affection."

"Affection?" Sam laughed. "If you think I alone killed Sonja, think again. *They* did her in. *Your* kind did that. What she was underneath the beautiful exterior caused the problem."

They did her in. Your kind... The insults ate away at Abby.

"Maybe I don't care what you do to me," she said. "But I have to understand what you did to her."

"It was self-defense."

"So I've heard."

"You don't believe it?"

"I'm not sure anything you say is believable, Sam."

"Because you're a monster, like your new friends, and have turned against me."

Abby shook her head. "They didn't make me this way, and they haven't hurt me. You, on the other hand, aimed a gun at my chest."

"Just like I'm aiming one now."

"So who is the monster here, Sam?"

Though she didn't see him, she heard him take a step. She sensed his fatigue. Possibly he hadn't slept or showered, waiting for her arrival.

"All those years meant nothing at all to you," she continued. "My work in the bar, my help with finding what you said were really bad guys, and my being around didn't endear me to you in any way that served to change your mind about how this has worked out?"

"I couldn't afford to like you," Sam said.

"Was that because you planned all along to kill me if I changed?"

"It was due to the fact that I loved Sonja more than anything on earth, and she betrayed me by pretending to be human."

Abby turned slowly, able to see Sam's outline as sunlight peeked through the window high up on the wall, and not quite believing her ears. Sam had made a confession, and it rang true. He had admitted to loving her mother, and that he hadn't been able to cope with what she was.

"Tell me about that, Sam. It's why I have come." She tried to stay calm with her heart hurting so greatly.

"Then you've come here for nothing, and walked right into my hands," Sam said.

"So, you'll kill me, and that's that? No lingering emotional ties I might not have been aware of, and no explanation to send me off with?"

"You've got to love it when things work out like that," Sam replied threateningly. He stepped forward a few paces to show her the raised gun. "I would have thought that you, perhaps better than anyone else in this business, know what a Lycan is worth."

"More than a wife, I'm guessing. But I doubt you'll get off so easily in court after murdering your daughter, too."

"You let me worry about that."

"All right," Abby said, voice cracking with shock as

Sam's insinuations about her mother kicked up horrible, lurid thoughts about what Sam might have done with her mother's Lycan pelt, and how pelts were removed from the bodies they covered.

She opened her mouth to shout, without having time to get anything out. The hallway filled with a clicking noise, like a slide of security bolts, and a trapdoor opened beneath her.

With a protest on her lips, Abby started to fall.

Chapter 28

Fifteen minutes to reach the bar. Too long. An ungodly amount of time wasted when Abby's life was at stake.

Cameron angled the Mercedes to the curb without bothering to parallel park, and opened the door forcefully with a crack of bolts. The street was relatively quiet at this time of day, which did nothing for his growing angst. Abby had to have gone in the building beside him.

He sniffed the air and rolled his shoulders. "She's here, all right."

There truly was something to this imprinting phenomenon. He felt Abby nearby. He inhaled her scent. Abby Stark had become a part of him, and he doubted if anyone knew the exact science behind such a connection.

Abby's thoughts infiltrated his at times as if they were his thoughts, making it hard to tell which was which, though she was curiously silent now. The sinking sensation in his gut told him she was in trouble.

He tried the front door of the bar and found it locked.

Anxiously, he looked the place over as he strode to the side, where a wooden staircase spanned the first floor, leading to a second. He took the steps three at a time.

The door at the top allowed him access to a narrow hallway brimming with Abby's sweet fragrance. Fear laced that sweetness.

He pounded on the first door he came to, ready to tear Sam apart with his bare hands. But no one appeared.

He moved to the second door and repeated the series of knuckle-to-wood blows. No one opened that door, either.

Running both hands through his hair, Cameron paced the hallway. No mistake. She'd been there minutes before. Scent didn't lie. He could almost reach out and touch her.

"Abby? Where are you?"

His voice sounded dull in the space, and angry.

"Abby?"

Nothing. But all that nothingness was a damn lie.

"Sam, you bastard. Miami PD. Show yourself."

The air moved slightly. Cameron whirled with both hands raised, but it was the floor that had moved—old wood settling beneath his weight.

He didn't have a warrant or a lawfully sufficient reason to kick down those two doors. Breaking and entering… Destruction of private property… Missing Lycan female…

He wasn't in uniform and didn't have his badge. "Shit."

After one more deep breath that produced spasms of anger in his chest, Cameron put a boot to door one and watched it splinter. The noise was deafening in the tight corridor.

Stale air met him as he stepped across the threshold. Two windows were closed in the small studio room. His eyes methodically searched the place for signs of struggle. This was Abby's apartment, he knew intuitively. The plain, unadorned room was well cared for. Any other time, he would have relished coming here to look around. This time, it didn't take long to understand that Abby hadn't been here lately.

"Next."

Back in the hallway, he raced to door number two and repeated the force of his foot. The door went down in one piece with a jarring thud to show him a larger room. One of a couple. Lots of furniture crammed the space. A separate kitchen lay off to the right. Nothing moved. No Sam, no sleeping hunters, no Abby. Cameron's wolf gave a whine of disappointment as he turned back to the hall with his hands fisted.

He was letting Abby down. What had Sam done to her, if, in fact, Abby had found him? Where had everybody else gone? Hunters didn't just disappear with sunrise. They'd be sleeping the late night off. Maybe they had a hotel nearby.

It would have been useless to call this in to the department. Nothing he'd say to other cops could remotely begin to explain the turn of events that hounded him. Although he was strong, able-minded and good at his job, he hadn't helped Abby here, and that realization hurt worse than the damn silver bullet had.

"Sam, you crazy son of a bitch. Where is she?"

Again, he ran both hands through his hair and stared at the deserted corridor. He stood motionless a few minutes more, searching with his senses, soaking in the essence of the place. Then, empty-handed and no better off than when he'd arrived, Cameron headed for the stairs.

Abby opened her eyes to darkness made dim by the light of a single bulb in an overhead ceiling fixture. She was on her back, on a big mattress pad that lay on bare concrete. She had fallen through the floor by her apartment, but to where? Her mind appeared to be muddled. Sam's bar took up the floor below her apartment, and the bar she knew every inch of looked nothing like this. Had she fallen into a basement or alternate storage space that she hadn't known existed?

She had hit her head hard enough to see stars. One arm rested painfully behind her, wrenched at the shoulder. Pretty sure she hadn't broken her back, Abby waited a few beats before attempting to sit up. When she managed, the injured shoulder hurt so severely she nearly blacked out.

Head in her hands, Abby tried to center her mental faculties, when nothing about the fall made sense. The pain shooting through her was muddying her reasoning skills.

She felt for the spot on her neck where she'd been hit by a dart the night before. Small prickles came from there that were nothing like the rest of her body's discomfort. She looked at the forearm she had sliced open with her knife, and felt a remnant of the deep muscle ache. But the wound had begun to miraculously heal, just as Cameron's bullet wound to the chest had, proving that as extraordinary as it seemed, it was hard to keep a werewolf down.

"Sam?" Her voice had a new edge. "What have you done?"

No reply came. Neither did an aspirin.

Hugging her arm to stabilize her shoulder, Abby looked around. The place did resemble a basement, with a workbench on one side attached to a large washbasin and a small metal counter. There were no windows. Stains marred the wide expanse of gray concrete floor. A wooden staircase stood opposite her that she couldn't reach because there were several metal bars in the way.

Hell, she was in a cage, and trapped. As that sank in, recent events began to make a horrible kind of sense.

"I'm a prisoner," she said out loud. "That's unusual, isn't it, Sam? Instead of killing me outright, you'll keep me as a pet for a while?"

The way her words fell flat in the enclosed room caused

her heart rate to spike. What did Sam use this room for, if not to torture werewolves?

What were all those stains on the floor?

"Is this how it ends? Did you predict this? Plan for it? I know about her, Sam. I know what my mother was, and metal cage or not, I want to know what happened to her. I won't rest until I do."

Nothing. No reply came, and there was no fresh breeze to make talking easier. Abby took a better look around. She cringed and scuttled backward when she saw the chains attached to the wall beside her. Darkened by some sort of coating—God, was it dried blood?—the chains hung from huge rings screwed into the wall at a standing person's shoulder height. They were made of silver.

The chains didn't swing. She did, as a whirl of vertigo spun her sideways.

Odors rushed at her from the floor as her face neared it. Abby tried desperately to get away from those smells, and to swallow the shout arising from the pain of her injured shoulder as she rolled onto her side. Words began to form in the fog to categorize the onslaught of scents. Musk. Urine. Blood. Lots of blood. Enough blood to create a river. Years of odors were here, piled layer upon layer. No amount of cleanup had removed them.

She covered her nose and fought off a gag reflex. Her throat filled with bile. Fisting her hands in her hair, she tore at the roots.

Then she brought her head up with a cry of alarm. Centered in those awful odors, she found a surprise—a remembered fragrance that she knew well. The pleasant, rosy scent that had comforted her in those years of loneliness. A ghostly drift of flowers.

Biting back a scream, Abby struggled to her feet, unable to make herself touch the wall with the chains, and instead using the cage's bars for support.

"Sam, what did you do?" she shouted. "You kept my mother here, you sick bastard, and dared to claim self-defense when she died?"

Anger shot through her, intense enough to pitch her against the bars. There she stayed, head lifted, queasiness roiling in her stomach. "Mother? I feel you here. What has he done?"

She moved her neck to shift the wave of vertigo and heard bones crack. The sound made her want to vomit. She couldn't hold back. Up it came…only it wasn't what she had expected. Not sickness, unless the term *Lycan* counted.

The oncoming blackness tossed her helplessly to the mattress as a torrent of pain reshuffled tolerance levels from acute to something far worse and her heart began to pump lava through her veins. The pressure inside her skull intensified until vision blurred. Her shoulders twitched repeatedly, as if testing the water for heaven knew what— some future realignment, maybe—and then muscle began to pull away from bone.

Abby screamed.

Sanity faded into the distance as the scream went on and on, leaving emptiness in its wake—a great, yawning emptiness that only one thing had the substance to fill.

The wolf's outline tickled hers before expanding. Light from the overhead bulb tortured Abby's closed eyes. Her arms burned as tendons stretched like taffy. But the really bad thing came from inside her.

Hatred was an emotion so pure, so hot, it vied with the concept of revenge. Hatred for Sam's sins and his transgressions against innocent victims, among the rest. Hatred for Sam hurting her mother, and for whatever time her mother had spent in this hellhole. Hatred for Sam not telling her about this, and for shunning her all those years when she felt lost.

Sam had admitted to feeding this kind of hatred to her,

along with the silver, hoping to ward off her changes until she had fully matured. Was this what she had to look forward to now? Silver chains in a basement cell?

Her disgust had an iron-like taste that coated her tongue. She didn't want to be a wolf, not like this. Bad thoughts had to translate to bad wolves. But emotion rushed upward from her gut like a living, breathing entity within the entity taking her over, straining to get out, pushing the limits of her stamina. She had nowhere to hide. There was to be no covering up her secrets in this awful place.

Sweat stung her eyes. Her borrowed clothes tortured her oversensitive skin, and she tore at them with her claws. The fact that she had claws barely registered as Abby pulled up her knees and curled into a ball on the floor, on fire, seeking the coolness of the concrete. But on the ground, with her face turned sideways, the foul odors quickly overwhelmed her senses.

The concrete carried a vibration. Someone was coming. Someone not wholly unexpected.

Adrenaline surged. Her injured shoulder exploded with pain as it jumped back in the socket, aided by the expanding musculature around it. Both arms shot out straight from her sides, the skin stretching, thickening. Her stomach twisted. She convulsed. All this happened fast, and automatically.

Blood, moving within her, took on a rhythm, flowing like a mysterious, underlying melody. It sang through her arteries and weaved through her heart's chambers, dragging long lines of pain behind that came and went in undulating waves.

Her lungs expanded as if she'd swallowed several helium balloons filled to capacity. Ribs cracked to accommodate the lungs. Vertebrae detonated at the base of her spine, setting off more explosions that worked their way up.

Abby's vision turned red. She panted with her mouth

open and raked her face with her claws as her body turned itself inside out and a dark cloud that had to be Death hovered, waiting to see if she'd come through.

The room turned. Her body lengthened. The bones in her face rearranged as if remolded by the fires inside. New teeth, as sharp as the claws, tore into her lower lip, adding more blood to the foul scene.

And then the pain stopped suddenly. The whirling darkness ceased as if someone had merely flipped a switch to the Off position. Discomfort receded like thunder rolling into the distance. The lightbulb over her head sparked, flared, dimmed, then winked on and off in the manner of a strobe light with its batteries used up.

No sound reached her, other than the random pulses of the electricity in that bulb.

Abby opened her eyes, afraid to move. She lay shaking on the floor, chilled, but saturated in sweat. Thoughts returned with an alarming clarity, though she had no v??? to prove their validity. Moonlight had not reached her i? this dank place, whether or not the moon was full, and yet...

I am a werewolf.

At last.

Like her.

The world didn't give her time to assimilate that fact. A door at the top of the stairs opened on oiled hinges. Abby didn't bother to get up, not certain she could, and if her legs would hold her. Footsteps on the stairs were loud and jarring to her enhanced hearing system. Whoever approached moved with a limp and smelled of sweat and whiskey.

"Sonja," Sam said, his voice low, his tone gruff with hidden innuendo and a hint of madness. "It's time to play."

Abby didn't know much, and though her body felt as if she'd just circled a drain, the one thing she did know was her name. And it wasn't Sonja.

Chapter 29

Cameron rapped on the door to the bar before pounding on it with both fists. "Not mistaken." Abby's scent clung to the place, and he was determined to find her.

The door had huge metal hinges too sturdy to break through. Although kicking it in would have been nice, Cameron stepped back and shouted, "Abby, do you hear me?"

Her scent had weakened. He cursed and headed back to the side staircase. Studying the building as he strode toward the steps, he noticed a peculiar anomaly in the building's structure—a wide gap in spacing between the windows on the first and second floors. He had climbed the equivalent of three flights of stairs minutes ago, and saw this as a viable clue.

He remembered the creaky floor in the hallway.

"Hell," he shouted, heading for the stairs. "Damn it all to hell."

Confirming his speculation, Abby's scent grew stronger when he reached the door leading to the hallway of apartments. But her scent had changed. Abby was alive, and different. Abby had taken on her wolf.

It was daylight. The sun was up. Had Sam tortured her into shifting? Lycans, Dylan had explained, possessed the ability to change shape at will, no moon necessary. How about according to someone else's will? What about the Blackout phase she'd have to go through, and might not survive?

"Abby!"

He felt along the walls, searching for a lever or other kind of switch. Finding none, he scoured the floor by digging his fingernails into grooves between the boards. One of the boards budged. He shouted, "Yes!" but couldn't pry up the piece of wood.

Anxiety was a bitch. Anger made him crazed. Jumping to his feet, Cameron stomped on the floor, letting whoever might be down there know he had discovered their hidey-hole.

When the cell phone tucked in his pants pocket rang, the hallway filled with the sound of alarm bells going off. He had no intention of answering, and turned for the door, wondering hopefully if Dylan Landau, who was so much more than he seemed at first glance, kept an ax in the trunk of that pretty silver sedan.

Abby sensed Cameron's nearness with a terrifying certainty. Her cells strained toward him. Her throat hurt with the need to shout. He was here, close. As for finding her, and what waited in Sam's lair...was that possible?

Cameron, she sent to him along the connection uniting them. *Stay away. It's a trap.*

Sick to death of this shit, she changed her position. She had swallowed a bomb and it had exploded, but she could deal. She had to open her eyes.

She saw Sam leaning against the wall with the basin, loading a dart into his weapon's chamber. The weapon looked similar to the ones she went after rabid dogs with to knock them out. She'd seen it before, the night before, in a hunter's hand.

With that recall, she swiped at the spot on her neck where the dart had struck. Last night, she'd had Cameron to help. No one was here to help her now. If she had never found this place, or known about it, Cameron wouldn't be able to. Cameron might be close, but she was on her own.

"I'm thinking it's too long until the next full moon," Sam said. "But look at you, all decked out and furred-up as if it were here right now."

Abby watched him carefully.

"Then again, we both know that Lycans don't need the moon to instigate changes. I first tested that theory here, in this spot, if you recall."

He set the weapon on the counter. He was, Abby realized without needing all of her senses to determine his status, totally mad.

"You wouldn't help me before, back then," he said. "Not with your kind. Nevertheless, you helped us to bag quite a few pelts. And what did I do in return, Sonja? I promised to take care of your spawn, and treat her like one of my own."

Abby glanced behind her at the wall of chains. Her heart pounded. She withheld a growl. Things were becoming clearer. Too terribly clear. Maybe the reason there weren't any pictures or photos of her mother in the apartments was because Sonja Stark had never set foot there. It was possible that Sam had hidden his madness all along, but how possible was it for him to have kept Abby's mother here, in this dreadful place, on purpose, and by promising that Sonja's daughter would enjoy the freedom Sonja never had?

There had been no marriage. That was the answer to the questions of her past. Sam and Sonja's union had been a sham, no more than a deal with blackmail at its core. Sam had used her mother to catch werewolves, just as Sam had used her.

Tears sprang to Abby's eyes and spilled over, trickling down her elongated face. How long had her mother been a prisoner, and watched over by this madman, when her daughter had been the cause? She had been the reason her mother complied with Sam's demands. Her mother had loved her enough to live like this, and to be treated like one of Sam's monsters.

For how long?

She wanted to know how her mother had lived in chains, and how many darts filled with sedatives had her mother endured.

The world spun around in slow circles, and Abby's mind went with it as tears continued to fall.

She had found the truth, at last.

"We'll have to address a new problem," Sam said as casually as if he were speaking about too many broken glasses in the bar. "Your new friend. What's his name? Oh yeah. Mitchell. Cameron Mitchell. Did you bite him, I wonder, in a fit of passion, to make him a wolf?" Sam crossed his arms over his chest. "You always were a cheater. After all, you had *her*."

Abby looked up at him, her anger rekindling, heat radiating off her in waves. Sam was mixing things up now, going between her mother and herself.

"Well, you're safe here, for now. Tonight, we'll go out. Just you and me. There might not be any Weres around, but Lycans are another matter, and when they see what I'm going to do to you, they might come running."

Again, Abby's vision turned red. In a swift, unplanned move, she got to her feet. Sam using her against Lycans like Dylan Landau was not in the realm of possibility. She wasn't Sonja. She didn't have to protect anyone here, and sure as hell didn't have to obey the real monster in this room.

Power soared through her. Her muzzle curled back to expose a mouthful of sharp teeth, some of them bloody from biting down too hard. With clawed hands, she took hold of the bars thinking that Sam had made one mistake too many. He hadn't locked her into those silver chains before taunting her with information she had spent most of her life searching for.

She was Sonja's daughter. Lycan. Strong.

And Sam was just a big demented bastard.

With Lycan power swimming in her veins and the musculature to back it up, she bent two of the metal bars back, stuck her head through the gap and let loose a growl that echoed in the room and wiped the grin from Sam's surprised face.

But the bars were too strong to get her body through. She couldn't reach Sam, or get free. She didn't want to think about how many times her mother might have tried.

And yet…

She looked up at the ceiling, where the cracks outlining the trapdoor were barely visible but there. Something had gotten stuck in that trapdoor on her way down.

She pulled her head back into the cage. Gathering what she could manage of her new strength, she launched herself at the bars. Using them as leverage to heave herself upward, hearing the ring of her claws against the metal, Abby propelled her newer Were bulk toward that ceiling in a flash of startling energy, hoping that trapdoor would help her escape.

"No damn ax," Cameron muttered. But there was a tire iron. He used it to beat at the wall between the two floors, causing some damage to the building's siding, though he didn't have to continue for long.

The door above him opened and a werewolf, furred-up in pure daylight, jumped toward him. Startled, he stepped back, but the wolf came right to him and put its face close to his.

"Abby?" he said, blindsided by her appearance.

She pushed past him, leaped from the stairs and took off. Cameron knew she wanted him to follow, but first he had to find Sam Stark, to see what the imbecile had done to make Abby shift.

He ran up the stairs and into the hallway, seeing that there was indeed a trapdoor, and that it was open. Abby had crawled up that way. Scrape marks scarred the floorboards.

He swung himself down into the hole and landed on his feet with his fists raised. No one met him. No one was there.

It took all of ten seconds to see the place, and figure out what had happened. What he saw made him sick. As Cameron headed for the stairs and wherever they'd take him, he flipped open Dylan's phone and dialed the emergency number. "Mitchell. PD. You might want to send a car to the following location and find the trapdoor."

He had no more time for explanations. There were only two places Abby would go, and he had to get to her before she chose.

The keys were in the Mercedes. He cranked the ignition, glanced quickly behind and was about to pull away when he saw her. God, he saw her…

Abby had pressed herself into a space between the building housing the bar and the one next to it, on the opposite side of the vacant lot. She crouched on her haunches with her head on her knees.

He reached her as she looked up, and yanked her to her feet. He pushed her back, out of sight of the street, and ran his hands over the new angles of her face. "Change back, Abby. Do it now. You're out of there, and I have you."

She looked at him with red-rimmed eyes that were still a deep emerald green. She panted with shock and the effort to restrain herself from doing as he asked.

"Abby. Listen to me. Do it now. I have a car. We'll drive away, and you never have to see Sam again."

Clearly she understood, and yet Cameron felt the power of the Lycan blood coursing through her dictate another direction.

"No," he said. "Not now. Maybe never. You cannot get to him. End it, Abby. Please. The police will find Sam and haul him in for creating a place like the one I saw in there. He will be out of the way. We can figure out what to do once you've rested, and after you let me know you weren't hurt."

The tears that ran down her face broke his heart. Cameron put his arms around her shaking body and waited, silently urging her to come back to him, so that he could take her away.

Her skin began to shrink. The fine hair covering the parts of her that were bare disappeared. This was nothing like his own reversal. The snapping of her bones back into place sounded like stepping on bubble wrap, and happened all at once, instead of in pieces. The extra musculature in her arms and legs streamlined, molding into limbs he had been familiar with on more than one occasion.

And there Abby was...in his arms, dressed like a street urchin, her tears falling from thin, pale cheeks to splash on his shirt.

God, he loved her.

She had been through hell, and had made it back.

"Come on," he said, taking her hand in his. "Time to go."

With a grip that no one on the planet could have made

him loosen, Cameron led Abby to the car, got her inside and climbed behind the wheel. He figured that five or six people might have seen her furred-up when they drove by, but there were plenty of wacky phone calls to the department, everything from alien spaceships to ghosts.

What difference would a lone werewolf beside a bar make?

Chapter 30

Werewolf gangbangers knew where he lived, which meant he'd have to relocate sometime soon. In the middle of the morning on a weekday, Dylan and the other Landau pack members would be at work, maintaining a distance from one another and from things that went bump in the night. They weren't apt to be up for another rescue today.

Motels were everywhere in Miami, plenty of them by the ocean offering scenery and fresh air. But he was minus his wallet, and Abby looked as if she'd been in a train wreck. She shook as if she'd been frozen in ice cubes. Her face was pale enough for the lacing of fine vessels beneath her skin to show as blue streaks.

He thought about taking her to the department, where she'd be surrounded by cops and safe, and he wondered what kind of questions might arise if he did, in the state they both were in.

No, as he saw it, there was only one way to go, and he had abused that welcome a few times already. However, Abby needed care, food and a shower, and Dylan had said the words *any time*, so maybe he'd be allowed to get through the gates. He'd head for the cottage on the property, or the garage, leave Abby in one of those secure places, then gather his stuff from home and find a new location to take her to, where she'd be comfortable and he'd feel relieved.

The Mercedes took the roads effortlessly. Cameron had automatically memorized the route, for personal reasons and to return the car. Abby rode in silence next to him, with her head against the seat. She lacked the energy to speak, he supposed. Perhaps she just wasn't ready.

The road took a turn through wide-open spaces, and then doubled back. Big stone gates appeared, closed. When he pulled up in front of them, the Mercedes emitted a beeping sound that brought a man out from behind one of the gates' statuesque pillars. After looking through the windshield, the man waved them on, and the gates opened.

So, the Landaus had guards. Wolf guards dressed in black, no doubt packing heat. Dylan's family wasn't taking any chances on intruders getting inside.

So far, so good.

Cameron had time to look around as the driveway meandered through a grove of trees. In the sunlight, the estate looked different—slightly smaller and less imposing. Freshly watered lawns sparkled. Flowers bloomed in beds along the driveway, adding pops of vibrant color to a place that had started out as part of a nightmare.

It all seemed so normal, so refined. Just another mansion among mansions that not too many people got to see up close. Its secrets seemed ludicrous bathed in yellow, but it only took a sideways glance at Abby for Cameron to remember how different and difficult life could be beneath any surface. Sam's building had a false floor, accessed by a trapdoor. Abby's beautiful countenance housed a wolf with the ability to shift without a full moon.

And Cameron Mitchell? He was a cop, a defender of the weak and a wolf. He was a man who wasn't really a man, in love with a woman who wasn't a woman.

Yes, he loved Abby, and dreaded every minute they were apart. He loved her so much that the word *love* didn't begin to describe his feelings. And this, Cameron thought as he turned the car toward the garage, read more like science fiction than reality.

So, what was the world coming to, and where would these things end? Well, a good start in that direction would be to help Abby deal. Help her over the hump that remained as a last temptation for trouble. Finding Sam Stark.

"I've never thanked you," Abby said, bringing his thoughts back around.

"For the ride, or the great bedside manner?" His joke, meant to lighten the mood, didn't result in a smile. "I haven't helped much," he added soberly. "I wasn't there today."

"How could you have been there? I left while you were sleeping."

"That doesn't make me feel any better about what just happened," he confessed without bringing up what he thought about the stupid, dangerous move she'd made by running out on him to face Sam alone.

"I had to go there," she said.

"I know."

"He kept my mother in that terrible place. I don't know how he killed her, or how he got away with it. I don't understand how anyone, crazy in the head or not, might keep someone in a cage."

"What about you, Abby? Tell me about you."

She fell silent, seeming to mull over his question.

"You shifted, and shifted back," he said, as if she didn't know that.

She turned her head toward him as they drove into the coolness of the garage. "Lycan. I get it. It's not about pelts or money for Sam. That's a cover-up. He's not like the rest. For Sam, it's about revenge."

"Revenge for what?"

"Loving someone he considered inhuman. Loving her so much, her Otherness drove him insane."

Cameron sensed Abby's reasoning powers hard at work. He wanted to hear about what had happened, and feared pushing her too far. Abby might be Lycan, and therefore a kind of werewolf royalty, but she was newer to this wolf business than he was. She looked thin, ragged and hungry. She looked haunted. Not in the way she haunted him, more in the manner of having had a ghost walk over her grave. Her mother's ghost.

She'd shared only pieces of what had happened to her. He didn't fully understand what she'd said, though he had a good idea about Sam's treatment of wolves after seeing that hidden room. Sam had likely hurt her mother before killing her. He had hurt Abby in ways that were going to be difficult to repair.

"They won't catch him," she said.

"We will. We'll do our best."

"He'll be waiting for me."

"Why? Hasn't he done enough?"

"I don't remember what my mother looked like, but I must resemble her. I probably smell like her. When Sam sees me, he sees her. He…"

"He…what?"

"He thought I was her. Am her."

"Your mother is dead. Surely he'd remember that."

"I'm not certain. He's unstable. I believe he won't rest until I'm in the ground with her."

"We will find him," Cameron repeated. "And then it will be over."

"Yes." Abby's voice had grown weaker. "Over."

Cameron pulled the Mercedes into its slot and shut off the engine. He didn't open the door. He liked things this way—just Abby and himself. The coolness of the garage offered a respite from the heat outside. Leather seats were the ultimate luxury for weary bones. Sooner or later, though, Abby had to be seen by somebody better able to help.

Although his thoughts raced, the interior of the garage was serenely quiet. A mint julep would have been a bonus, or a cold beer. Cameron had no idea when he had last eaten a meal, and doubted if Abby had had enough sustenance in the past seventy-two hours to sustain her for much longer. She had been slender before all this had started. Now, she was rail-thin. The bones of her shoulders jutted out beneath her shirt. Her jaw had the quality of carved marble. Looking at her hurt him in ways he obviously had yet to discover. If anything more happened to her, he didn't know what he'd do.

Good thing full-on humans didn't have to contend with this imprinting thing, or insanity might rule the masses.

And heaven help him, with that last thought, it was clear that he had begun to differentiate between what he had been, and what he had turned into.

"We need to see if Dylan's mother is at home," he said at length.

"I don't want to talk about what happened," Abby said.

"I'm guessing you won't have to. If my instinct is correct, everyone here has secrets and is adept at keeping them. They won't bother to pry into anyone else's."

Abby faced him again. "Are we a pack now? You and me?"

"Only if I can be the leader."

Abby smiled briefly. Because of that smile, Cameron figured she'd be okay. Gauging the magnitude of his relief over that was next to impossible.

He would keep things light and honor her timetable for providing him with more pieces to the puzzle that consumed her. Impatience was a cop's daily staple, and had to be overcome. Abby had to have her mental space, for now. Physical space was altogether different. This cop planned on sticking to her like glue, or gluing her somewhere safe, while he picked up his weapon, his wallet and his badge, items he'd need in the search for serial torturer Sam Stark.

"Time to go in," he said as he opened the car door, hoping against better judgment that he'd get to carry her again, and for a few minutes more keep her close to his heart.

Abby had never felt so weightless. If a stiff wind had blown, she might have drifted away. The heaviness of her wolf had been decreased, or dispersed…whatever the hell it did when not showing itself. But the wolf hadn't gone completely. She felt its nearness. On her fingers, the phantom imprint of claws made her nerve endings tingle.

In a self-protective gesture, she reached for Cameron's hand, relieved when his fingers closed over hers. Handholding was a human thing, and she desperately wanted to feel human.

Cameron led her over the grass, taking a shortcut to the house. The scent of the freshly mowed lawn seemed to her like heaven, and drowned out the stench of Sam's cage. She wanted to lie down and roll in the grass, cover herself with greenery, immerse her senses in normal, decent, everyday smells. Many kinds of animals did this, and she now understood why.

Nearing the house brought on anxiousness, a slight movement of the beast within her, as well as a ton of regret. She had been offered help here, and had run away in search of her destiny.

Finding some of the answers to the questions she'd asked added light to the dark hole of her past, yet a few questions remained. Why had Sam killed her mother? How had he done it? Something had finally pushed him into the abyss.

Sam had to be taken off the streets.

Landau's front door opened before they had reached the steps leading up to it. A gray-haired Were woman that Abby barely remembered advanced. Dressed in pale gray slacks and a matching silk shirt, their hostess extended a hand first to her, then to Cameron. Gray eyes, inquisitive and wide, gave her a quick once-over.

"We don't like to intrude. Are we welcome at this hour, Mrs. Landau?" Cameron asked.

"Of course you're welcome here. We hoped you'd make it back sometime today," the woman replied in an aged alto. "Dana has been calling every half hour. I hope you need breakfast, because everyone left this morning without eating, and the food will go to waste."

"Breakfast," Abby repeated. The word had a foreign ring to it.

"Do you always eat breakfast together?" Cameron asked, voicing the question she'd been thinking about.

She was fascinated by the idea of a family—or in this case a pack—spending time together over a meal of any kind, or for that matter, any reason, as if they liked one another, and as though they got along. She had ached for that kind of closeness, dreamed of it her whole life.

"Only when there are things to discuss," Mrs. Landau replied. "My son and his mate often stay on the property, in the cottage by the wall. The others drop in fairly regularly. We usually have a houseful."

"Is your husband at home?" Cameron asked.

"He's in court today."

"Court?"

"Yes. He's sending down judgments all afternoon."

"He's a judge?" Cameron asked, then blinked as if he'd asked a stupid question. "Of course. Judge Landau. I've heard the name."

Abby hadn't, but Cameron's hold on her hand produced a small electrical charge that passed from his fingers to hers, letting her know the judge was somebody special and well-respected. Cops might have to know things like that.

She wouldn't have been able to come here on her own, Abby realized as they followed their hostess into the house. The silk and the pearls, the black shutters and the wide expanse of lawn, were a glimpse into a world far removed from hers.

Breathing in scents of polished wood, grass and faint traces of lemon brought up the dichotomy of other recent odors: blood, fear, metal bars and silver chains. She wasn't sure if she could afford to leave those terrible remembrances behind for the time it took to eat a piece of toast served on a china plate.

On the threshold of the Landau house, Abby turned to glance at the sky, needing no wristwatch to tell her how many hours there were until nightfall. Her wolf's intuition had all the aspects of a well-oiled sundial.

And then what? Why did she suddenly fear the dark?

"What is it?" Cameron asked with his mouth close to her ear.

"I'm a freak."

"Welcome to my world."

The way his lips brushed over her hair, the familiar warmth of Cameron's breath, made her heart and her wolf jump. The truth? She wasn't alone. And she had never been a weakling. Now wasn't the time to forget that.

She also had her knife. Sam, who didn't have the benefit

of wolfish senses, hadn't picked up on the blade strapped to her leg.

She had more questions—a bucket full. But glad to have the support of Cameron's hand on hers, Abby closed her eyes as she entered the home of Sam's enemies, her body soaking up the wild wolf vibes underlying its contradictory genteel exterior, her inner wolf beginning to claw at her insides, craving freedom now that it had had a taste of what freedom was like.

Buttered toast wasn't going to satisfy either of them.

Chapter 31

Cameron entered the room assigned to Abby without bothering to knock. She would be expecting him.

He had observed how restless she'd been all day, while awaiting the return of the others in the Landau pack. She had paced continuously inside the house and across the grounds, making sure of his closeness with guarded glances, though she didn't have to look at him to be assured of that.

They both were aware of the bond tying them together, as well as the exact distances separating them most of the time. That special sense of togetherness had deepened after her first shift, as if there were now four beings attached at the hip and securing the bond, instead of just two.

Cameron heard water sounds that came from the adjoining bathroom as he entered her space. Abby would probably relish a shower and be trying to cool off, unused to full-on Were heat in a city that topped a hundred degrees on a daily basis.

He didn't envy her the months ahead of getting to know her wolf side. But Abby seemed to have passed through her Blackout phase with few visible scars to show for it. He wondered how bad it had been, without wanting to linger on the thought. She had shape-shifted in a cage, and had managed, which said a lot about the toughness of her character.

Maybe he'd join her in the shower.

Quietly, Cameron closed the door behind him and looked around her room. Abby's old clothes lay in a pile on the floor. She'd want to burn them, and he couldn't fault her on that.

New clothes were spread out on the bed next to the rumpled blankets she had tried to curl up on. A shirt, some loose pants, fresh underwear in an unopened plastic package and a pair of rubber sandals that might have been close to her size were yet another offering from the Landau family.

A tray sat on the nightstand, with a bowl of melting ice and a pitcher of the tangy lemon drink he had chugged at breakfast in an attempt to coat his blazing insides. Abby had eaten nothing. Drank nothing. This worried him.

He glanced up, and looked to the bathroom door, relieved to sense her there. For a minute, he'd been unsure.

Cameron leaned against the doorjamb, searching the bathroom, knowing that for he and Abby privacy was no longer an issue. The shower curtain was clear. The small room was devoid of frills of any kind. This kind of sparseness would suit Abby, he thought. Her apartment above the bar had been modern and spare.

Feeling a bit like a voyeur, he watched her from the doorway, able to see every angle and line on her ultralean body. She stood under the showerhead with both hands on the tile wall, motionless, allowing the water to cascade over her. Rivulets ran down her shoulders, over her breasts and belly and between her thighs. In spite of the hurt inside her, and having been mentally abused, she was the sexiest female he had ever seen.

And she still wore the silver knife, in its sheath, strapped to her calf.

After making a sound he hadn't planned on making, Abby turned her head. Through the flimsy barrier of the shower curtain, their eyes met with a stunning, fiery impact, igniting sparks that spread through him.

He had been physically desirous of her before she formally acknowledged him, but grew harder when she did. This wasn't the time to show her what he thought of her, of course, and yet he wanted nothing more. It was always that way when he saw her.

"Abby," he said. "I…"

She turned fully, and swept the wet hair back from her face. He saw hunger in her expression that matched his. Maybe she needed to be lost in the sheer physicality of their union, and to exert pent-up energy that had nowhere else to go. He sure as hell hoped so.

He drew back the curtain, and didn't reach to turn the water off. A light spray of water hit both him and the floor.

She reached out to him, grabbed hold of the front of his shirt and tugged. Like everything else here, the shirt belonged to someone else, but it was too late to worry about that, and how many he'd already borrowed. The look in Abby's eyes did him in. The way she wanted him overruled everything except the need to be mates.

Fully clothed, minus the shoes he'd taken off to stretch out on the bed in the room next to hers, Cameron slipped into the shower with Abby. As the water soaked him, her fingers worked his buttons. Not slowly or carefully this time, but more like a woman who refused to wait for any kind of foreplay.

She tore the shirt from his shoulders, resting her mouth

on each patch of bareness she uncovered. With her sharp little teeth, she bit down on his flesh with a force that made him growl.

He took her face between his hands and held her motionless for several agonizing seconds. Then Abby's hands continued in her goal of getting him naked.

His shirt dropped to the tub in a sodden heap of blue and white stripes. She went for his zipper by sliding her hands over his wet skin, pausing on the indentation on his chest where the bullet wound remained but had miraculously begun to heal, then she circled that wound with her lips.

She shook him off when he reached for her, silently asking for control of this, for now. His zipper came down in a soft grating of metal on metal. His pants, somebody's khakis, melted to the tub. He stepped free of the tan puddle one foot at a time, content for the time being to give Abby the lead in the direction of this encounter.

But he confessed to her, "I have to move." And his breath came in rasps. "I can't hang on for long, Abby."

She smelled like oranges and soap. Her hair, with its edgy black tips, hung to her shoulders in a gleam of copper. Large green eyes bored into his.

"Payback," Abby said. "At least in part."

"You owe me something?"

"Maybe not yet."

He reached for her, unable to resist the thrash of the blood pounding inside him. Slick with the sheen of moisture, Abby slipped from his grasp in a downward slide until her knees hit the floor. Her head angled toward his engorged, raging proof of how much she affected him.

When her mouth took him in, Cameron howled and curled his fingers in her hair. He hit the wall, tasted the water on his lips, wanting to push Abby away in order to regain his equilibrium, while also wanting to do nothing of the sort.

"My turn," he whispered, dragging Abby up by the arm-pits and setting her on her feet. "My damn turn."

He kissed her deeply. It was a long, deep, hungry devouring for what, in the end, could only be satisfied in another way.

He'd had her before, but this time seemed new. He had been between her legs, had tasted her with his mouth, had made love to her, front and back. The difference here was that all the cards were on the table. Abby had been brought up to date about herself. Secrets had been shattered. The only thing remaining was the effort of this moment, and how long it might last.

In order to have that moment and have Abby completely, Sam Stark's hold on her mind had to be forgotten, had to fade as a bad memory.

He drew her closer with his hands on her backside, in a firm grip. Her breasts flattened against him. Her heart beat frantically. She tilted her head back when his kiss lightened, and allowed her room for a breath.

Her lips parted.

"Don't," he cautioned. "Don't say a word."

Her skin was slippery, and partially covered in foam. That suited him just fine. Lifting one of her legs, he caressed the place where her thigh met the velvet folds of her sex, watching her closely for every twitch, every wince, every blink, she made.

He found raw emotion etched on her beautiful face that was personal enough to be heartbreaking.

He thought about stopping this, and about allowing her to vocalize that emotion. But she rubbed against him seductively.

"I'm still stronger, little wolf," he whispered. "So, is this what you need?"

In place of a nod, she reached between them and found something to wrap her fingers around. Her smile taunted him. Her quakes of excitement produced a sultry, smoldering heat. And though he was stronger, taller, heavier, Cameron was certain of his imminent defeat.

The lick of her tongue across his lower lip nearly sealed the deal. One long lick from corner to corner threatened to end the standoff. Abby's fingernails did the rest, scraping slowly over him as she raised her hips a fraction of an inch—enough to give him a clear picture of her needs.

He took her. Without waiting for her reaction, he took her again. Unvoiced shouts formed on her lips. Growls rose from his chest. Each stroke he made created more feelings of ecstasy.

And when she growled back at him savagely, he paused, electrified by the sound.

He came in a fiery explosion that rocked them both— his breath suspended, his eyes closed, his chest heaving.

Time seemed to stop. All sound ceased except for the force of the water hitting the back of his neck.

When Cameron opened his eyes, his forehead was resting against the tile, and his hands were on the wall, on either side of Abby. Her head rested on his arm. He would have given her a medal if she had been able to move.

"Like I said," he ventured teasingly with vocal cords that weren't quite working properly. "My turn."

Abby leaned her head back to look up at him. "Oh no," she said.

He quirked an eyebrow before realizing something was wrong. Abby's face had drained of the color it had only just found. Her head twitched on her long, graceful neck.

He recognized those signs.

Cameron spun her out of the shower, glancing to the window to find that the day had fled. The room beyond the bathroom lay in the shadows of an enveloping darkness, and he hadn't noticed. But Abby had.

The first crack came from the vicinity of her spine, followed by the pop of her rib cage expanding. Abby's eyes were wide and fearful. Her lips were bloodless.

"Come on," Cameron said, pulling her to the door. "Hell, Abby. Can you hold back?"

"Can't."

But Cameron wondered, as he ran for the window to close the shutters, if that was entirely true, or if Abby sensed Sam Stark out there in the night, and was going to fur-up to meet him.

Chapter 32

Abby heard shouts coming from behind her as she landed on the lawn in a crouch, on her werewolf haunches, as the rest of her transition took place.

Electricity sparked across her nerves. Pain streaked through her like well-aimed bolts of lightning come to ground. Her racing heart didn't seem capable of keeping up with the changes, since fear also had it thundering. Pure, unadulterated fear.

Cameron landed beside her, having climbed down from the second floor by using the trellis. Others were coming, rounding the house as if her change had tripped some sort of silent alarm. Six people, all of them in their human co-coons, all of them concerned, headed her way. Abby felt their hearts and their pulses alongside hers, though Cameron's heartbeat was dominant, hammering at her as if she had swallowed his heart whole.

"Abby!" Dana Delmonico called to her.

This was, she supposed, a freaky party, where she had become the central theme.

"Here," Cameron answered in her place, because she had lost the ability to speak, along with her outer shell of humanity.

Dylan Landau reached her first, gliding to a stop a few feet away. Dressed in a gray suit and matching tie, his expression was thoughtful.

Without saying anything to her, Dylan's gaze moved to Cameron. "You're naked, Mitchell." Dylan yanked off his jacket.

"I don't think that jacket will do much good," Delmonico said, pulling up alongside the pair. "Unless he puts his legs in it."

Abby growled her displeasure over the gathered crowd. The word *freak* became part of her internal buzz.

"I think he's out there, nearby," Cameron said.

"Sam Stark?" Dylan asked.

Abby didn't recognize the other Weres. The detective who had lent her his leather jacket hadn't shown up. All the Weres present, except for Dana Delmonico, were males. Abby had no idea how many of them possessed the same knack she had for changing without a full moon.

Anxious, she got to her feet and began to back away from the group. Cameron followed, circling around to stand behind her, unconcerned about being naked, his only concern for her. Abby closed her eyes, fearing that if she looked too closely at Cameron, she might completely lose her mind.

Dylan sidestepped the rest of the group, glancing toward the wall and sniffing the air. Then he loosened his tie in a motion reminiscent of the man of steel stripping off his glasses to reveal what lay beneath the disguise.

"Stark's in the park," Dylan said.

Everyone present looked to the wall as if they possessed the ability to see through the stone.

"He can't possibly know where she is," Cameron said.

"Maybe not, but he thinks she will find him," Dylan warned.

And Dylan was right. For Abby, a whiff of Sam is what had brought on the change. She had located him from inside the house. Her wolf had immediately responded, possibly out of self-defense, and possibly out of a need for justice to be served.

She turned. Sighting the wall at the edge of the lawn, and ready to meet Sam once and for all, she figured she might be able to dodge a silver bullet in her new wolf form, and a medication-tipped dart, but she couldn't ask Sam the questions still in need of answers unless she changed back in his presence.

Okay. That was dangerous. Seriously dangerous.

She looked to Cameron longingly, and he seemed to pick up her thought. "No," he said adamantly. "We'll call it in. Let the cops have him. You can ask anything you want of him after that."

The suggestion was reasonable, perfect, aside from one small thing. The hatred she felt for Sam had become like a separate being, and that being was chained to her wolf. Revenge was a ravenous parasite that Sam had called forth from its slumber. Sam had tortured her mother. Sam had killed her mother.

If she couldn't have Sam and the answers she needed, she'd have to be put out of her misery. And though she might be strong at the moment, she had never been stupid. The Weres facing her weren't going to let her go to her death alone.

She howled. Cameron returned the sound with a human equivalent.

"Wait," Dylan said. "Just give me five minutes. Three. All right, two at most. Let me call the others."

Of course, she had no intention of waiting, or allowing anyone here to fight her battle with Sam.

The silver knife pulsed against her calf as if it, too, wanted satisfaction, as if parts of the moon itself had been caught up in the blade. Abby touched the handle of the knife and felt the power of its burn. Her palm sizzled, branded by the touch, but she rode those things out, conquering the pain as deftly as she had in Sam's death cage.

She would fight silver with silver, if she had to. She'd pit a werewolf hunter against the one thing he despised most. She'd set a wounded daughter against a false father, and use her mother's ghost to do so. And if she survived...

Leaving the thought unfinished, Abby spun on both heels and raced for the wall.

She ran, heading for Sam's scent in the deepening dark. The beast she carried infused her with a fair amount of courage, but her pulse beat mercilessly in her throat. Sam had always instilled fear in those around him, and she was no exception. He alone had the ability to frighten her. She had no doubt that he'd try to use that fear against her again.

Maybe, though, that fear now worked both ways.

Sam had scuttled from the torture room before she'd gotten clear of the cage. All he'd had was the dart; at least, that was the only weapon she'd seen. Against the sheer force of her anger, a dart might have been more of a nuisance than a worry.

But Sam hadn't been quick enough to use the dart on her thick werewolf hide. When he'd seen her escape route, he had run away. He'd been a coward in the face of possible defeat.

What about tonight? Would he run? Would he surround himself with hunters to bolster his courage?

Sam wouldn't come after her unprepared, not after seeing her stretch the metal bars out of shape. Strength came with the fur suit, along with a hefty dose of intimidation factor. Her muscles sang with newly found power. Surges of strength flickered in every muscle and cell, producing massive amounts of energy. But she couldn't use these things to take Sam down. And if she killed Sam, she also would be a murderer.

Sam's mantra rattled around inside her head.

The only good werewolf was a dead werewolf.

Growls of protest bubbled up as Abby slowed. Sam's scent grew stronger as she neared his hiding place, but the night itself seemed another kind of enemy, tempting her with a bombardment of scents and smells.

Each fresh scent existed as a trail she wanted to follow. Each led somewhere else. She had to close them all out, ignore all but the trail she needed to take to stick with the goal. Her life, her soul, depended on this meeting.

A life force hit her sight radar, appearing suddenly in the form of a wavy infrared outline. Her wolf gave an inward roar. She let that roar out. She had tracked her prey, and found it.

She headed toward the outline, unable to think about how she'd get Sam to talk. Pin him to the ground or against a tree? Roar in his face. Use her claws to put more fear into him, before she changed back to Abby? Once she shifted back, Sam would again have the upper hand.

Years of living in close proximity to Sam Stark left no leeway for doubt. She smelled his clothes, his hair, his skin and the distinct odor of gun metal. Rifle, she guessed.

And there he stood, with his legs apart and his body braced, near the intersection of two merging walls. She hadn't gone far to find him, and had not misjudged the voracity of the emotions radiating off him in waves. Sam was filled with red-tinted hatred and blackened disgust. His steely determination was very much like a slap in her face.

If Sam hadn't seen her, she had the advantage of surprise. With that flash of insight, Abby realized that wolves had always possessed that kind of advantage. Given the sensitivity to smell and the heat-seeking radar, it made no sense that hunters had been able to take down so many Weres, so easily—unless those Weres had believed themselves to be invincible.

Sam waited for her, soaked with the aura of an executioner. His calmness made him doubly dangerous. She hadn't considered that he might have a night scope on the rifle, but it didn't matter now. The end had come.

Abby paused a few yards away and waited to see what he'd do. His image filled in. She now saw the scope that allowed him to view her, as well, and that pretty much evened things out.

"Abby," Sam said. Not a question. He had his sights on her.

She growled in reply, and the sound carried.

"You had to come," he said. "Beast blood makes all of you do stupid things."

Did you shoot my mother? Hunt her down?

She didn't have the ability to demand answers for those questions, and had an eerie feeling that those answers really weren't something she wanted to hear. The image of her mother running in the dark, being chased, hunted and about to lose her life made her sick. Sam had silver bullets in the rifle. She stood very still, wondering why he didn't just pull the trigger and get this over with.

Another growl rose, scary but insufficient in getting to the heart of the matter of her mother, and of what Sam might do next.

"She was Lycan," Sam said, continuing to aim. "Not bitten, though that wouldn't have mattered much, either.

She had a ring of scar tissue on her left arm in the shape of a set of teeth. I found out that's a sure sign of the moon's wolf cult. So I had to take care of that."

Abby's hatred, pent-up and boiling, leveled out. Sam was talking about his wife, not her. At the moment, he didn't believe they were one and the same. He had just filled in some of the missing information she'd been searching for, but she wanted to understand the rest.

Go on, Sam.

"I took you both in," he said. "Imagine my surprise when the full moon arrived."

This didn't sound good. Abby growled again, unable to hold her sadness back.

"In the end, she faced me just like you are. If she had run away, she might have had a chance. If she had stayed a monster, she might have lived. But she wanted to be assured of your survival. She said if indoctrinated into my cult, instead of hers, you might never change. If kept from the moon after puberty, you might never realize what you are. I made sure of that on all counts, for as long as it lasted, and your inner awareness of monsters came in handy."

Yes. I only hunted for you the nights before a full moon, supposedly to see who was around. To see what wolves prowled the park grounds.

Hell...you almost had me. If I hadn't met Cameron, I might have remained ignorant of my birthright.

Her hands fisted. The claws brought up blood.

"So, here we are, Abby. You have destroyed my livelihood and brought cops to my door. I don't lose much if I pull the trigger. You, on the other hand, lose a lot."

Sam was a crack shot. No way he'd miss at this range. She'd have a chance of surviving the silver bullet, as Cameron had, if help arrived quickly. But she could not maintain the shape that might save her. More gaps had to be filled in, and she needed a voice.

Abby wasn't sure how to go about that reversal in this situation. Outside of the bar, at Cameron's urging, the shift had happened on its own, without any real conscious thought. Did she have the power to will one shape into another? If hatred kept her in fur, that hatred hadn't dimmed by much.

She opened her hands, pictured the claws retracting. Nothing happened.

Why not shoot, damn you!

What are you waiting for?

"I prefer shooting monsters in the back," Sam said. "It's less personal that way. Any time you want to run, I'll do the honors. You can't possibly want to live like that. Look at you, Abby. You are a beast. You're one of them. Now that you've changed, you'll always be a freak."

One claw pulled back into a fingertip with a painful sting. A second claw followed. At that rate, a reversal might take all damn night, and she had only seconds before Sam's patience gave out and his madness took over.

"Run," he advised. "I can't stand the sight of you. Never could actually."

At last, more confession. Sam had despised her from the start.

A whiff of heat-filled air reached her as Abby stood her ground. The earth moved beneath her feet. She didn't dare turn her head or turn around to see who was coming. Weres. She didn't have to guess who.

Waves of adrenaline coursed, drawn from the stagnant pool of her motionlessness. The oncoming Weres were nearing, fast. In another minute they'd find her.

Must. Change. Back.

No matter how close that silver bullet was, Abby closed her eyes and reissued the demand.

Change back.

A third claw retreated, then three more. Her face began to feel soft and gummy, as if the bones had started to melt.

"Haven't I said enough?" Sam asked. "Run, Sonja. I command you to run. I can't look at you. I can't stand the sight. You tricked me, and that happens only once to a Stark."

Sonja.

Sam's madness had prevailed, maybe so that he didn't have to face murdering another family member that had disappointed him to the point of desperation. In Sam's crazy mind, he might imagine himself to be reliving what had gone down before.

Abby's chin shifted without sound. Bones at the base of her neck began to realign. Pain echoed internally with a series of metallic sounds. Patches of red-brown fur sucked back into her pores.

She refused to double over or shut her eyes again. She watched Sam, counting the seconds. *Three...four...*

Leaves overhead rustled. She heard the sounds of running feet, mixed with the crackle of her rib cage decompressing.

"Sam Stark?" someone shouted. But his aim remained locked to Abby.

Figures moved, running as fast as anything Abby had ever seen. But they wouldn't be protected without a full moon overhead.

Please. Not Cameron, Abby thought before Cameron appeared, calling her name. He didn't reach her in time. Dana Delmonico moved like lightning to stand in front of her...just as Sam fired.

Chapter 33

Dana didn't fall back. Her arms were spread wide to cover Abby, but she couldn't have taken the bullet.

A roar filled the night that shook the trees and everyone still standing. The sound came from the furred-up beast that had raced to protect Dana.

Sam's bullet had pierced that werewolf's hide, but the werewolf lunged forward to rip the rifle from Sam's hands before Sam knew what hit him. And Cameron pushed Sam face-first to the ground, with a knee on Sam's writhing back.

It happened so fast. In a moment removed from time, and without the carnage that could have resulted from Sam's demented rampage—a rampage Abby had not expected to survive—it was over. Truly over.

Abby looked down at herself as Delmonico tossed her cuffs to Cameron. She also found herself buck naked, without one hint of a wolf showing.

She shook so hard her teeth hurt.

Then she was running.

She moved toward where Sam lay hog-tied with his hands behind his back. Her knife, drawn from its leather sheath, was in her right hand.

She straddled Sam's body, holding the knife high, pulling at the collar of his shirt. "You bastard!" she cried. "Did she run, as you asked her to? Did my mother give you the satisfaction of shooting her in the back? Is she a pelt on some other bastard's wall? A trophy?"

"No," Sam said. "Her pelt hangs above my bed."

Her knife never came down to sever Sam's murderous flesh. It remained suspended, motionless, frozen, until Cameron took it from her and tossed the blade to the grass.

Cameron pulled her to her feet and spun her around. "It's over," he said. Then he called over his shoulder, "Dylan? What do you need?"

"A new chest," Dylan, in man form, replied, getting to his feet with Dana Delmonico's help. "Good thing I know where to get one."

"He wore a vest," Delmonico said. "And it was the strangest-looking duo I have ever seen. Sort of like a high-fashion runway featuring fur and Kevlar. However, the combination seems to have worked its magic."

"Vest?" Cameron said.

"Just so happens I know a cop who had a spare," Dylan said with hardly a disturbed breath.

The moment of levity that should have seemed out of place, didn't. After what felt like a lifetime of holding her breath, Abby finally exhaled and found her voice. "I didn't kill him."

"No." Cameron tightened an arm around her, crushing her to him while he tore off yet another borrowed shirt. "You didn't. No one thought you could."

"I shifted."

"One of many more, by the looks of things," he said gently. "Next time, though, can you give me a sign?"

"They'll take him away?" She loathed saying Sam's name.

"Yes. It really is over."

"Not quite," she countered, pulling away from Cameron, ignoring her nakedness.

She went to where Sam still lay. "You loved her," Abby said. "You loved my mother. You knew there were decent Weres among the bad, and yet you murdered a beautiful soul."

She didn't actually expect Sam to address that, with his face in the dirt and the monsters he hated standing guard.

"It isn't over," Sam said, contradicting Cameron. "It will never be over, whether I'm loose or not."

"Oh, you won't be loose," Cameron confirmed. "And we'll take another look at that self-defense judgment in your past, to see how you managed it."

"Too late," Sam said smugly. "And if you go for my business in trafficking rare-animal pelts, I'd like to see you explain what those pelts are, and where they came from."

A chill wafted over Abby. Sam couldn't be freed. Ever. Because he was the monster.

"I believe the secret floor and the cage it holds might take some explaining on your part," Cameron said.

"As will the blood staining it," Dylan tossed in. "Also the stockpile of weapons in three storerooms behind the bar."

Cameron nodded his head. "Forensics teams are going to tear up the floor in that secret room, and they're going through your apartment right now. What will they find, Stark, in light of those things? Enough to hold you for a very long time, I'm thinking."

Sam became uncharacteristically silent.

"Where is she?" Abby said to Sam. "What did you do with my mother's body?"

He did not reply. But he had confessed to her about her mother's pelt—an awful confession she'd never forget.

"Did you keep it because you loved her?" Her voice was as shaky as the rest of her. "Just answer that."

Sam said nothing. Of course, he'd know not to speak of those things here, with cops standing over him.

Abby couldn't think about her mother's pelt being among Sam's things. She would never be able to see it.

Detective Wilson and another Were stood him on his feet. "Time to go, Stark," Wilson said.

"I'll tell them about you," Sam hissed. "I'll sic them on all of you."

Dana Delmonico shook her head. "Going for the insanity plea, huh? We'll see how far that gets."

Abby again felt Cameron's arms enfold her. She desired more than anything to give in to his heat and his nearness and his unconditional support. She fought back tears of anger and regret. But she had one more thing to say, and had to say it. "Thank you. All of you. Will you ever be able to forgive me?"

"That depends," Dylan replied.

Abby turned her head.

"On what?" Cameron asked.

"On both of you agreeing to join the pack, so that we can keep an eye on you."

Abby sensed Cameron's relief. She heard him draw in a long breath. "Abby?" he said.

But she was beyond speech. One more word and the tears would fall. She had lost nothing in this fiasco, and had gained a new family. She had a mate she loved more than life itself. The puzzle of her mother's death had been solved—as much as she wanted to hear about, anyway, wanting to forget the nightmares that had plagued her all this time.

"I think they need some alone time," Wilson said, eyeing the pair.

"I was thinking the same thing," Delmonico agreed.

"Shall we book this sucker, Dana?" Wilson asked.

"The pleasure is all mine," Delmonico said.

Without another word, they hustled Sam off, leaving Abby wrapped in Cameron's arms. They stood entwined for several minutes more as silence returned and Abby's shaking eased a little.

Then Cameron spoke. "You're naked," he said, a comment so unexpected Abby nearly laughed in disbelief. The smile felt so damn good.

"Completely naked," he added.

"Is that the only thing you have to say to me after all of this?" Abby asked.

"No. But it's a start." He took a moment to go on. "The pack will be expecting us at the Landaus', I suspect. But I'd rather wait awhile. How's that for a confession? From now on, I'd prefer you wore no clothes every night, even in a public park. And when you do get dressed, I'd prefer my clothes next to your bare skin, in lieu of not having that skin pressed to mine."

Tilting her head back, Abby looked up at him. When her eyes met his, he gave her the dazzling smile that captured her on that first night and haunted her still.

"Furthermore," he said, "you might be a werewolf princess, or some such thing, but just so you know, I wear the pants in this family."

"I see that you're wearing them now," Abby said.

He smiled a devastatingly gorgeous and revealing smile...

And Abby, satisfied, but still hurting on a level that only the Were beside her could take care of, smiled back as she reached for his zipper.

* * * * *

MILLS & BOON®

n o c t u r n e ™

AN EXHILARATING UNDERWORLD OF DARK DESIRES